Glastonbury

Glastonbury

Brian L. Porter

Published 2014 by Creativia
Paperback design by Creativia (www.creativia.org)
ISBN: 978-9526823829

'Glastonbury' is dedicated to the memory of Enid Ann Porter (1914 – 2004). She loved and supported me in my work throughout her life, and to Juliet, whose daily support keeps me going through the darkest times.

Acknowledgements

'Glastonbury' owes its existence not just to the words that appear on its pages, but to the efforts of a number of people who helped along the way. In particular I must say a big thank you to the dedicated group of readers around the world who read and critiqued the book, word by chapter, chapter by chapter, as it progressed. They are Graeme S. Houston, (Scotland), who was responsible for the wonderful cover design for 'Glastonbury', Jean Pike, (USA), Malcolm Davies, Ken Copley and Sheila Noakes, (UK), and of course the book's fiercest critic of all, my wife Juliet.

My appreciation also goes to Sue Chapman, the proprietor of Meare Manor Guest House in Glastonbury for allowing me to use the name of her establishment as one of the prime locations in the story.

Also by Brian L. Porter

- A Study in Red – The Secret Journal of Jack the Ripper (*Winner, The Preditors & Editors Best Thriller Novel Award, 2008*)
- Legacy of the Ripper
- Requiem for the Ripper
- Pestilence
- Purple Death
- The Nemesis Cell
- Avenue of the Dead
- Behind Closed Doors
- Kiss of Life

Short Story Collections

- After Armageddon
- A Binary Convergence (with Graeme S Houston)

As Harry Porter

- Tilly's Tale
- Dylan's Tale
- Wolf
- Alistair the Alligator

Brian L. Porter's short stories have appeared in numerous journals around the world, both in print and digital formats. More information can be found by visiting the author's websites at

http://www.inspectornorris.webs.com
http://www.astudyinred.webs.com

Contents

Introduction

Glastonbury! The name itself conjures up mental images of the England of long ago. Here in the heart of the ancient county of Somerset, stands the home of the first above-ground Christian church in England, the ruins of a centuries old abbey, and the whole town is overlooked by the imposing Glastonbury Tor, with the crumbling remains of St Michael's chapel standing at its head, overlooking the swirling green countryside that surrounds the town. Glastonbury throbs with legend; it is said the bones of Joseph of Arimathea were laid to rest here, as were the mortal remains of the legendary King Arthur. The Arthurian connection is strong in Glastonbury with many believing it to be the site of Arthur's Camelot. Could it have been the home of the famed round table? Did the Knights who formed that noble group, Gawain, Lancelot and Co. really tread this ground? Was the Holy Grail really brought here all those years ago? Is it still here, buried in some long forgotten secret niche known only to those whose bones have long since crumbled to nothing beneath the marshes and mires that once swirled around the Tor, once an island rising up from the wetlands of Somerset, and now cast adrift upon the land-locked plains of South-West England?

For many, Glastonbury is a hallowed place, a town where history and the present exist hand in hand, where the souls and the ghosts of history encroach every so often on the lives of those who exist in tandem with their memory, and who walk where they once walked, talk in the quiet places they once conversed in, and who tread lightly when the sun goes down and the moon rises over the forbidding and compelling hill that stands as an eternal sentinel over the town and keeps its secrets hidden from those who would pry too deep.

Into this land of myth, magic and legend comes a small group of professionals, hired by a mysterious and wealthy entrepreneur who professes to have acquired a map that will reveal the hiding place of one of the most magical and famed emblems of Arthurian legend. For Joe Cutler, Winston Fortune, and Sally Corbett, fame, wealth and riches could be just around the corner, but first they have a job to do, a job that will lead them into far more dangerous corners of this place of myth and legend than they could possibly have foreseen. As the rain falls on Glastonbury they wait and prepare their equipment for the job ahead, and a new Glastonbury mystery waits to be unravelled.

Prologue

A pale and baleful moon looked down upon the green landscape below as the five men moved silently across the wet and marshy surface of the field. Apart from the leader who walked ahead the other four were burdened by the weight of the load they shared between them. The load had felt heavy enough when they'd started; now it grew heavier with every step. Their arms felt leaden, their muscles ached, and a great sigh of relief issued from each of the four when the leader stopped, raised his hand and uttered one word:. "Here."

They slowly placed the heavy, lead-lined boxes upon the grass and untied the shovels that were strapped to the top, adding to the weight. Under the orders of the tall man who'd brought them to this spot, they began to dig, first cutting rectangular sods of turf from the ground, pieces that would later be fitted back into place to disguise the burial place. Next, they dug deep, almost as deep as the height of a man, a task made easier by the softness of the earth, but also harder by the degree of fatigue they suffered.

Two hours later it was done; the last pieces of turf were carefully re-laid to cover the traces of the burial. They were well away from any regular byways and it was unlikely anyone would find the place before the turf had knitted itself back into place. To all intents and purposes, the hole was perfectly hidden, its contents safely interred in the earth.

With the moon as sole witness to the burial of the heavy lead-lined boxes and their contents, the five men looked back just once as they left the field, their leader taking time to pause and mark the burial site on a map he carried tucked into his belt. Soon, the men had gone, the field lay silent and only the moon would know that they had been in this place that night, and of course, the moon would never tell.

Chapter 1

A faint grey wash of daylight breaking through the crack in the curtains signalled the coming of morning. Joe Cutler stirred beneath the warmth of the duvet, listening to the steady drip of raindrops falling from the gutter to the ground below. Rain, bloody awful rain, third day in a row. No work again, they couldn't do a thing as long as this damned rain persisted. He and his team needed dry weather, solid ground beneath their feet, not the soggy morass that presented itself as long as this perpetual downpour lasted. Even then, when it finally stopped they'd have to wait for the ground to dry out before they could recommence the job, and the more time they lost the more money they lost.

Capshaw was paying them to get results, not sit around checking their equipment day after day, and Cutler's frustration was mounting. It was possible, of course, under normal circumstances to work in the rain, but the low-lying ground in this part of England meant that three days of steady rain had turned the ground into a veritable quagmire, and any attempts to achieve results were doomed to failure. No, Cutler knew he was destined for another irritating and annoying day of relative inactivity, with nothing but the company of his two friends and employees and the sights of Glastonbury to fill what should have been his working day.

Tempted for a moment to pull the duvet back over his head and return to the land of dreams, Cutler thought better of it, and swung his feet over the side of the bed. He stretched, then ran his fingers through his well-tousled hair. Standing, he walked to the window and opened the thin curtains, allowing his eyes to take in the sight of the miserable downpour that had brought operations to a standstill. In the distance, the ruined tower of St. Michael was visible atop the legendary Glastonbury Tor and reminded Cutler just why he was here.

After a hasty shower in the tiny shower room, (Mrs. Cleveley's Guest House wasn't exactly the Hilton Hotel), Cutler made his way down to the dining room for one of the landlady's superb home-cooked breakfasts. At thirty pounds a day for bed, breakfast and evening meal, Cutler certainly wasn't complaining about the standards of cuisine or comfort at the guest house, though with the bill for all three of them running at just over six hundred pounds a week, Capshaw's two-thousand-pound advance certainly wouldn't last long if the rain refused to let up.

The others had beaten him to it. As he walked into the well-lit dining area on the ground floor, the smiling faces of Winston Fortune and Sally Corbett greeted him from a table positioned under the large bay window that looked out upon the street.

Cutler made his way over to them and sat down next to the large Jamaican, who had become not only a trusted employee, but one of his closest friends. Sally Corbett sat opposite the two men, a cup of coffee in her hand.

"I don't know what the hell you two have got to look so happy about," said Cutler, in response to the smiles from his friends.

"Good morning to you, too, boss," came Sally's response .

Brian L. Porter

"Yeah man, like, how are you today?" Winston Fortune added.

"How am I today? You dare to ask me how I am today? Hell, Winston, we've been here for three days now, and apart from walking around the gift shops and sheepskin factory shops, and checking and rechecking and calibrating and recalibrating every damned piece of equipment in the van, we've done bugger all, and you ask me how I am today?"

"Wow, someone got out of the wrong side of the bed today, that for sure," said the big Jamaican.

"This rain can't last for ever, boss, we'll get the job done, we always do," said Sally, the youngest member of the team, and at five feet and half an inch tall (she always stressed the half-inch), by far the shortest. Sally Corbett was twenty-four, pretty in an academic sort of way, and purposely kept her hair cut on the short side, as much of her work involved being stuck in dirty holes in the ground, which would have made long hair wholly impractical. Cutler held his hand up to interrupt the flow of the conversation as Mrs. Cleveley came striding towards the table, smiling as always.

"Hmm, yes, the usual please," said Cutler as Mrs. Cleveley greeted them heartily, inquiring if they wanted a full breakfast.

"Right, Mr. Cutler, two boiled eggs, toast and coffee it is then," and she scurried off back towards the kitchen.

"As I was saying," he continued, "Capshaw is paying us to find the bloody thing, not sit on our backsides all day. We started off with a two-week contract to do the job and this will be the third day we've lost already. May I remind you, my wonderful employees, that the advance I received is going to pay for this wonderful lap of luxury in which we're currently ensconced, but once I've paid the marvellous Mrs. Cleveley for our two week stay, there won't be much left to go around unless we do something to earn our fee?"

"But Capshaw will still pay us, won't he, boss?" asked Winston.

"Sure, he'll pay us. But do I need to remind you that we only get a flat fee if we see out the job and find nothing. The big bonus is only payable, if we actually find what he's looking for."

"Yeah, like that's going to happen" joked Winston.

"You know, I have to agree with Winston on this one, I think you've really flipped this time," jibed Sally.

"Listen you two doubters, I've seen the original document; he showed it to me spread out on his desk. I've no reason to doubt his sincerity or belief that the thing is genuine, and if it is and we can solve the puzzle of its location, we'll share in the rewards that such a find will bring. You've both seen the copy he gave me, I know it's not the same as having the real thing in your hand, but believe me, that document was old, very old."

"These things can be faked, you know," said Sally.

"Sure they can, and maybe someone made a mint by selling old Capshaw a dummy document and then doing a runner," Winston continued.

"Listen, I don't think a reputable man like Malcolm Capshaw would be taken in by a fake document. He's very wealthy, very knowledgeable and from what I've heard, not a man to cross in either his business or personal life."

"So you think it's the real deal then, eh, boss?" asked Winston.

"If I didn't, we wouldn't be sitting here now, waiting for the bloody rain to stop would we, you moron?"

"Rain, rain, go away, come again another day," Sally sang the old childhood rhyme.

"Don't come back at all," Cutler snapped as he looked out the window at the incessant precipitation that seemed to be drowning his prospects of achieving what his cohorts already thought of as being wildly impossible.

Brian L. Porter

Mrs. Cleveley chose that moment to arrive at the table with two plates of scrambled eggs, ordered by Winston and Sally before Cutler had made his entrance.

"Here we are, my dears," the landlady chimed in her sing-song Somerset accent. "Yours will be along in a minute, Mr. Cutler. They say the rain'll stop later this morning, I just heard it on the radio."

"I hope you're right, Mrs. Cleveley, I really do," he replied quietly as she scurried off to fetch his breakfast.

Twenty minutes later the three of them gave up their seats under the window and made their way to Cutler's room, where he unlocked his briefcase and removed the copy of the document Malcolm Capshaw had presented him just two short weeks ago.

"Right then, let's just go over this again, in the hope that the rain does stop and the ground dries out enough for us to start the search sometime tomorrow."

"You're the boss," said Winston as he stretched his large frame out along the edge of Cutler's bed.

Sally sat demurely at the foot of the bed; her legs tucked under herself as Cutler unfolded the document and placed it on the bed where the three of them could see it clearly.

The paper he placed on the bed was a photo of something that definitely *looked* old. Most of the wording was indecipherable to the three of them, being written in what today is referred to as Old English, though the words seemed to have a hint of French or perhaps even ancient Latin to their untrained eyes. Whatever the words were, they were faded enough to make most of the script unreadable, perhaps even to an expert in languages. What made the document so interesting and potentially valuable was the one word which was still quite visibly etched in centuries old ink towards the end of the first line at the top of the document.

As the other members of the Strata Survey Company looked on, Joe Cutler, owner and chief survey engineer of the company he'd started three years ago traced the index finger of his right hand slowly across the page. His finger stopped directly below the word that had convinced him to take the job when Capshaw had called him and invited him to a meeting in his office. Hell, if they were successful, it would put him and his company on the map big time, he knew that such a find would bring him instant recognition, and the contracts would come pouring in.

"You know of course, that most people don't even think Arthur existed and if he didn't then this is just a wild goose chase," Sally pointed out.

"Will you just listen?" Cutler replied. "If Capshaw was convinced, then for what he's prepared to pay us for succeeding, we at least ought to try."

"Okay, boss man, we're all ears," said Winston as he waited for Cutler to speak. "Go ahead and tell us again just how we're going to find King Arthur's Excalibur!"

Chapter 2

Two weeks earlier Joe Cutler had sat waiting outside the office of Malcolm Capshaw. He'd responded to a phone call three days previously, inviting him to a discussion with the millionaire, one which might lead to his company making a large sum of money and enhance its professional reputation at the same time. Cutler had been unable to resist the invitation, even though Capshaw's secretary had been less than forthcoming about the nature of the job her boss had in mind for Cutler's team.

Now here he was, sitting on a leather sofa in a palatial office in Stratford-on-Avon, with Capshaw's secretary looking over her glasses at him as he fidgeted uncomfortably on the squeaky polished leather. She looked around thirty years old, dressed in a smart, dark blue business suit, her long dark hair tied back professionally. Her shoes were of the highly glossy patent variety and her make-up could have been applied by a professional at a beauty parlour. Cutler found himself wondering if she performed more than secretarial duties for her boss; she looked the type.

The telephone on her desk buzzed and she listened to her boss via an earpiece hidden discreetly behind her left ear.

"Yes, sir, he's here. Of course, Mr. Capshaw, I'll show him in now."

She rose from behind the desk. She was taller than Cutler had imagined as he'd watched her sitting behind the desk. She stood almost as tall as he was, which he found a little intimidating.

"Mr. Capshaw is ready for you now, Mr. Cutler," she announced, somehow managing to make Joe's name sound like an insult. She led him through a heavy oak panelled door that led to what appeared to be a sort of air lock, with another identical oak door about five feet further on. Cutler realised this aided in sound-proofing Capshaw's inner sanctum, and also prevented anyone eavesdropping through the door.

The secretary didn't knock at the second door, she simply opened it and ushered Cutler through into the thickly carpeted office of Malcolm Capshaw.

"Thank you, Charlotte," said the man sitting behind the large desk at the far side of the office. "That will be all for now. Do come in please, Mr. Cutler."

Charlotte seemed to disappear on silent heels and the door closed equally silently behind her, leaving Cutler alone with Capshaw. The office was huge and Cutler couldn't make out the face of the man behind the desk until he drew nearer. The sunlight brightly glittered through the large plate glass window directly behind his host. As he moved closer he saw that Capshaw was a broad thick set individual, dressed immaculately in a suit that must have cost at least five hundred pounds. Capshaw was clean shaven with a good head of hair, expertly groomed, and Cutler guessed he was probably around fifty years of age. He had the steely, determined look of a man used to getting what he wanted, his eyes were grey and deeply penetrating in their gaze, and Cutler thought it might not be a good idea to cross a man like Malcolm Capshaw.

Capshaw motioned to Cutler to take a seat and immediately proceeded to the matter in hand. He obviously hadn't got where he was in the world by wasting too much time on small talk.

"I have a proposition for you, Mr. Cutler, one that may prove quite lucrative for you and your company."

"Can I ask you how you heard about us, Mr. Capshaw?" asked Cutler, always eager to know how word of his professional services passed from one person or client to another.

"That's hardly important, is it, Mr. Cutler? The fact is I researched your credentials and decided that you and your people are the best qualified to do the little task I have in mind for you. Either you want the job or you don't, it's as simple as that."

"Well yes, of course, Mr. Capshaw. It's just that I don't know anything about the job yet. Your secretary was a little, er, shall we say vague when she called and asked me to meet with you today?"

"Ah yes, good old Charlotte," said Capshaw with a smile. "Always efficient you know, never says more than she has to in order to get the job done. That's what I like in a woman, or in a man, come to that."

"Of course, I can agree with those sentiments, Mr. Capshaw. So, the job?"

Without further preamble Capshaw stood up and walked around his desk, gesturing for Cutler to follow him. They walked across the office to a large planning table, which held various papers and what appeared to be a number of large scale maps, all neatly arranged. There was a briefcase at one end of the table and Capshaw swung it around so that the locks faced him, rolled the numbers on the combination locks and then snapped the case open. From its interior, he took hold of and removed a rolled up document that had a yellowed, aged appearance. Cutler didn't need telling that he was about to view something that hadn't just come from a digital printer.

"This, Mr. Cutler, is the reason I asked you here today. This document which recently came into my possession is the clue that will lead us to solving one of history's greatest secrets. Tell me, have you ever been to Glastonbury?"

Cutler narrowed his eyes. "You mean Glastonbury, Somerset, as in rock concerts and such?"

"No, Mr. Cutler. I mean Glastonbury, as in the history of Christianity, the Holy Grail, King Arthur, *and such.*"

"Oh no, Mr. Capshaw," Cutler said, shaking his head. "You don't want me to get involved with some improbable and highly unlikely grail quest, do you? If that's what this is all about, I'd rather we didn't waste any more of each other's valuable time. I think you've been reading too many novels and I wouldn't be interested in getting involved in anything like that, not even for the lucrative sum you seem to be hinting at. There's no such thing as the Holy Grail, I'm sure of it. It's just a wonderfully romantic historical fantasy."

Capshaw pursed his lips. "This is not about the Holy Grail, Mr. Cutler. I'm talking about King Arthur."

Cutler drew a deep breath. Capshaw might be a millionaire entrepreneur and renowned financial speculator, but he suspected he'd definitely got his sums wrong this time.

"Oh come on, Mr. Capshaw. With all due respect, there's no proof that King Arthur even existed! Just what part of the Arthurian legend do you want me to get involved with? His body was supposedly found centuries ago and as far as I know, that was later proved to be a hoax perpetrated by the monks at Glastonbury Abbey."

"King Arthur *did* exist, Mr. Cutler. I'm convinced of it, and this document will help to prove it to you. I can't reveal to you where it came from or how it came into my possession, but a lot of people have died over the years to protect it and the information it holds. I'm a wealthy man as you already know, and the money itself is not of great importance to me. I thought you would appreciate a large cash injection into your business. You're building a very good reputation in your field, Mr. Cutler. Imagine how high your stock would rise amongst your potential clients if you could put on your CV that you were instrumental in leading the team that finally revealed the burial place not of King Arthur himself, but of his great sword, Excalibur!"

Cutler stared at him, incredulous. "Excalibur? You're not serious, surely? That's just so much myth and legend, for sure."

Capshaw held up a hand. "Give me fifteen minutes, Mr Cutler, that's all I ask. If you're not convinced there's a possibility I might be telling you the truth by then, you can leave my office and we'll forget we ever met. The job will go to one of your competitors and the future success and prosperity of another survey company will be assured as opposed to Strata Surveys."

Cutler knew he couldn't just walk away without giving Capshaw the chance to state his case. He couldn't take the chance that the man might be right, though everything he knew told Cutler the Arthurian legend was just that, a legend. Still, fifteen minutes wouldn't hurt; after all there was the fee to consider.

"Fifteen minutes, Mr. Capshaw. I'm all ears," said Cutler, and he bent over the planning table as Capshaw spread the document out before them.

An hour later, Cutler was back outside in the fresh air, walking along the cobbled path that followed the bank of the River Avon. He wondered if William Shakespeare had ever walked along this bank of the river, not on this path of course, which was quite modern. His mind was still refusing to take in everything he'd learned in the last few minutes. The document Capshaw had showed shown him was centuries old. At least, Capshaw said it was, and he was more of an expert on that sort of thing than Cutler was. There was no doubt that it had been written by someone with a grasp of the language of a millennium ago, nor was there any doubting the location described by the map attached to the document. Though the topography of the terrain and the very nature of the land had changed in the last thousand years, Glastonbury was still Glastonbury. If the map and the text were genuine, then there was every chance that the fabled sword used by the presumably mythical King Arthur was buried somewhere near what was today known as Glastonbury Tor, a site that would have been an island many years ago. Was it possible therefore that King Arthur had actually existed? Had the history of the Dark Ages failed to record the accurate story of his rule? Could Glastonbury really have been the Avalon of legend, as many have supposed it to be over the years? Had truth and legend somehow become so intertwined that the reality of those long-ago days had been lost in the swirling mists of time, until the story of Arthur had become just that; a story, with the truth being hidden behind a veil of myth, superstition and legend? Had it all been a cleverly orchestrated deceit by those who had reason to keep the facts of Arthur's life and death a secret from those who followed him?

Suddenly, Joe Cutler found himself asking questions he wouldn't have been capable of formulating a short time ago. Somehow, Capshaw had convinced him that there was a real possibility the sword of King Arthur actually existed. He knew that if he and his team were to find it, and Capshaw kept his promise to ensure it became a national treasure, the publicity would assure his company's future, aside from the sizeable sum Capshaw was offering for the work of locating the artefact.

As for Capshaw, he'd managed to convince Joe he was truly an entrepreneur, and a benevolent one at that. He was a true patriot, and he wanted England to have positive proof of this important part of its heritage. He would make nothing from the find himself, though again, the publicity wouldn't do him any harm. Plus, he would be able to bask in the glory that would attend the fact that he was the man who'd organised and effectively led the team that discovered Excalibur. He'd told Cutler he wanted to see Excalibur behind glass in the British Museum, brightly illuminated so that all could see it, perhaps with his name on a plaque on the case, alongside that of Cutler and his team, of course.

Joe Cutler patted the breast pocket of his jacket, ensuring the envelope containing Capshaw's two-thousand-pound advance was still there. He'd taken the job, for better or worse Capshaw's secretary had handed over the envelope as though she was paying the window cleaner, with a look of disdain on her face. Cutler was, after all, merely the hired help.

To hell with her Cutler thought as he arrived back at the riverside car park where he'd left his rather dirty Toyota pick-up. *The stuck up little bitch. Now all I have to do is sell this bloody madcap scheme to the others.*

Chapter 3

Cutler figured he'd done a reasonable job of selling the scheme to the others; otherwise they wouldn't be sitting on his bed in room 3 of Mrs. Cleveley's Rowan Tree Guest House, discussing their plans for the next few days. It hadn't been too hard to convince Winston of the possibilities exhibited by the project. Perhaps it was the romantic soul of his Caribbean background that had led the big Jamaican to think a search for the sword of King Arthur might make a pleasant diversion from their usual fare of surveying jobs for building contractors or gas pipe-laying companies and the like. Either that, or the prospect of the fame and fortune coming their way if they were successful convinced Winston Fortune that his boss might not be totally crazy and they might just find what they were looking for. As Winston had pointed out; the client must have good reason to believe in his cause, otherwise, he wouldn't offer them a big fat fee to carry out the search, would he?

Sally Corbett had been a little harder to convince. Younger and definitely more cynical and sceptical than Winston, she'd laughed aloud when Cutler first told her of Capshaw's quest, and the part they were expected to play in it.

"Excalibur?" she'd exclaimed. "You really have lost it this time, boss! You're surely not serious, are you? Who is this Capshaw guy anyway? Has he just escaped from a loony bin, or what? I thought you had more sense than to fall for something like this, I really did."

"Look, Sally" he'd replied patiently, "I ran a check on Capshaw. Seems like he's rich beyond anything you or I could ever dream of being. He's made a fortune from property speculation and from playing the world's financial markets. Stocks, shares, futures, they're all like bread and butter to him. He's donated vast sums to charities over the years, particularly to those with an artistic connection. He also invests in projects around the world to recover historical artefacts. He's funded a whole range of archaeological expeditions in the last ten years, and he definitely isn't the sort of man to waste his, or anyone else's time on wild goose chases. If he believes in the existence of King Arthur and Excalibur, and he thinks he can find it with our help, then I'm not going to refuse his money without at least giving it a good try."

"Did you see the original document then?" she'd demanded.

"Yes, Sally, I did, and what's more, I believe it's the real thing. Capshaw was very secretive about where and how he got hold of it, but I couldn't doubt his sincerity for a minute. Anyway, he's paying the bills, and our wages for the job, so what have we got to lose by going along with him, eh? Come on, Sally girl, where's your sense of adventure?"

She'd eventually given in to his persuasion, though in truth, she could hardly refuse to go along with him in reality. Sally had the greatest of respect for Joe Cutler. After all, he'd given her a job when she'd abandoned university without a degree, after she'd suffered a long spell of depression when her twin sister had been killed in a horrific hit and run road accident while on her way to visit their sick mother in the hospital. Sally and her twin, Maggie had been more than close. They'd shared that special bond only identical twins possess, including the ability to second-guess each other's thoughts, and 'see' the same things in their minds simultaneously. Losing Maggie, Sally felt as though a part of herself had died along with her sister. Deeply distraught, she'd ended up packing her things, walking out of the halls of residence at Oxford University, and disappeared into a world of her own for almost a year. Unwilling to return to university, she'd plucked up the courage to start job hunting. Seeing herself as little more than a failed geology student, she hadn't held out much hope of securing a job within her chosen profession. When she'd seen the advertisement for a survey team assistant in her local newspaper, she'd applied just to see what would happen. At the interview, Joe Cutler's down-to-earth approach had been a surprise, he'd refused to see her lack of a degree as a problem, and she'd been totally over the moon when he'd told her he'd rather have someone knowledgeable and prepared to get her hands dirty, than someone whose head was filled with too much theory and a sense of their own importance.

Two days after the interview, Sally received the telephone call that had made her the third member of the team now sat waiting to begin their unlikely quest to discover King Arthur's long-lost sword. They worked well together, and Cutler appreciated everyone's personal opinions. He wasn't the sort of man who imposed his own ideas, merely because he was the boss. If they could devise a better way of doing something, or had an idea which might help get the job done quicker without compromising safety or accuracy, Cutler was always ready to listen. He might be nearly twice her age, (she thought), but Sally knew she was ever-so-slightly in love with the man who paid her wages, not that she'd ever dare to admit it to him, or anyone else, of course.

"Hey, boss. Look." Winston was pointing at the window. "If I'm not mistaken I could swear that it's getting brighter out there."

"Looks like Mrs. Cleveley was right. The rain's easing off and the sun's trying to come out," Sally concurred.

Sure enough, as Cutler stared hard through the wet pane of his bedroom window he could just about see that the clouds were beginning to move away from what had appeared to be their permanent mooring over the town and were gradually giving way to a pale blue and brighter sky blowing in from the east. A broad smile broke out on his face as he turned back to face the others.

"Well, folks, it looks like our luck's in. If things dry out just enough, we'll be able to start laying out our search grids first thing tomorrow. Now, let's go through everything one more time, shall we?"

Sally and Winston groaned, and Sally took the liberty of playfully throwing their street map of Glastonbury at her boss.

"Slave driver," she laughed at him as Cutler ducked.

"Okay, boss man," said Winston, sounding resigned to the inevitable. "Let the lecture begin."

Cutler removed a whole mass of papers from his briefcase along with a beautifully leather bound book, the page edges deckled with gold. It was a thick and heavy volume containing almost everything known about the legend of King Arthur, Camelot and the Knights of the Round Table. Whether fact or fiction, virtually everything ever written on the subject was contained within this one concise work of literature, and Cutler had been left in no doubt as to its value when Capshaw had entrusted it to him. They'd studied the text so many times over the last few days, and now the time was near when they would put what they'd learned to good use. If Excalibur really did exist, then with the information contained within the pages of the book, together with the information on the document furnished by Capshaw, Joe Cutler knew that he and the others would find it. They just needed to sift through the myths, find the facts, forget the possibility of failure, and make sure they followed the trail to wherever the sword was buried.

As the sun broke through the clouds and shafts of golden light suffused the room, he made himself comfortable, leaning back against the headboard of the bed. Having made sure he had Winston and Sally's full attention, Cutler began to read aloud from what, until now, they'd thought of as nothing more than the 'legend' of King Arthur.

Chapter 4

"So, let's see I've got this right then, boss," Winston said, after an hour of intense listening and discussion. "Camelot wasn't here at Glastonbury, but it *was* at Cadbury, and Glastonbury was the ancient Avalon, right?"

Cutler nodded.

"And Arthur died of wounds he received at the battle of Camlann in the year 542, and was carried back here, where his body was interred somewhere in the area?"

"Whereupon," Sally joined in the conversation, "Sir Pelleas, husband of Viviane, otherwise known to history as The Lady of the Lake, took it upon himself to bury the sword Excalibur in a place apart from the body of Arthur, to prevent its discovery and the possibility of it being used by his enemies against the forces of good that Arthur had stood for. Pelleas was afraid that Arthur's enemies might attempt to disinter his corpse and remove the sword if it were there, and use it as a rallying symbol for those who would follow the pretenders to his throne."

"Looks like you guys have got it," said Cutler, that irrepressible smile spreading across his face again.

"And you say that all this is true?" asked Sally.

"No, Sally, the book says it's true, Capshaw says it's true, and his tame historical expert says it's true."

"Ah yes, boss, the expert. When the hell we s'posed to expect the great man, anyhow?" Winston wanted to know. "Wasn't he s'posed to be here by now, man?"

"He was busy translating some old medieval manuscript, according to Capshaw. It was taking longer than he expected, but he should be here any day now. He's apparently spent months checking the facts, and Capshaw is convinced he knows what he's talking about. He's managed to separate a lot of the fact from the fiction and he'll be here to help us once we get the Ground Penetrating Radar up and running. His name, by the way, is Walter Graves."

"Good name," said Winston.

"Very appropriate," Sally giggled.

"Lay off, you two."

Cutler smiled as he spoke. He wouldn't swap the two of them for anybody else. He could trust them implicitly, and he knew that despite their apparent scepticism regarding the search for Excalibur, deep down they were probably just as excited as he was at the prospect of making such a momentous discovery. If they really did find the sword of King Arthur it would turn history on its head. All the doubters would have to run and hide and bury their cynical heads in the proverbial sand of their inaccurate and out-of-date text books. If Arthur really did exist, live and die within the shores of Olde England as legend tells, then the history books would have to be re-written, new lessons devised for school history courses, and all those childhood games he remembered playing about the Knights of the Round Table, riding to save damsels in distress, would take on a whole new meaning.

Joe Cutler glanced at his watch and realised that the signals his stomach was sending to his brain indicated lunchtime was imminent. "Okay, guys. Let's leave it there for now. It's time to eat. How's the outside world looking, Winston?"

Fortune moved over to the window and surveyed the busy street scene outside The Rowan Tree. Cars were gleaming again as sunlight reflected from their highly polished paintwork, the grey mantle of the previous three days replaced by a bright and cheerful picture postcard scene as Glastonbury took on the look of an archetypal historic English country town. People were no longer dashing along the street with their heads down to avoid the rain; the umbrellas had disappeared, and it was as if the pavements themselves were filled with a new vibrancy, coming awake after slumbering through the drowning torrents of the last three days.

"Hey man, de sun is shining, and all's well wit' de world" he said in a gross self-parody of his own Jamaican background.

"Stop playing around, Winston," Cutler said, always aware that as far as Winston Fortune was concerned, racial stereotypes were a waste of time and he was always the first to have a little fun at his own expense when it came to regional or national accents. He was comfortable with his own birthright, and in fact, he was a grand master when it came to imitating almost any accent on the planet. The former Special Forces operative was also a brilliant linguist, able to speak English, French, German, Spanish, Dutch and Japanese fluently and could speak a fair bit of Farsi, Hindi, and Mandarin Chinese to boot.

"Sorry, boss, but yeah, it's cleared up a lot, and people are even walking around out there in their shirtsleeves, so it must be warming up quite a bit, too."

"Tell you what," said Cutler. "What do you say I treat us all to a decent lunch at that pub we had a drink in last night? Then we'll take a stroll around the abbey and maybe take a walk up to the top of the Tor, sort of reconnoitre the area a bit before we start work in earnest?"

Twenty minutes later, the three of them were seated at a table in 'Ye Queens Head' hotel on Glastonbury High Street. Lunch was a light-hearted affair with Winston and Joe inventing various jokes about the 'days of old when knights were bold', and there was much speculation as to character and personality of the historian, Walter Graves. Sally wondered aloud what use he would be to their search, and Cutler pointed out that his historical knowledge might mean the difference between them finding Excalibur, or possibly unearthing a medieval toilet.

The food was excellent, Winston devouring a twelve-ounce sirloin steak, garnished with chipped potatoes, onion rings and garden peas in no time at all. Cutler enjoyed gammon and eggs, while Sally tucked in to a generous helping of spaghetti bolognaise. Cutler never ceased to be amazed at young Sally's ability to eat large meals without ever seeming to gain weight. He guessed most women would be envious of her talent for eating and staying slim without the need for dieting or overly vigorous exercise. They shared a bottle of very good Australian Chardonnay and finished off with a pot of coffee between them.

They walked the meal off by taking in the sights of the abbey ruins and, as they'd arranged, a walk to the top of Glastonbury Tor, from where they had a superb view of the surrounding countryside. Great swathes of green seemed to disappear into the far horizon as they stared out across the Somerset countryside, each lost in their own thoughts for a time. It was impossible to stand at that point and not be awed by the sheer weight of history and legend that emanated from that great mount, and from the very brickwork and stone of the town that lay sprawled in the shadow of the Tor. It was as if something intangible hung in the very air above Glastonbury, a secret shrouded in the mists that often swirled around the grassy top of the Tor. Would they have the knowledge and the skill to find something that until now had been nothing more than a legend in their minds? Was it possible that in a few days' time, one of them could be holding aloft the famed 'Sword in the Stone" of fairy tale fame? Could the fairy tale become reality; a material item to be seen, touched and felt by human hands for the first time in over a thousand years?

Time would tell, and as Joe Cutler, Winston Fortune and Sally Corbett began the long walk down from the Tor and back to The Rowan Tree, a companionable silence fell over the three friends as each kept their private thoughts hidden from the others. Little did they know that each had similar thoughts. The money they'd receive for a successful search would be great, but to actually find Excalibur? Despite any sceptical reservations any of them had harboured to begin with, each of them knew that locating the fabled Excalibur *really would* be something to tell their children about one day.

Chapter 5

After their brief foray around the town, the three members of the Strata team made their way back to the guest house. The company van was parked in Mrs Cleveley's private car park at the rear of the building. Winston and Sally spent a couple of hours rechecking that all their equipment was in working order, while Cutler went up to his room to make a few phone calls. The final and most important one was to the fourth member of the Strata Survey team, the hub around which all of Cutler's tiny empire revolved, Mavis!

White-haired widow Mavis Hightower was fifty-eight years old, highly opinionated, remarkably efficient in every respect, and totally protective towards Joe Cutler. She'd worked in the office of Strata Survey Systems for the last three years and now basked in the highly important title of 'Office Manageress', bestowed upon her some time ago by Cutler in recognition of her efforts in keeping the business afloat from an administrative perspective. There were no staff to manage, of course, just a desk, a computer and a filing cabinet, but whatever she did, Mavis did it well! Though her appearance gave her the look of being everyone's favourite maiden aunt, Mavis was a skilled administrator, an expert with a computer and a first class bookkeeper. Whenever they were away 'on site', Joe checked in with Mavis every day, to make sure that everything was okay in the office, and to let her know that she hadn't been forgotten about while he and the team were away 'having a good time', as she always referred to their jobs away from home. Though she wouldn't admit it, Mavis appreciated those calls more than anyone would ever know, the loneliness of living alone was often unbearable, and her part in the survey team's operations was her lifeline, small though her involvement might be. The nice thing about Joe Cutler, as she'd always tell anyone prepared to listen, was that he had the knack of making people – making *her* – feel important.

"Everything's fine, Mr. Cutler," Mavis assured him when Joe made his usual daily call to the office. "No new job requests since yesterday, and I'll make sure any potential clients are put on hold."

"That's good Mavis. I know you think I'm an old woman…"

"Oh no, that's my job, Mr. Cutler," she joked.

"You know what I mean," Joe laughed. "If I didn't check in with you every day, you know you'd only worry."

"Quite right I would," Mavis agreed. "Now, you know things are in good hands here, all ship shape and Bristol fashion. I promise to be professional and positive with any potentials, and tell them you and the others will return in a fortnight. Hopefully you'll have a diary full of work by the time you finish up in Glastonbury"

"You make me feel quite surplus to requirements, Mavis" Cutler smiled as he spoke.

"Well you did hire me to take care of the office, Mr. Cutler and that's just what I'm doing."

"And very well you do it too," he replied.

"Now, off you go, and give my love to Sally and Winston. I'm sure you've more important things to do than gossiping on the telephone with me."

Suitably reassured, but somehow feeling like a naughty schoolboy who'd just been chastised by the headmistress, Joe said his goodbyes to Mavis, leaving her to do what she did best.

Mavis Hightower smiled as she replaced the phone on its cradle. She really did appreciate Joe's daily calls and knew he did it not just for work purposes but because he liked her to feel included in whatever the team were involved in. That was just one of the reasons she loved her job with Strata Survey Systems.

Satisfied that all was well back home, Cutler joined the others as they cleared away the last of the equipment and helped lock everything up for the night.

"Mavis says hi to you both," he said cheerfully to Sally and Winston as the big Jamaican locked the Transit's rear doors.

"Mavis doesn't say 'hi' to anyone, boss," Winston pointed out with a grin. " 'Hello', maybe, or even 'Good Morning', or 'Nice to see you', but 'Hi'? Never."

Cutler chuckled. "Yeah, well, that's what she meant anyway."

"How is she?" Sally cut in.

"You know Mavis, as bright and breezy and super-efficient as ever."

"Any work waiting for us when we get back, boss?" Winston asked.

"Not yet."

"Geez, we'd better make sure we make a mint out of this one then, hadn't we?"

"A fortune for Mr. Fortune," Sally joked.

"And why not? Why not indeed?" asked Winston.

"There'll be no fortunes for anyone if we don't get a good night's sleep tonight," Cutler intoned. "I want everyone early to bed after dinner, and we'll be up at six in the morning. As soon as we can, I want us to start laying out the first search grid."

"No problem, boss," Winston said.

"What about the historian?" Sally asked.

"That was one of the other phone calls I made. I spoke to Capshaw's secretary and she said Mr. Graves should be arriving sometime tomorrow. She couldn't, or wouldn't say exactly when, so if he turns up after we've gone in the morning, he'll just have to wait until we get back, or come looking for us."

"You don't like her at all do you, boss?" Winston asked.

Since taking on this job, Cutler had made no secret of his dislike for Capshaw's snobby secretary. "No, Winston, I don't. She's a self-important, over-made-up little cow, if you want my true opinion."

"Well, Capshaw must see something in her," Sally pointed out.

"Must be a great secretary," Winston suggested.

"Yeah, and the rest. I think she does a bit more than just typing and taking calls," Cutler sneered, his meaning clear.

"Joe Cutler! You're nothing but a sexist, overbearing, male chauvinist pig," Sally snarled. "Just because she looks good, you think she can't be good at her job, and that Capshaw only keeps her there as window dressing, or to keep him company between the sheets."

"You said it, Sally, not me," Cutler grinned.

"Really! You men can be so bloody irritatingly predictable sometimes!" she snapped.

"Hey, Sally girl, calm down," Winston urged. "The boss told us what she was like when he met the great Mr. Capshaw. I don't think I'd like that lady too much either if I met her, and that ain't got nothing to do with how she looks. Heavens sake, girl, I haven't even seen her and I'm developing a distaste for the woman."

Cutler cut the friendly banter short.

"I'm going for a shower. I'll see you two for dinner in an hour. We'll meet in the bar, okay?"

The others nodded in agreement and all three were soon en-sconced in their own rooms in the Rowan Tree. Sally took the time to languish for a while in a hot bath surrounded by about a twelve inch covering of luxurious bubbles. After washing and drying her hair, she changed into a simple white blouse and grey skirt and sat reading a trashy romantic novel for half an hour before making her way downstairs to join the others in Mrs. Cleveley's small, but well-stocked, bar for a pre-dinner drink.

"Hey man, what do you know? Mrs. Corbett's little girl, she got legs!" exclaimed Winston when he caught sight of Sally entering the bar in her evening attire.

"Ha, bloody ha," Sally sneered. "I do have other things to wear apart from my working gear, you know."

"You look real good, girl, real good," Winston said. "Hey, boss? What d'you think about our little Sally, eh? She looks real good, don't you think?"

Cutler raised his head from the newspaper he'd been studying as he sat at the bar and nodded in agreement with Fortune, then hurriedly lowered his gaze back to the page he'd been reading.

Sally knew Joe felt a slight embarrassment whenever Fortune in-dulged in his little performances with her, and she didn't press him for a verbal answer to Winston's query.

"I see you got me one in advance," she said instead reaching out to take the glass sitting at Cutler's side.

"Hope I got you the right thing," Cutler said as she took a sip of the gin and tonic.

"Mmm, just the thing, thanks. Anything more to report from the office?"

"No, I didn't bother to call Mavis again. There was nothing hap-pening earlier, so I didn't see the point. I'll check in with her tomor-row as usual, see if there's anything new on the books."

"Hey, man. Can we forget about work?" asked Winston, with a large grin on his face. "Now that she's finally arrived, let's eat! I'm starving!"

That was the last they spoke of the job until they'd finished their meal that evening. Not wanting to risk any upset stomachs the following day they'd all stuck to a simple meal of roast chicken with fresh vegetables and new potatoes. Mrs. Cleveley had done them proud. The food was superb and they were soon back in the little bar once again being served drinks by the landlady's daughter, Claire.

"So, tomorrow we start in earnest, eh, boss?" Winston said.

"Yes. The sooner we get underway, the sooner we stand a chance of making you that fortune, Mr. Fortune," Cutler replied, his own inhibitions slightly relaxed by the amount of wine he'd consumed at the dinner table.

"So what's with the historian, boss? Tell us again why we need Mr. Fuddy Duddy," Sally interjected, completely changing the direction of the conversation.

"I've told you," said Cutler, "We might have the document and the map and the book, but we need help in pinpointing exact locations as described in the old papers. The whole topography of the land has changed over the past thousand years; what was an island then could be a hill now, or a river might now be a gorge, or a former field could be buried under a modern housing estate. Graves will help us translate the old markings and texts into something approaching a modern layout of the old representations. That way, we won't be shooting totally blind. At least, that's Capshaw's theory."

"So why we startin' tomorrow, without the big, bad history teacher to guide us, then?" asked Fortune, lisping into his native accent once again.

"Simple," said Cutler. "We lay out a starting grid in the general direction indicated by what we know from the document, and start eliminating the areas we can easily identify. Even Graves can't be too specific, according to Capshaw. There've been too many changes in the land since the sword was originally buried, to pinpoint a location with certainty, so we'll 'cut' the land into parcels and work outwards from the town. Graves will guide us as best he can when he gets here, but the real work is still down to us."

"Sounds to me like having him here will be next to useless," Sally offered. and then concluded, "If he can't tell us where the sword is, and doesn't have a clue where we should be looking, then I don't see the point of his being here. I know it sounds negative, but apart from being able to read Old English, he doesn't sound as if he's going to be a lot of help on a dig in a wet and muddy field."

Cutler sipped his drink. "Look, Sally, Capshaw is paying Graves, the same way he's paying us. If he thinks he can help us, that's up to him. He should at least be better at deciphering the old text than any of us would be, and he should be able to point us in the right direction. As for starting without him tomorrow, at least it'll give us the chance to field-test the equipment and eliminate part of the search area."

"What about the authorities, the local council, the countryside commission, or whoever toes we'll be treading on by carrying out this search? Has Capshaw got them in his pocket as well?"

"Probably, Sally, I don't know. He told me that we wouldn't have any problems with the local authorities. As far as they're concerned we're representing Capshaw Enterprises searching for early Christian artefacts in the hope of unearthing physical evidence to support the theory that Joseph of Arimathaea visited Glastonbury."

"And they believe that old chestnut of a story?"

"Whether they do or they don't we just get on with our jobs, and leave the behind the scenes politicking to Capshaw. If he says there'll be no local interference then we have to believe him. He's the money man after all."

"Bet he's bald," said Winston suddenly.

"Who?" asked Sally.

"Graves. Bet he's old, bald and walks with a stick."

"That's a sweeping conjecture, Winston," said Cutler. "Just because he's a historian doesn't mean he has to be old."

"Or bald," said Sally.

"Anyway, we'll see tomorrow with a bit of luck," said Cutler, trying to bring the conversation to a close. "I think it's time we all thought about hitting the sack. Like I said, I want us to get an early start tomorrow."

The others concurred with Cutler's suggestion and the three friends made their way up to their respective rooms in a spirit of wine induced conviviality. Within twenty minutes all three were tucked in their respective beds, the prospect of a hard day's work the next day conspiring with the effects of the wine to send them all into a deep and pleasant sleep.

As the moon traversed the night sky over Glastonbury, Cutler dreamed of knights and damsels and the steely glint of a wondrous sword. In his mind as he slept he already visualized the prize they were about to launch their search for. In the dream, unfortunately, just as he reached out to take the sword from the unknown hand that offered it to him Excalibur exploded into a myriad of fragments, shards of shining steel flying off in all directions as the mighty sword disintegrated before his eyes. It was a dream Joe Cutler was to remember much later, but for now he slept on, and no other dreams appeared to disturb his sleep that night. If they did they quickly became nothing more than forgotten memories.

Chapter 6

Meare Manor Guest House is situated on St. Mary's Road, some three miles from the centre of Glastonbury in the pretty village of Meare, and was once the summer residence of the abbots of Glastonbury Abbey. Rebuilt in 1802, and more recently fully renovated, it afforded a finer touch of luxury than Mrs. Cleveley's welcoming little Rowan Tree. With complimentary port and sherry included in the room package Graves felt it added a touch of welcome refinement to his task, and after all, he considered himself to be a refined man.

Walter Graves checked in to the Manor early on Thursday afternoon, long after Cutler and his team had left the Rowan Tree to begin their first day's 'real' work on the search for Excalibur. He could have been extravagant and booked one of the Manor's rooms with four-poster bed, but decided instead on a regular double bedded room. It would suit his purposes adequately, he didn't intend on spending too much time in the room anyway. Contrary to Winston Fortune's assessment of his appearance Graves was neither old nor bald, and certainly didn't need a stick to assist in walking. In fact, anyone casting more than a cursory glance at the man who now sat relaxing in his room at the Manor would have probably placed him in his mid-forties (he was fifty-three), and might have been forgiven for thinking him to be a retired professional soldier (which he was), rather than a so-called stuffy old historian. Graves stood six feet two with a full head of dark wavy hair, and a muscular and tanned body that belied his years. His interest in things historical and his subsequent acquisition of his academic credentials had followed his service in the Falklands War, after which he'd resigned his commission and followed his heart rather than his mind when it came to his future career choice.

Over the years things had changed a little for Walter Graves and he now found himself doing a certain amount of free lance work in addition to his normal duties as a part-time tutor in history at one of the country's lesser known seats of learning. He didn't like Malcolm Capshaw and under normal circumstances he wouldn't have dreamed of working for the man, but Capshaw knew a little too much about certain aspects of Graves's past, and the ruthless businessman hadn't been afraid to use a few threats in order to coerce Graves into going along with his plans for the Glastonbury job. Having worked for the man once before, Graves knew better than to try to turn Capshaw down. As he rose from his chair and pushed his emptied suitcase under the bed and out of sight, Graves decided to do his job and no more, then get the hell out of Glastonbury and as far away from Malcolm Capshaw as he could, hoping that this would be the last time he'd be forced to work for the man.

Capshaw had given him precise instructions as to the nature of his responsibilities once he arrived in the town, and Graves now opened the briefcase he'd left lying on his bed. He removed his own copies of the document and the map supplied by Capshaw, as well as two volumes of historical texts he brought from his own personal library to help with the task. There was also a note book, bound in worn thin red leather, with dog-eared pages and a well crushed spine. Cutler and the others would have been surprised to know that the notebook dated from a mere sixty five years ago, and contained no reference whatsoever to Excalibur, King Arthur or the history of Glastonbury. It was, however, vital to Graves as far as his part of the search was concerned. Finally, he removed from his briefcase the one object that would have caused Cutler, Fortune and Corbett to freak out and probably have felicitated their early departure from Glastonbury, money or no money. The Ruger P89TH Two-Tone 9mm semi-automatic pistol with its comfortable rubber handgrip may not have been the world's most powerful handgun, but it suited Graves admirably and had never yet let him down. He ran his fingers over the cold steel of its barrel, and then turned the gun over in his hands with the practised movement of a professional. After checking that the magazine was full he replaced it with a satisfying clunk as it clicked into place. Making sure the safety catch was on Walter Graves placed the gun in the specially reinforced and adapted inside pocket of his jacket. He stood and checked in the mirror to ensure that there was no tell-tale bulge, and two minutes later he was out of the room, leaving his key at reception, and getting into his black BMW 525 which sat gleaming where he'd left it in the Manor's car park on his arrival. A quick drive and he was in Glastonbury. He found a car park in the centre of town where he left the BMW and then made his way on foot to the Rowan Tree using a local tourist map as a guide.

As he made his way through the throng of early morning shoppers and tourists along the streets of the old town, Graves took time to look around him and study the beauty and workmanship that made many of Glastonbury's buildings a joy to behold. His learned eye would flit from side to side, taking in the panoply of historic (and less than historic) buildings that decorated the highways and byways of the ancient town.

The sun was shining, the grey wet weather of the previous three days had given way to a warm spring day, and Graves felt the sun's warmth upon his back as he walked. His mind switched off from the sounds of the passing traffic; he heard the sound of a blackbird as it sent its serenade bursting forth from its perch on the guttering of a bookstore. He heard the bird but managed to filter out all other sounds as he took pleasure from the sound of nature and shut out the noise and hustle of the street. Graves was good at that, driving unwanted sounds and intrusions into another dimension, leaving his mind clear to focus on the good things in his life. Even in the midst of the battles on the Falklands all those years ago his mind had managed to block the sounds of Argentine bullets as they whizzed above his head, Graves hearing only the sound of cormorants as they wheeled above the battle, screaming their displeasure at the man-made cacophony below.

Ten minutes after parking the car he found himself looking up at the small guest house currently serving as temporary home to the staff of Strata Surveys. Though not quite exhibiting the ambience or 'Olde Worlde' charm of Meare Manor, he found it clean and welcoming, the tiny reception area quiet and airy. As he approached the desk he was greeted with a polite and cheery 'Good morning, sir. Can I help you?"

Mrs. Cleveley had popped up like a glove puppet from behind the desk.

"Sorry," she said, slightly breathlessly, "I was just looking for something, what can I do for you, sir?"

"I'm looking for a Mr. Joseph Cutler and his associates from Strata Survey Systems."

"Oh, I'm sorry. They left very early this morning, barely had time for breakfast. Mr. Cutler said they'd be back sometime around five."

Graves checked his watch. It was 3.50 p.m. Not too long to wait and he could do with a drink.

"Do you have a bar here Mrs…er?

"It's Mrs. Cleveley, sir, Annette Cleveley. Yes we do have a bar, but I'm afraid it doesn't open until we start serving evening meals at five. There's a good pub on the corner if you turn left out of the door, though. They're open all day."

"Thank you, Mrs. Cleveley," said Graves, smiling his most charming smile. "I'll take a little walk and return after five. Perhaps you could tell Mr. Cutler I've been asking for him if he returns before I do."

"Certainly, sir, who shall I tell him was asking for him?"

"Oh yes, of course, I'm sorry, I forgot. My name is Graves, Walter Graves. He's expecting me."

"Are you part of his exciting scheme then Mr. Graves?"

"Scheme?"

"Yes, you know, looking for things to do with that Joseph of Arimathaea from the Bible."

"Oh yes, Mrs. Cleveley, I'm a part of that alright. I'm just here in an advisory capacity though. I'm a historian."

"A historian? Well, I never!" she exclaimed. "I don't think I've ever met a historian before. That must be very interesting, Mr. Graves."

"I assure you it is, Mrs. Cleveley, though it can also be quite boring at times as I'm sure my students would be only willing to testify to."

"Oh, I'm sure that's not so at all," said Mrs. Cleveley, already enthralled by the academic air that seemed to ooze from every pore of her visitor.

"Anyway, I'll be back before too long," said Graves as he turned to leave.

Mrs. Cleveley gave him her widest smile and said a cheery, "See you soon then, sir," as Graves made his way through the door, "and I'll be sure to tell Mr. Cutler you've been looking for him."

"Thank you," called Graves, already on the second step that led back onto the street. An hour of peace and a couple of whiskies would do him no harm as he waited for Cutler and his minions, he thought as he made his way to the local hostelry recommended by Mrs. Cleveley. There'd be plenty of time to catch up with Cutler.

As he sat sipping at a fine malt whisky a few minutes later, he took time to pull a piece of paper from the opposite inside jacket pocket to the one that held the Ruger. Stapled together was a three page résumé on the life and times of Joseph Albert Cutler. It was all there from birth to the current day, his parents' names, his father's job at the old ironworks and his premature death from lung cancer at the age of just forty five, and his mother's death three years ago. Cutler's college education and professional qualifications were listed in detail, as were his various romances over the last ten years. As for his business dealings, they took up most of the third A4 page, and it was clear that the man was good at what he did. There was a short section on the credentials of Fortune and Corbett and Graves could see why Capshaw had chosen Strata for the job. Even before he'd met the man he found himself quite liking Joe Cutler, he hoped it would stay like that and that he wouldn't be called upon to take drastic action in the pursuit of his end of Capshaw's quest.

As the second whisky disappeared warmingly down his throat Walter Graves rose from his table, patted the Ruger through the fabric of his jacket in a reflex gesture to be sure it was safely tucked away, left the pub, and made his way slowly back to the Rowan Tree. It was only just after five and he hoped to catch Cutler before he disappeared to his room for a bath or shower. He wanted to see the man, take stock of him after a hard day in the field, rather than when he was refreshed and alert. In short, Walter Graves wanted to get a measure of the man at the lower end of his physical spectrum. That was always the best way to judge a potential adversary!

Chapter 7

A hubbub of laughter announced the return of Cutler and the others as they bounced through the door of The Rowan Tree. They had shared a long day setting up and testing the ground penetrating radar system. After ensuring it was working as it should they had made a tentative start on the job. Cutler placed a yellow metal box on a tripod in the centre of the designated search area, which was little more than an area of marshy wasteland five miles from town. The box contained a lens, through which Cutler scanned the area, guiding Corbett who was holding a red and white survey rod with a knob on top. When he was satisfied with the various positions he spoke to Sally through a microphone attached behind his ear, and instructed her to insert a series of marking pins in the ground that would serve as reference points. These would serve as control points, and Winston Fortune busied himself attaching long lines of string between the poles, gradually marking out a grid they would follow when the survey began. By walking along the grids with the radar in hand, they could survey and map out the whole of the search area in a few hours.

Accurate to about two thousandths of an inch, the GPR system enabled the search team to identify 'anomalies' in the ground terrain. For example, if a tree had stood for hundreds of years and then been uprooted at some time in the past, and the hole where it had stood filled in, the radar would enable a trained operator to say with a high level of confidence that a tree had once stood there. Likewise, if a body had been buried in the ground, the shape of the grave, whatever its depth would show up on the radar, and Cutler had more than once used this part of the GPR's arsenal to help the police in searching for murder victims. In this case, according to Capshaw's document, they were searching for a wooden box, centuries old, that may or may not have degraded beneath the ground, which contained the long lost sword Excalibur. Despite their earlier scepticism all three of the Strata Survey people were now focused upon the job on hand and would apply the highest levels of their professional skills to follow the clues that may or may not lead them to their goal.

Having drawn a blank, but satisfying themselves that everything was working as it should, Cutler, Corbett and Fortune had packed up their equipment for the day and made their way back to Mrs. Cleveley's guest house. On the drive back to town Winston had been amusing himself and the others by attempting to compose a rap based on the Lady in the Lake legend. It was his hilarious attempts at this composition that was the source of the mirth that accompanied their arrival back at the Rowan Tree.

Annette Cleveley greeted them with her usual air of bonhomie as they burst through the front door of the Rowan Tree, and informed Cutler that they had a visitor, a Mr. Graves waiting for them in the bar. Cutler and the others stopped giggling and looked at each other as she announced the news of Graves' arrival.

"At last," said Winston Fortune.

"About time," Sally echoed.

"Well then, let's see if your advance appraisal of Mr. Graves was on the mark Winston," said Cutler as they made their way to the small bar where they found the historian seated at a table in the far corner of the room.

"Wrong," whispered Sally to Winston Fortune as they took in Graves's appearance.

"Very wrong I admit," replied Winston grinning from ear to ear. "He's got hair, no stick, and he's nowhere near as old as I thought."

"Just goes to prove that you don't have to be an old fossil in order to be an expert on them," said Cutler quietly as they approached Walter Graves.

Graves, his head buried in a book on the history of Glastonbury, sensed rather than saw their approach, and quickly closed the book. He looked up once they neared and spoke in that most charming voice of his: "Mr. Cutler and associates I presume?"

Cutler nodded, and quickly introduced the others to Graves, who rose to his feet and shook hands with Cutler and Fortune, then in a gesture worthy of one of the Knights of the Round Table themselves, he reached across, took Sally Corbett's right hand in his own, bowed towards her, and kissed the back of the hand very gently before gesturing to them all to sit and join him. Sally was impressed with his old-world courtesy, and smiled at Graves as she took her seat.

"I'm sorry I wasn't able to join you sooner," said Graves, looking directly at Joe Cutler. "I hope Mr. Capshaw explained the reason for my tardiness in arriving in Glastonbury."

"Oh yes, he explained it quite adequately," said Cutler. "We weren't able to do much until today anyway. The weather's been against us I'm afraid."

"And how did your day go?" asked the historian.

It was Winston Fortune who cut in with the answer to Graves's question.

"Well, we know that all our equipment is working at its optimum capacity, and we know that the ground is soft though not too boggy despite the rain, but as for the search itself, we found zip, nada, nothing, man, know what I mean?"

"Not that we expected to find anything straight away, of course," said Cutler. "I just selected a parcel of land that I believed to be in the general vicinity of the search area as best as I could decipher from Capshaw's map. We could have been miles off track in reality, but I thought it best to start somewhere. Now that you're here, Mr. Graves, perhaps you'll be able to guide us a little more accurately."

"Exactly, Mr. Cutler. I must say that I admire your endeavour and I know that you must be keen to make progress as soon as possible. As I said, I apologise for not being here sooner, but now that I am here, we should start the work in earnest."

"You're not quite what we expected," said Sally suddenly, still smiling at Graves as she spoke.

"Ah, Miss Corbett, but then who is always as expected? I think perhaps you were expecting some old fossilized semi-geriatric with a beard and leather reinforcements on the elbows of an old tweed jacket, and thick spectacles dangling from a chain around his neck. Am I right?"

Sally blushed.

"I'm sorry, I didn't mean..."

"Please, don't apologise, Miss Corbett. I'm quite often a surprise to those I work with for the first time. I assure you, however, that my credentials are more than satisfactory for the job on hand. I am a bona fide professor of history, though I came late to the profession. I was a professional army officer you see until I gave up the military way of life to follow my one true calling. I'd been a history buff since I was a child and my father took me to The British Museum one day. I begged and begged of him to take me again, and I suppose I must have visited the museum at least a hundred times before I was fifteen years old. I was totally enthralled by the past, but for some reason my life took a different path after leaving school and my first love was left on the back burner until I'd lived out my youthful years and indulged in more warlike pursuits. After the Falklands, though, I decided to go to university, get my degree, and the rest, as they say, is history."

Graves laughed at his own words, as did the others. He'd managed to put them at ease in the space of a few minutes. He knew that his short potted history of his life would do the trick, it usually did, and he smiled again as he addressed Joe Cutler.

"Perhaps you'll allow me to join you all for a meal this evening, Mr Cutler, after you've all showered and changed, of course. We can maybe discuss our plan of action for the search over a good meal and a couple of drinks?"

"We'd be delighted," said Cutler. "We can all get to know each other a bit better. After all, we'll be working closely together for the next couple of weeks, won't we?"

"That's settled then." Graves clapped his hands together much in the way as they would have expected a history professor to do. "I'll let you go now, and meet you here in an hour if that's alright. I've some calls I have to make and I'm quite comfortable sitting here enjoying a good whisky."

Graves reached into his pocket and took out a mobile phone which he sort of waved at the others, as if to show them he really did have some calls to make.

"Well, we'll see you soon then," said Cutler as he rose and led the others towards the door way.

"I shall look forward to it, Mr. Cutler," smiled Gravesas they left.

As the three of them made their way to their respective rooms to wash off the grime of the day, Graves keyed a number into his phone, sat back in his chair with his whisky in one hand and, hearing a voice reply at the other end of the line, he spoke quietly and professionally to the man who answered.

"Hello, that you, sir? It's Walter Graves here. I've arrived in Glastonbury."

He listened as the other man spoke.

"Don't worry; I know what I'm doing. I'll get the job done, don't you worry about that, and no, sir, they don't suspect a thing."

Capshaw said something at the other end of the line and Graves simply replied with a "Yes, sir," before hanging up and relaxing once again, taking another sip of his whisky. He made a couple of other calls to no-one of particular connection to the job in hand, his broker, his bookmaker, and a friend at the college he taught at, and then spent the rest of his time waiting for the others by sitting and admiring Mrs. Cleveley's daughter Claire as she worked behind the bar. As attractive as Claire was, however, Graves wouldn't allow himself to entertain any thoughts in that direction, not while he had a job to do. He couldn't help thinking though, as Claire moved around the room clearing empty glasses from a few of the tables in her white blouse and short black skirt, that the landlady's daughter had a dammed fine pair of legs.

Cutler and the others arrived exactly an hour after they'd left the bar, and Graves turned his thoughts away from Claire and back to his professional responsibilities. He smiled and rose as they entered the bar. He reached out his hand once again, greeting the Strata Survey team as if they were old and valued friends. Sally even took his arm as they walked the short distance to Mrs. Cleveley's dining room, and the four of them enjoyed a splendid roast beef dinner before returning once again to the bar, where the evening's real work took over and the conversation turned to things ancient and mysterious.

Chapter 8

By the time Graves left them it was almost eleven p.m. and by then their minds were alive with the tales he'd told them of those by-gone days that many believed to be nothing more than myth. They'd been enthralled and intrigued by the names of some of the Knights of the Round Table; names like Sir Aglovale, son of King Pellinore of Listinoise, Sir Bors, King of Ganne (Gaul), and Sir Dagonet, the court jester. Graves had been totally enthused by his rendering of his stories, which included tales of Sir Palamedes the Saracen and Sir Ywain the Bastard. Sally had found some of the names quite amusing, particularly the last one, though there were other, less fantastically named Knights such as Sir Daniel, Sir Lionel and Sir Gareth.

Graves had told them of Avalon, Camelot, Viviane the Lady of the Lake and Tintagel, Arthur's birthplace, and had related all he said to them in terms of the words being fact as opposed to legend or fiction. If what he'd told them was true, (and of course it had to be if they were to succeed in their search), then a great part of English history had been submerged into the dark mists of time, buried in Dark Ages myth and legend. The big question was why? Even Graves hadn't ventured a speculation on that one, though he did have a theory that he'd told them he might share with them as their work progressed.

Cutler and Graves had agreed that the four of them would meet at Meare Manor the following morning at eight. The manor was on the way to the first search area pinpointed by Graves as being of possible interest to them. He'd explained that the map provided by Capshaw had been drawn up over a thousand years ago, and as they all knew, the topography of the land had altered appreciably since then. Not only that, but the scale of the map was in some doubt, and some of the directions and positions of markers on the paper were not as he had expected them to be. In short, the map itself was something of a puzzle, a conundrum, with indistinct and possible misleading entries contained within it, perhaps to prevent an 'unauthorised' person from discovering its secrets. He thought that only those with special knowledge and authority in Arthur's day would have been able to decipher the map without any trouble, and he made it clear to Cutler that though he was an authority on the subject, even he would have difficulty directing them to a precise burial location.

"That's precisely why Mr. Capshaw enlisted the services of your company, Mr. Cutler," Graves had informed him. "If it was as easy as ABC he could have simply sent me along with a team of diggers and we could have gone straight to Excalibur's burial place and dug it up. No, we need you and your ground penetrating radar system. I'll do my best to guide you to every possible location and the rest will be up to you. I have to try and re-orientate the map into today's geographical topography, which is not as easy as it sounds, I assure you, as there have been so many changes over the years."

"Hang on a minute," Sally had butted in. "What you're saying is that it's possible that Excalibur is buried somewhere beneath a twentieth century housing or industrial development, and if that's the case we'll never find it below tons of reinforced concrete or an asphalt road."

"That is indeed a possibility, though a remote one I assure you, Miss Corbett. From my study of the map I'm reasonably certain that the sword is buried well away from today's built up or paved areas. I have every reason to believe that Excalibur is located well outside the boundaries of modern-day Glastonbury. Had I thought differently I would have told Capshaw that there was high chance of failure and it would have been unlikely that he would have financed the search on that premise."

"So we were wasting our time with today's search?" asked Winston.

"Not at all, Mr. Fortune," Graves replied. "Mr. Cutler and your good selves made an informed deduction based on your own reading of the document and the map, and you may well have stumbled upon Excalibur on your first try. At least you know that everything is working correctly, and we can also discount that locale from our search area, so the process of elimination has begun. Don't think for one minute that you've wasted your time, I assure you that both Mr. Capshaw and I appreciate the start you've made even if you were barking up the wrong tree, so to speak."

The evening had broken up soon afterwards and after Graves had departed Joe Cutler and the others sat in the bar for a while discussing their new temporary associate.

"Well, he certainly seems to know what he's talking about," said Sally Corbett, "and he fervently believes in the Arthurian stuff by all accounts."

"I'm not sure I trust him, man," Winston Fortune replied, a deep frown engraved on his brow. "Somethin' about the man just doesn't sit right with me."

"I'm with Winston I'm afraid, Sally," Joe continued the conversation. "He may know his stuff, and I don't doubt his credentials, they're too easy to check if we wanted to, but there's something about him as Winston says. I can't put my finger on it, but it seems as though Capshaw has taken Mr. Walter Graves far deeper into his confidence than he has me, and that's a little worrying. He seems too close to the man for my liking."

"But what's to be suspicious about a historian?" asked Sally. "Surely you can't think he's up to no good?"

"I'm not sure what he's up to, Sally, but I just think we should keep a close eye on Mr. Graves."

"I agree with the boss man, Sally girl," said Winston. "Can't quite fathom it, but he smells of something other than college libraries and old parchment."

"I think you're both being positively absurd," said Sally as she got up to leave the bar. "He's a perfectly respectable and likeable man, and I think you're being very disrespectful towards him. After all, he's here to help us find the sword. What can possibly be wrong with that?"

"Nothing, Sally. Nothing at all," Joe Cutler replied. "It's what else he might be here for that worries me."

"Oh, don't be silly," she said as she walked towards the door. "I'm going to bed. I'll see you two at breakfast."

"Goodnight, Sally," said Cutler, and Winston echoed his words as Sally disappeared from view.

After she'd gone Winston turned to Cutler and said, "You really think there's something fishy about him then, boss?"

"I'm not sure, Winston. Maybe it's just the way he kept gawping at Sally's cleavage, or staring at Claire's legs whenever she came out from behind the bar. I just think he's an old lecher, and I don't think I trust him one little bit. I don't think he's quite as warm and genuine as he makes out. When I looked into his eyes I felt as if there was something a bit cold and unnatural about Mr. Walter Graves."

"What you expect, man, with a name like that?"

"Oh no, Winston," said Joe Cutler, in his parting shot for the night. "Whatever is wrong with our Mr. Graves, it goes far deeper than that, far deeper than I'd care to imagine."

"Now you're scaring me, boss man."

"Sorry. I'm probably just being paranoid. Just go get some sleep, we'll feel better in the morning, and start afresh."

They parted on that point, going to their rooms, where both Cutler and Fortune soon fell asleep. Cutler slept well as usual, though for Winston it was a night beset by dreams, dreams of things he'd rather not talk about when he rose to meet the dawn the following day.

Chapter 9

Malcolm Capshaw replaced the phone on its cradle, reached out and switched off the lamp beside the bed and plunged the room into darkness. As he settled back into a comfortable position the warm and semi-slumbering figure beside him stirred into wakefulness.

"Is everything okay?" asked a sleepy Charlotte Raeburn.

"Mmm," Capshaw relied. "That was Graves. He's spent the evening with Cutler and his people. They seem to be well-hooked on his historical scenario and let's face it, why should they doubt him? He's got all the papers and documents, the map, and he is a history professor after all. He thinks they're well primed for the task ahead. They should carry out the search for Excalibur in good faith. They won't know a thing until it's too late. He's a good man is Walter Graves. I couldn't have picked a better man for the job."

As a personal secretary Charlotte Raeburn was about as compliant as Capshaw could wish for. Despite her cold and unfeeling exterior, she was efficient, totally reliable, and able to keep her mouth shut. As such, he was able to take her into his confidence knowing that Charlotte would assist his plans in any way she could in order for her to continue to be paid the lucrative salary with which he rewarded her. There was also of course the small matter of keeping his bed warm at night, and providing him with the use of her body whenever the mood took him.

Capshaw in turn saw nothing wrong in using Charlotte's body for his personal sexual gratification. He paid her enough, after all. She was good at her job, yes, but then so were a hundred others out there. He had only to call any reputable secretarial agency and for the money he was offering he could take his pick of the best secretarial staff in the country. The thing he liked about Charlotte, if Malcolm Capshaw could be said to like anything, was her unfailing loyalty and willingness to 'turn a blind eye' to some of his more nefarious business dealings. Not only that, but she was more than willing to assist him in return for him providing her with a lifestyle she could otherwise have only imagined.

From Charlotte's point of view, she knew that he probably thought of her as little more than his private whore, which she knew herself to be, but at least Capshaw's sexual demands weren't excessively demanding so far, and the whole thing was usually over quickly. Charlotte had had three lovers in her life before working for Capshaw, and two of them had also been her employers at the time, and she saw nothing wrong with providing such 'personal' services for her boss as long as the financial rewards were adequate.

She'd been with him long enough by now to know almost every aspect of Capshaw's business empire inside out. All of his dealings, both legitimate and not quite so legitimate were recorded in her almost computer-like analytical brain, and Charlotte had managed to make herself almost indispensable to the man who now lay beside her. She was enough of a realist, however, to know that if ever the time came when Malcolm Capshaw felt the need to dispense with her services, he would be as ruthless with her as with any of those unfortunate business associates who had had the misfortune to fall foul of the millionaire business man in the past. She hadn't known of the shady side to Malcolm Capshaw when she'd first taken the job as his secretary. She was now far too deeply involved with his empirical aspirations and dealings to be able to take the risk of baling out, not that she wanted to at this time. She just hoped that if ever the time did come when Capshaw wanted to terminate her employment her payoff would be of the financial rather than the painful kind.

It was Charlotte who had found and suggested Strata Survey Systems as being the ideal choice for the current task. A small but highly regarded company, they advertised the fact that they used the latest state-of-the art ground penetrating radar in their work, and that client confidentiality was top priority. She'd checked out the credentials of Joe Cutler and those who worked alongside him. He'd inherited a sizable legacy on the death of his mother, and had left his previous employment with a large multi-national corporation specialising in international contract work to set up his own business. They'd even done work for various police forces in the short time the company had been in existence, so no-one would suspect them of being involved in anything other than a highly legitimate and worthwhile historical search project when the time came for them to begin digging around in the Glastonbury countryside. Cutler had done well for himself and had recruited good people to work with him. She'd also found Marchant, the private detective who'd carried out an in-depth investigation into Cutler's past. If it were ever needed, Capshaw was armed with a full and comprehensive dossier on Joseph Cutler that ran from his childhood to the present day.

Blackmail was only one of many avenues that Malcolm Capshaw was prepared to resort to if he felt it would help him achieve his goals in life. After all, that was precisely the way he'd first managed to bring Walter Graves on board for a job that had entailed a little more than the usual expertise exhibited by a history professor. When a rival entrepreneur had threatened to beat Capshaw to the site of a hidden hoard of Nazi gold secreted beneath the dark and gloomy waters of a Norwegian fjord, Capshaw had enlisted the help of Graves in misdirecting the rival team's expedition while his own divers raised the horde from its actual resting place. When Graves had at first shown a degree of reluctance to become involved with the venture Capshaw had informed Graves that he was in possession of certain documents relating to the unauthorised shooting of two Argentinean prisoners of war during the Falklands campaign some years previously for which Graves had been ultimately responsible, though no charges had been brought at the time. Capshaw was sure that the authorities would be interested in Graves' secret past, as would his current employers. Faced with the threat of exposure of the sorry episode that had convinced Graves to leave the army and enter a more peaceful world of employment, he had reluctantly accepted Capshaw's commission and travelled to Norway as instructed and succeeded in delaying Capshaw's rivals long enough for his employer's people to find the gold and have it flown back to England, where it was soon secretly 'fenced' through various international dealers and the proceeds added to Capshaw's personal fortune.

Unfortunately, the man who had first stumbled upon Graves's past whilst carrying out a background check on him for Capshaw, a private investigator by the name of Silas Bowling, somehow got wind of the fact that Capshaw had come into a large sum of money that had something to do with Graves' involvement with the millionaire businessman. Foolishly, Bowling had tried to extort a larger fee from Capshaw as a means of buying his silence in the affair and Capshaw had made sure that Graves would be forever tied to him by sending the former army officer to ensure the detective's permanent silence. Much to his own disgust, Graves had been compelled to bring his Ruger 9mm out of retirement, and Silas Bowling was later recorded at an inquest as having been killed by 'person or persons unknown' as he walked from his office to his car one dark and stormy night.

That was why it had been important for Charlotte to find a new and reliable private investigator, one who wouldn't ask too many questions, and who would do the job he was paid for without coming back for more. Marchant had fit the bill perfectly, and if there were a next time Capshaw knew that he would be a reliable and worthy occasional employee.

Capshaw turned towards Charlotte Raeburn in the dark. He'd made love to her earlier that evening, and Charlotte fully expected that now he'd received the telephone call from Graves, he would be ready to drape his arm over her as usual and fall asleep until the morning. Tonight was different, however. His arm didn't drape across her, instead his hand came to rest on her breast, and Charlotte knew that Capshaw needed her again. Though unusual, it wasn't unheard of for him to require the use of her body twice in one night. Obviously, the thought that his latest scheme was officially underway had served to excite something in her boss, and Charlotte knew there would be no putting him off, not if she wanted to keep her job at any rate.

As he squeezed her right nipple enough to make her wince with the sharp pain he induced in her breast Charlotte murmured in a mock display of arousal. She'd rather go to sleep, but then she felt his hand straying down towards her belly and beyond, to that warm and tender region between her legs, and she reached out and felt him growing harder by the second. Knowing that she had no choice and wanting to get things over with as soon as she could, Charlotte Raeburn rolled dutifully onto her back, opened her legs, and as the heavy figure of Malcolm Capshaw lowered himself onto and into her and began an animalistic grunting and thrusting, she could do no more than lie back and think of the big fat pay cheque that would be deposited in her bank account the very next day.

Chapter 10

After returning to his room at Meare Manor and making his call to
Capshaw, Walter Graves placed the Ruger back in his case, locked
it securely for the night and poured himself a large brandy from the
bottle he always carried with him on his travels. After stripping to
his undershorts and removing a pile of papers from his briefcase he
climbed into bed and placed the brandy glass next to the bottle on
the bedside cabinet. Before going to sleep that night he wanted to
run through everything once again. He needed to make sure that the
fabric of truth, half-truth and downright lies that he and Capshaw
had woven together would hold up to the closest scrutiny by Cutler
and his people. Though he doubted that Cutler had the intelligence
to see through the subterfuge he wanted to be certain that there
was no chance of any of the Strata Survey people suspecting their
search for Excalibur was anything but genuine.

He'd checked and verified everything a number of times before
arriving in Glastonbury, but Graves was a meticulous and methodical man. It never hurt to check again! The map and the historical
document were beyond Cutler's range of doubt, of course. Produced
at a great expense for Capshaw by Giovanni Santorini, one of the
best forgers of historical artefacts known to the underworld, they

would pass inspection by any but the most learned of scholars, and fool many. The rest of the story had been put together so expertly that Graves himself could almost believe in the authenticity of the task that had brought Cutler and his people to the ancient town. After reading through the mass of papers he'd assembled to add credence to this latest episode of misdirection and misinformation Walter Graves was satisfied that every 't' had been crossed and every 'I' dotted. Unless Joe Cutler were a better historian than Graves himself was, there was no way that the survey master was going to be able to decode the fact that their search was a blind, a feint designed to cover up the real reason for their presence. Knowing that to be an unlikely occurrence, Graves was content to place his papers back in the briefcase and settle down for the night.

As he lay in his bed waiting for sleep to come he reflected for a moment on the double deception he and Capshaw had finally decided upon. In order that Cutler and his team kept quiet about what they thought to be the real reason for their search, the two of them had invented the idea of informing the local authorities that they were searching for proof of the visit and subsequent death of Joseph of Arimithea in Glastonbury. The Biblical connection had served to gain a degree of co-operation from those authorities, far more than they would have given to a search for an item belonging more to legend than to reality. This would also ensure that by making Cutler and his people believe they were involved in a small but necessary misdirection themselves in order to keep sightseers and treasure hunters at bay, the silence of the three surveyors was virtually guaranteed.

A smile played across Graves's sleepy face as he thought of the double misdirection ploy. It was probably his best yet, and though he might hate working for a man like Capshaw, he couldn't help but feel pleased with himself at the thought of his proficiency in this particular field of expertise. This was yet another the fourth job he'd been coerced into performing for Capshaw, and he had to admit to himself, so far it was probably his best yet!

Just before sleep finally took him for the night Graves thought of the one weak link in the chain as far as Cutler and his people were concerned. If anything went wrong with Graves's plan and Cutler caught on to what was really happening, then Graves would have no choice but to exploit that weakness.

"Such a pretty girl, Miss Sally Corbett" thought Graves just before he fell into a sleep that would last until his alarm clock roused him the next morning. He hoped that if and when the time came, he wouldn't have to hurt her too much or cause her too much discomfort. That, of course, would be up to Joe Cutler and Winston Fortune.

Chapter 11

Three days of searching had so far yielded very little. The radar had enabled Cutler to locate two old prams concealed in the marshy ground, a doll buried by some poor little girl who had presumably been playing a game and forgotten where she'd put it, a number of tree holes and a line of smaller holes which indicated where several fence posts had at some time in the past been hammered into the ground. They had found not one single artefact of any age, certainly nothing to suggest that anything from the time of King Arthur was deposited in the area. Despite the hours they'd put in and the work involved, a sense of disenchantment fell over the little team.

"You'd have thought we'd have found *something* at least," said Winston Fortune as he sat disconsolately in the rear doorway of the van parked at the bottom of a gently sloping hill about three miles from the Tor, not far from the tiny hamlet of Glastonbury Heath.

"Not necessarily," said Graves, seated more comfortable on a camping chair he'd brought expressly for the purpose of these impromptu field conferences. "As I told you, after Sir Pelleas returned the mortally wounded Arthur to Glastonbury and the King's subsequent death, a conclave of senior Knights met and decided not to bury Excalibur with the King. They made this decision for two reasons. First, had they done so it might have led to a case of grave robbery with the Dark Age equivalent of the pyramid robbers looting the King's grave in order to get their hands on the legendary sword. Secondly, by burying the sword in a place unknown except to a few trusted and chosen Knights the chances of Arthur's enemies getting their hands on Excalibur were reduced to a minimum. Had they done so, and I think I've told you this before, they could have used Excalibur as a symbol through which to rally support for some pretender to Arthur's crown. Excalibur was placed in a lead-lined wooden chest, almost a coffin of its own, and taken to a burial place in Livara by the Knights Sir Geraint, Sir Palamedes, Sir Sagramore le Desirous and Sir Gingalain under the command of Pelleas, and Excalibur was laid in a place known only to the five of them. Each of the Knights vowed, under pain of death, never to reveal the location of Excalibur's 'tomb', and so the great sword was lost and disappeared into the mists of time and legend."

"Why is there no mention of this 'Livara' in any other known record of the Arthurian legend?" asked Cutler joining in at last.

"Probably because, apart from it being the burial place of Excalibur and thus part of a closely guarded secret, Livara played no significant part in any other aspect of Arthur's life, or that of the Knights of the Round Table," Graves replied.

"And there's no mention of a 'Livara' on any known maps of the time," Cutler continued.

"Again, that's no surprise," said Graves. "Livara was quite possibly nothing more than a hamlet, or maybe something smaller, a settlement of no more than a couple of houses. There were no accurate maps at the time we're talking about, and most of those that did exist are no longer in existence. Livara could also have been a code name given to Excalibur's burial place by the Knights to disguise its real identity."

"Now I think we're getting into the realm of fantasy land," said Fortune, feeling less confident by the minute. He was beginning to believe the 'wild-goose chase' theory again.

"I agree with Winston," said Sally, "Let's not start getting into the world of codes please, Mr. Graves. I think you've been reading too many modern sensationalist novels."

"I don't mean a code in that sense, Sally," Graves replied, "but remember, you've seen the copy of the Excalibur document. It was written by Gareth, Sir Pelleas's scribe, and it's almost certain that as the location of Excalibur was such a closely guarded secret Gareth would have done his best to disguise the true location as he could. He recorded the event because it was his job to do so, and almost all the events of the time were recorded in one chronicle or another, but it would have been more than his life was worth to reveal the true hiding place of the sword."

"That makes sense anyway," said Cutler, his response surprising his companions a little. "If the document was a fake then I'd have expected the precise location to be clearly marked and named. The fact that this Gareth character has hidden the name behind a veil of mystery does add some credence to its authenticity to my way of thinking."

"I'm glad you see it that way, Mr. Cutler," said Graves. "Believe me when I say that I have every confidence not only in the document and the map, but in your combined abilities to locate the burial place of Excalibur. We shall succeed, I know we will."

"And exactly what use is the map when it refers to a topography that no longer exists?" asked Winston, still showing signs of scepticism.

"It's true, Mr. Fortune, that the land has changed much since the days of Arthur," Graves replied, " but the map is still important to us because it points us in the general direction of the burial site. Much of the land around us may have been under water in Arthur's day, and there may have been any number of small islands jutting out of the various marshes and bogs that existed then. It's even possible that Livara was such an island. If so its name would have disappeared many centuries ago as the land dried and new communities sprung up, bigger and more modern. It would have become historically redundant as many small places have become redundant as mankind developed and progressed. Some of those islands may even have sunk into the marshes, and their remains may still lie beneath the ground we now walk on. I'm asking you to have a little faith, that's all. Trust me, please. After all, the reason for me being here is to act as a guide and historical researcher, to solve the mystery of the jigsaw and put the pieces of Gareth's puzzle together in a modern context. If I can do it we'll succeed. If I don't then it won't be for the lack of trying."

"Well, Winston," said Sally, "I say we give Mr. Graves a chance. After all, we've barely scratched the surface yet, so to speak. We've got over a week left to go before we report to Mr. Capshaw, so why don't we just get on with it"

"That's just what we're going to do, Sally," said Cutler. "We're professionals, after all, and we've been hired to do a job. I intend to do it to the best of my ability, and I expect you both to do the same."

"Oh wow, the big bad boss man comin' heavy," said Winston in his best Jamaican accent.

"Yes, boss, keep your hair on. Winston was only expressing an opinion," added Sally, a little shocked at Cutler's uncharacteristically heavy-handed outburst.

"I know that, Sally. Sorry if I was a bit sharp, Winston. I guess the frustration is getting to me a little as well."

"Hey, no sweat, boss man."

Graves added: "Mr. Cutler is quite right in what he says. We should remember that we're all being paid to do this job, and we'll do it a damn sight better if we stop bickering and try to work together as a team."

After a lunch of sandwiches and hot coffee from a thermos flask brought by Sally Corbett, they spent the rest of the afternoon in a companionable silence, each working at their allotted tasks, the radar showing nothing more interesting than it had all morning. It was Joe Cutler who brought the working day to an end as they completed their sweep of the area they'd marked out for that day's search. Graves agreed that they could do no more that day, it was too late to move on and begin marking out the parameters of the next search grid, so they packed up the equipment and went their separate ways: Cutler and his team to The Rowan Tree, Walter Graves to his rather more upmarket accommodation at Meare Manor.

After a hot shower and brandy in his room, Walter Graves put his feet up on the bed and phoned his employer with his daily report on their progress.

"At least each time we come up empty handed we eliminate another part of the grid," he spoke into the receiver.

"Quite true, Mr. Graves. I have absolute faith in you and your ability to get the job done. I never expected instant success. If I had I wouldn't have needed to employ Cutler and his people. Speaking of them, how are you getting along with them? There's no chance of them working this out before we find it is there?"

"Don't worry. Cutler is actually being quite supportive of the whole enterprise, which surprises me a little. Then again, he's quite intelligent, and in their case I think his intellect will work against him. The 'facts' as I've presented them are highly convincing, so much so that I could probably convince a roomful of scholars of the truth of the document. Cutler wouldn't think that anyone would go to such great lengths to deceive him, so it's a safe bet that he believes in what he's doing. The girl is no problem either, in fact I think she might be quite attracted to me, which is always a help. She'll probably reach a point where she'll believe anything I tell her. No, it's the Jamaican that may be a problem. Mr. Winston Fortune is a little harder to convince than the others. I thought he'd be the most romantic of the three, the easiest to convince, but I think he's bordering on the side of scepticism. I may have to take action in that direction if he becomes a problem."

"As I said, Mr. Graves, you have my utmost confidence. If you think the Jamaican is a problem I'll leave it to you to deal with in your own, how shall we say, innovatively constructive fashion?"

"Of course, just leave it to me," said Graves. As usual he never mentioned Capshaw by name on the telephone. It was an in-built reflex to the possibility of eavesdroppers, and one which Capshaw both understood and admired. Walter Graves was probably the only man on the planet who could get away with conducting an entire conversation with the millionaire without using the deferent *Mr. Capshaw* at some point.

As Graves was conducting his conversation with Capshaw, the Strata Survey team were enjoying a quick drink in the bar at The Rowan Tree before going up to their rooms to wash and change.

"So, what *was* the point of all that vehemence today, boss?" Fortune asked, knowing full well that Joe's outburst carried some hidden meaning. He'd known Cutler and enjoyed his friendship long enough to know that Joe's outburst was completely out of character, and that for some reason he'd used it as means of closing down the topic of conversation at the time.

"Yes, Joe, do tell," added Sally. "You were trying to tell us something, weren't you? Something that you didn't want Graves to catch on to?"

"My, my, you two are becoming a pair of mind readers, aren't you? Yes, there was something, though you'll probably think I'm being stupid when I tell you."

"Hey, man," said Winston, with a huge grin on his face. "I might think you're a bit of a slave driver sometimes, and you like to play the big boss on occasions, which you are of course, but never ever in this whole wide world would I think of you as being stupid."

"Me neither, do tell," added Sally.

"Well, okay then, here goes. We've been with Graves for three days now, and I wonder if any of you two has noticed the same things I have."

"What 'things', man?" asked Winston.

"Come on, Joe, spit it out," said Sally Corbett, the impatience of her youth beginning to show.

"It's not much to base a suspicion on I'll admit," said Cutler, " but you see, I just don't think he's entirely genuine. There's nothing wrong with what he's telling us, that much I'll admit. I've no real reason to suppose there's anything 'iffy' about the job itself, but you see, I've been watching him very closely at times when you two have been placing markers or working away from the control point, and he seems to keep himself quite well away from me and the actual work until we complete a section of search area. Add to that the fact that he seems to spend an inordinate amount of time on his mobile phone, talking to God knows who, and what that has to do with the search is anyone's guess, but, guys, and this is where you'll think I'm stupid, I just can't believe in or trust a so-called historian who turns up in the field every day wearing the most expensive Armani jeans!"

Both Winston and Sally broke into peals of uncontrollable laughter at the seemingly preposterous reason for Cutler's suspicions regarding Walter Graves. When they finally managed to straighten their faces, Cutler added the final card to his hand.

"Oh yes, there was something else. I sort of came up behind him earlier today, and he was little surprised when he heard me approach. He turned to face me quite quickly, perhaps a little too quickly, and as he turned and his jacket flew open for a second, I could swear I saw the butt of a handgun protruding from the inside pocket."

Winston and Sally looked at Cutler, and then at each other, followed by a long unbroken silence. This time there was no laughter.

"It was Joe Cutler who finally broke the silence.

"Listen," he said. "I've got an idea. Let's all get changed and then meet in the bar. We'll talk some more over dinner. Graves is safely tucked in his room this evening. He told me he has some research to do to finalise the parameters of the next search grid, so we'll have plenty of time to talk."

Nodding to their boss, Fortune and Corbett rose with him and made their way back to their respective rooms.

Chapter 12

After showering and changing out of their work clothes the three workmates once more joined forces in the bar. Joe Cutler bought Sally a half pint of lager, Winston a large rum, and a whisky for himself and within ten seconds of them settling around the small table in the corner of the room Winston raised the subject that had merely been placed on hold while they'd been apart for the last hour.

"So, boss, you're sure the guy is carrying a gun?"

"Like I said, I can't be a hundred percent sure, but I could almost swear to you that it was a gun of some kind."

"Maybe it was something else," said Sally. "There must be other things that could look like the handle of a gun, Joe."

"Like what, Sally? I can't think of anything that springs to mind."

"I'm sure I've read of things like cameras that have pistol grips," Sally suggested.

"I think you're clutching at straws, Sally girl," said Winston.

"Well, even if it is, he might have a good reason for having it," she continued.

"Oh yeah, sure," Cutler intervened. "I can't think of a single valid reason why a history professor should be walking around the wilds of Somerset carrying a handgun, can anyone else?"

"Why don't we ask him about it?" asked Sally, somewhat naively.

"I can just imagine it," said Cutler. "Excuse me, Mr. Graves, but could you please tell us why a nice, innocent history professor like you is walking around with a nasty big handgun under your jacket?"

"There's no need to mock, you know," said Sally. "It was just a suggestion. The whole thing sounds preposterous to me, that's all."

"It sounds preposterous and potentially bloody dangerous to me," Winston added. "Like the boss says, Sally, I think we might have reason to be more than a little suspicious of Mr. Graves."

"You said earlier that you had an idea?" Sally asked, looking hopefully at Cutler.

"Yes. First thing in the morning I'm going to call Mavis. I want her to run a thorough check on Mr. Walter Graves. Perhaps she can find out something about him that'll throw a bit more light on why he's sporting a weapon when he's supposed to be here conducting a search for a historical artefact. We all know how resourceful she can be. She seems to know everyone who's anyone and has a whole load of internet connections. If there's anything shady about our historian Mavis will find it, I'm sure of it. Secondly, I want us all to keep a close watch on Graves while we're on-site from now on. He doesn't seem to do much apart from talk on his mobile phone so if any of us gets the chance to do a spot of eavesdropping I won't be complaining about their bad manners. I'm also going to get Mavis to send copies of Gareth's Chronicle and the map to various trustworthy bodies that might be able to give us a second opinion on the potential authenticity of the documents."

"Wow, you really have been thinking this through haven't you, Joe?" Sally said, obviously impressed with her employer's reasoning and proposed course of action. "Anything else?"

"Whatever we do, we mustn't let Graves think for even a minute that we suspect him of anything underhanded or malicious. Above all, we mustn't give him any reason to prove to us that he really does have a gun in his pocket, so please, both of you just go about your jobs as though nothing's changed. Be nice to Graves, or at least in your case, Winston, a bit respectful. It wouldn't do to suddenly change and become his best friend. I'm sure he knows you're a little unsure about him anyway."

A big grin burst across Winston's face at this last remark.

"Oh no, boss, and there was me thinking I'd been the epitome of friendliness from the moment we met the great Walter Graves," he said in mock horror.

The laughter that followed from all three of them helped to lighten the tension that had gripped the little band of surveyors from the moment Joe Cutler had mentioned the gun.

"Are you sure Mavis will be up for a bit of private eyeing, boss?" Winston continued.

"Up for it? Bloody Hell, Winston, she'll be like a dog with a new bone if I know Mavis. There'll be no stopping her when she gets the bit between her teeth, you wait and see. I feel sorry for Graves if he is a bit shifty. Mavis'll track down any skeletons in his closet like a veritable Miss Marple."

There were more giggles, this time from Sally who suddenly put on a thoughtful face and asked: "You don't think it'll put Mavis in any danger do you, boss?"

"Hell no, Sally. She'll be doing it all from the safety of the office. What possible harm can come to her there?"

"Maybe the man's got connections," said Winston.

"Who with, the Mafia?" laughed Joe.

"The C.I.A.?" said Sally, joining in the frivolity.

"Maybe he's a drug baron," volunteered Winston.

"What the hell would the C.I.A. or a drug baron want with Excalibur?" asked Cutler, still in a humorous mode.

"Well, what would the Mafia want with it?" asked Sally

"Touché," said Cutler, a wide grin on his face. It was as though all the tension he'd been feeling had now fully lifted.

"You're in a better mood now than you were ten minutes ago that's for sure."

"I know, Winston. Maybe it's the whisky, or maybe the company, or maybe I'm just feeling a little foolish at my wild theories about Mr. Graves."

"Hey, you just listen," said the big Jamaican, reaching out and placing his paw of a right hand on Cutler's arm. "You ain't saying nothing that I haven't been thinking myself. Maybe not in quite the same way as you thinking it, but it's been there anyway, in the back of my mind. Something about Graves doesn't add up, and I agree with you, it needs checking out."

Sally suddenly thought of something.

"Can I just say one thing?" she asked.

"Go on, Sally," said Cutler.

"Well, Joe, you went to Stratford and met with Mr. Capshaw, didn't you? You told us he'd had Strata surveys checked out before offering you the job, yes?" Cutler nodded. "You'd think therefore that he would also have had Graves checked out before hiring him, wouldn't you?" The nod again. "The point I'm getting at is this. If Graves checked out, and he must have done for Mr. Capshaw to hire him then we're left with only two options."

"Which are?" asked Winston.

Sally continued. "Well, first of all, if we assume that Graves is really who he says he is, then Mr. Capshaw could well be aware of the fact that he carries a gun, which would raise one or two questions about Mr. Capshaw if you don't mind me saying so."

Sally paused and took a deep breath as the two men seemed to hang on her words, waiting with baited breath for her to continue. They both leaned in towards her as she continued, and her next words really did take their breath away.

"The second train of thought that I came up with is the really scary one, though. What if *our* Mr. Graves isn't the *real* Mr.Graves?"

You could have heard the proverbial pin drop around the table as the two men allowed Sally's words to sink home. A full twenty seconds passed before Joe Cutler broke the silence.

"Phew. That's one hell of a theory, Sally. Your mind certainly works in a devious way sometimes, I have to hand it to you."

"Just one thing, Sally girl," said Winston. "Why the hell would anyone want to impersonate Walter Graves? That's what you're suggesting isn't it, that our Graves is an impostor?"

"Why, to get their hands on Excalibur, of course," she exclaimed. "Someone could have killed Mr. Graves, taken his briefcase with the papers and documents, and be using us to locate the sword so that they can steal it for themselves. You know, maybe someone being paid by an unscrupulous art collector or something like that."

"Wow, Sally, that one sure came from left field," said Cutler. "Just to be on the safe side I think I'll ask Mavis to try and get hold of a picture of the real Walter Graves. That might satisfy us in that respect at least."

"And what about Mr. Capshaw? Shouldn't we let him know that there might be something not quite right with Mr. Graves?"

"Whoa, now hold on, Sally. Let's not go quite so fast, okay? You said yourself that Capshaw might know that Graves has a gun, and if he does that tends to suggest that Capshaw might be a bit on the crooked side, too, doesn't it?" asked Fortune.

"Good point, Winston," said Cutler thoughtfully. "Listen, I don't think we can do anything until we know a little bit more. I did have

Mavis get some details on Capshaw before I went up to Stratford to meet him, but maybe I'll ask her to dig a little more while she's looking into Graves."

"You know, I don't like to say this, but things are becoming a little scary right now," said Sally.

"Hey, look, Sally, I'm sure it's nothing really. Maybe I just over-reacted to something I thought I saw today. Let's not jump to any conclusions until we know more, alright?"

"If you say so, Joe," she said, her eyes darting from one man to the other as worry lines appeared across her brow. Sally was sure she'd stumbled upon some dark, hidden aspect to the man they knew as Walter Graves.

Taking her silence for acquiescence to his last statement Cutler moved to bring the evening back onto an even keel.

"Come on, let's eat," he said, draining the last of the whisky from his glass.

The others followed Joe quietly into the dining room, but the meal that evening was eaten almost in silence. It was as though an air of gloom and despondency had descended upon them that wouldn't lift until they'd solved the riddle that bore the name of Walter Graves.

Chapter 13

Immediately after breakfast the following day Joe Cutler made a call to Mavis Hightower who as always was at her desk in the Strata Survey Systems office bright and early. After explaining to Mavis his exact needs with regards to Walter Graves and Malcolm Capshaw and receiving an enthusiastic and entirely expected response in the positive from his office manager, he turned his attention to the map and the chronicle supposedly written by Sir Pelleas's scribe Gareth. Not being in any way connected with the world of ancient history or historical artefacts, Cutler was faced with a dilemma. How was he to ascertain whether the documents were genuine or not if he couldn't find a reliable source of verification?

It was Sally Corbett who came up with the solution he was seeking as he sat in his room explaining the problem to her and Winston Fortune immediately prior to them leaving to meet Graves in order to begin the day's search.

"Lucius Doberman," she exclaimed, almost as if Cutler and Fortune should know exactly what she was talking about.

"Eh? Come again, Sally," was all she received by way of response from Cutler.

"Lucius Doberman," she repeated. "He was a professor of history at university when I was there and he had, er, shall we say, something of a 'thing' going for me. I wasn't interested, of course, and it would have been very unprofessional of him to become involved with a student anyway."

"But you weren't there to study history, so you could have got away with a liaison if you'd wanted to," said Winston.

"As I said, I wasn't interested in him in that way. He was tutor to one of my best friends, Helen James, and we used to meet socially now and then. He was very young for a professor, much younger than Graves, in fact, but he was thought to be something of a genius in his field. If I approach him he might be willing to take a look at the documents for you, Joe."

"Time is short, Sally. I haven't the time to go up to your old college and show them to this professor of yours. He'd have to work with fax copies or something like that and we need a fast appraisal."

"We can do better than that, boss," said Winston. "All we have to do is copy them onto the laptop and send them to Doberman over the internet, right, Sally?"

"Of course. Shall I ring him, Joe? As long as he gives me an e-mail address we could have the documents to him in less than an hour."

"We don't have a scanner with us," said Cutler.

"No, but I'm sure Mrs. Cleveley will have one in her office. If it won't work with the laptop she might let us use her computer to send the document via e-mail to the laptop and we can send it as an onward transmission to the professor."

"My God, Winston, the girl's a genius! Make the call, Sally. I'll go and have a word with our accommodating landlady."

Thanks to the co-operation of Annette Cleveley and the use of her scanner and computer, and following a call from Sally to Lucius Doberman who professed himself only too happy to help, the team were less than half an hour late in leaving the Rowan Tree for their rendezvous with Walter Graves, and the copied documents were probably already in the hands of Sally's old friend, thanks to that wonder of technology, the internet. Cutler had called the historian to explain that they had been delayed by a flat tyre on the van, and he'd had no hesitation in accepting Joe's excuse, merely suggesting that Cutler 'got his finger out' and made his way to the prearranged meeting place as soon as possible.

As Winston drove the van the ten miles to the day's scheduled search area the conversation turned to Sally's old friend Lucius Doberman.

"So, old Lucius didn't take much persuading then, eh, Sally?"

"None at all, Winston. In fact, when I told him what it was about he quite jumped at the chance to get involved."

"I don't suppose it had anything to do with the fact that the man still has the 'hots' for you, did it?" asked Cutler, grinning like a Cheshire cat.

"He probably does, that's true, but he's also quite brilliant, and he was relishing the chance to view what may be precious historical documents and give us his opinion on them. When I told him that there was the chance we might unearth Excalibur he was a little sceptical at first, but at least he's prepared to view the documents with an open mind. He's promised to get back to you as soon as he can, boss."

"What about his academic duties?" asked Winston. "Won't he have lectures or tutorials and stuff to deliver? He might not get a chance to look at them until later in the day, if at all."

"Universities aren't like schools, Winston. He doesn't work non-stop all day like a school teacher. Don't worry, he promised he'd look at them today, and he will."

"Did you mention Graves?" asked Cutler.

"I thought it best not to."

"Very wise, Sally," he continued. "You never know, they might know each other and that could make things awkward for us."

"I doubt they know each other, there isn't some big history professors club you know," she continued, "but something just made me keep him out of it for now."

"Probably safer for Doberman," said Winston. "Where did he get a name like that by the way? Sounds a bit of a dog to me."

"You've got a thing about names haven't you, Winston?"

"I just think it's humorous, Sally girl, that's all."

"That's rich, coming from someone called Fortune," she grinned.

"I think she's got you there, old friend," said Cutler.

"*Okay*, I'll shut up about it. I still think it's a weird name," he mumbled to himself as his voice trailed off.

"Next left, Winston," Cutler shouted as they approached a junction, travelling a little too fast for his liking.

Fortune quickly applied the van's brakes and the rapid deceleration threw the three of them forward, their seatbelts tightening as they held them in place in their seats.

"Sorry, boss, my mind was somewhere else for a minute."

"Never mind, just get us there safely. It's about a mile along the road, on the left. There's a track that leads to a small wooded area. That's where we're supposed to meet Graves."

Five minutes later they pulled up in the designated place to find Walter Graves standing beside his BMW, which, despite the state of the ground still managed to look as though he'd just driven it out of the showroom. The black bodywork positively gleamed in the morning sunshine, the reflection of the sun's rays gleaming as they refracted from the highly polished metal surface. Bearing in mind Cutler's view of the suspected weapon the previous day, it gave Graves the look of a Mafia hit man waiting for his victim to approach. Graves stubbed out the cigarette he'd been smoking on the ground in front of him and waved to the approaching survey team.

"Morning everyone," he called cheerfully to Cutler and the others.

"Good morning, Mr. Graves," Cutler responded as the others nodded and grunted their own greetings.

Cutler whispered to his companions.

"Remember what I said. Keep it normal."

"What a beautiful day we've been given today. Who'd have thought we'd had all that rain just a few days ago. Look how green the trees are, and the grass. At least nature has taken advantage of the downpour."

"I didn't think you were much of a nature lover, or an outdoor kind of person, Mr. Graves," said Sally.

"Ah, there you go, Miss Corbett," he replied. "I suppose you think I must spend all my time in dusty old libraries or my rooms at the college wrapped up in one or another historical research project and never seeing the light of day. In actual fact I quite enjoy the outdoors. I've even been known to enjoy the odd hiking weekend in the past, in the right company of course."

"I only meant…"

"I know exactly what you meant, Miss Corbett," Graves continued. "I assure you I'm just as happy out of doors as I am under cover. Not only that, but my knowledge of the natural world might serve to surprise you one day."

"I'm sure it could," Cutler interrupted. "Don't you think that we should be getting on with the job in hand, though?"

"Ah, I'm glad to see that you're keen to make progress, Mr. Cutler," Graves smiled at Joe. "Here's a copy of the grid I've prepared for today's search."

He handed Joe a sheet of A4 paper on which he'd drawn a perfectly scaled map of the area they were about to survey. While Winston prepared the radar Sally and Joe removed the marker poles and central control unit from the van. The wooded area they passed through on their way to the new search area was small, as Cutler had indicated from the road map. Barely a hundred metres square, he guessed that the trees, a mixture of oaks and horse chestnuts had been planted to provide a protective windbreak for the open space beyond. The only way to reach that space was by following the well-worn path that led through the small area of forestry. As they emerged at the furthest point from the small parking space they were amazed at the panoramic view that opened up before them. Unseen from the road due to the lay of the land and the fences that prevented entry apart from the way they'd come, the view that presented itself was nothing short of breathtaking. As far as the eye could see a swathe of green stretched into the distant horizon. Fields, marshland and gently rolling hills merged into a vista broken only here and there by the ragged lines of hedges and occasional dry stone walls. Tiny patches of colour sprang from small clusters of wildflowers dotted around in the swathes of green, and as a gentle breeze washed quietly across the land and the grass stalks bent their heads in reverence to it, it was as though the grassland had become a waving, undulating sea of green. Suddenly, from the field immediately in front of them, a skylark rose from the deepest growth of long grass and soon hovered high above them, its song reaching out across the blue of the sky to enthral and entertain its tiny human audience. Seconds later, it turned and wheeled in the clear blue sky before quickly disappearing from view.

"Wow, man, that's some view," said Winston Fortune, amazed at the sheer beauty of the vision that met his eyes.

"I hardly knew England still had such places of unspoilt beauty," added Cutler.

"It looks like it's barely changed in centuries," came from Sally.

"Ah, but that's the whole point you see, Miss Corbett," said Graves. "It has changed, and those changes are what have made our task all the more difficult. Where once ponds or lakes lay, there now exist the fields you see before you. Where forests of great oaks and pines once flourished, man has sought to render them redundant, and has cleared the way for fields of crops to grow to sustain the ever burgeoning population. Hills have shrunk, or grown and many Dark Age settlements have been buried beneath the progressive march of modern civilisation."

"You make it sound like an impossible task," said Cutler.

"Not impossible, Mr. Cutler, just difficult. That's why Mr. Capshaw chose those he considered best qualified to get the job done successfully."

"That leads me to a question, Mr. Graves," Winston suddenly cut in.

"Please, ask away, Mr. Fortune."

"Why us? After all, we're surveyors not archaeologists. Wouldn't it have made more sense for Capshaw to hire a team of qualified archaeologists to conduct his search? Surely they would have known what to look for and how to go about it in a more methodical manner than us?"

"Ah, but that's where you're wrong, Mr. Fortune. On the surface you may have a point, but you have to bear in mind that most archaeologists have very fixed minds, despite what you may think to the contrary. To try to convince a senior member of that profession of the authenticity of the project would have taken too long as far as Mr. Capshaw was concerned, and then there would have been the added problem of the students."

Glastonbury

"Students?"

"Yes, Mr. Fortune, students. You see, archaeologists generally work on their own, so when a project comes along that requires field searches like this, and certainly where some form of digging or excavation is likely to be needed, such men will invariable turn to the student fraternity. Archaeology students would have been recruited to carry out the donkey work of the search under the guidance of some archaic old member of the intelligentsia and I can assure you that those students would have soon developed what I call a 'loose tongue' syndrome, probably over a few beers one night in the pub, the secret would have been out in no time and the whole search area would have been inundated with treasure hunters and the like. No, Mr. Capshaw knew exactly what he was doing when he hired your employer here to conduct the search for Excalibur, with me as your guide and provider of historical reference."

"So you're the archaic intelligentsia, and we're the donkeys, eh, man?"

"Well, not quite, Mr. Fortune, but yes, in a way that's true I suppose. Though I must say that you and your friends are being paid a far greater sum of money for your time and effort than a group of long-haired students."

"Okay, everyone, enough chit-chat, let's get to work." Joe Cutler had heard enough. He wanted to get the day's search underway.

It took less than forty-five minutes for Sally and Winston to position the markers and pins under the direction of Cutler who manned the central control point.

Before beginning work in earnest they gathered at the van, where Sally poured coffee for everyone from the two flasks she'd brought along that morning.

"Well, here's to success," said Graves, raising his coffee mug high in the air.

"Mmm, success," added Cutler, as the others merely stared at Graves.

"Tell me, Mr. Cutler, if for example an old pond or lake or river bed lay beneath the land in front of us, would your radar be able to detect it? You see, here on the old map there are a number of settlements marked that are obviously long gone, consigned to history's recycle bin, and then there are a number of streams and ponds and at least one larger body of water marked, none of which appear on today's maps. If we could find one or more of them we would have a definite point of reference that could point us in the exact direction of Livara."

"Well, it's not quite that simple," Cutler replied. "If there was a pond for example, and it simply dried up or was drained for some reason and left to nature's own devices, it's highly likely that it would have simply become overgrown with the natural vegetation that already existed around it. In such a case the radar would be unable to pinpoint it, as the infill would have been perfectly natural and the pond would have been purely reclaimed by the land. Such natural infill would be extremely hard to detect, if at all. On the other hand, if that pond had been drained and then filled in artificially by rocks or some sort of structure, or by having something 'alien' buried in the resulting void and then covered over, then yes, the radar would give us a reading and we would have a possible site to investigate. Is that clear enough, Mr. Graves?"

"Quite clear, thank you. I think I see what you mean. Your ground penetrating radar is able to detect and indicate changes in the natural lie of the land where artificial means have been used to effect that change, yes? Natural changes would give you no reading?"

"Basically, yes," said Cutler. "The map shows several ponds and streams as you say, but the likelihood is that they simply dried up and disappeared over the centuries, at least they did if I'm any judge of the natural way of things. Our best bet, if we don't stumble directly onto the swords' burial place is to perhaps find evidence of one of those settlements shown on the map. If there were structures anywhere on this land in the distant past and they've since been overgrown or become buried as the land dried out and the vegetation or arable settlement took their place, then we stand a chance of finding something."

"Capital, Mr. Cutler, just capital. That's what I like to hear, a positive way of looking at the problem. So, let's get started everyone, shall we? We've got a sword to find."

"What's with the *we*?" asked Winston five minutes later, as he and Cutler carried a pair of heavy spades over their shoulders as they walked back down the path through the wood. "Have you noticed that it's us who are doing all the carrying, man, while he just sits and watches?"

"As you said, Winston, we're just the donkeys."

"Ha, bloody ha, boss, that's what I say, ha, bloody ha."

"Oh come on, Winston. Where's your sense of humour?" asked Sally, bringing up the rear and carrying a small hand shovel and a knapsack containing spare batteries for the radar handset.

"I'll tell you where it's gone, Sally girl," he remarked as he looked ahead to where Walter Graves was waiting at the edge of the open land. He nodded in the direction of the historian and spoke softly as he continued.

"Until we know for sure exactly who or what that man up ahead really is, my sense of humour has been sent on permanent sabbatical. I'll let you know when it comes back, okay, girl?"

"Whatever you say, big man, whatever you say," said Sally.

Thirty minutes went by as Winston walked the grid along the strings laid out earlier. As the sun rose higher in the sky and the day grew warmer he suddenly stopped, checked that he was reading what he thought he was reading and spoke into his the mouthpiece of his communicator.

"Boss? Hey, boss, you there, man?"

"Yeah, Winston, what is it?"

"I got a reading, boss; I got a reading, man. I think we've found something. Fetch those spades man!"

Chapter 14

"New suit, Charlotte?"

"Yes, Mr. Capshaw, do you like it?"

"Very nice indeed, Charlotte. Come closer, there's a good girl."

It was eleven thirty in the morning. Capshaw had no appointments for the next hour and Charlotte had a good idea what he had in mind as she approached the desk. The dark blue two-piece skirt suit carried an expensive designer label. Worn as it was today, with the open necked cream silk blouse that set the colour off perfectly, Charlotte knew full well that she could only afford such luxuries as a result of the hugely inflated salary paid by her employer. Even so, even for Charlotte it was sometimes hard to do everything that was expected of her in order to earn it.

"Closer," Capshaw ordered as Charlotte stopped about a yard from his desk. "Here, next to me."

Charlotte did as told. Though she had few qualms about sharing Capshaw's bed when called upon to do so, she often felt uncomfortable when called upon to give in to his demands within the confines of the office. She always harboured a fear that someone would walk in on them one day and find her in the midst of the sexual act with her boss. She had some self-respect left, not much, but enough not to want to be found with her clothes in disarray and a panting Malcolm Capshaw between her legs in the middle of the day.

Capshaw's right hand moved slowly up the inside Charlotte's leg, slowly savouring the feel of the nylon as he slowly pushed the hem of her skirt upwards and his hand moved higher until he reached the bare flesh where her stocking top gave way to the naked flesh of her thigh. He grunted, and Charlotte inwardly shuddered.

"Open," he commanded in a voice not to be argued with.

Slowly, she opened her legs as far as the confines of her skirt would allow. Capshaw's fingers began to probe between her legs. In accordance with Capshaw's instructions Charlotte wasn't wearing any underwear. As his fingers pushed into the warm wetness of Charlotte's private places the sound of the telephone ringing in the outer office gave her the opportunity she needed.

"Mr. Capshaw, the telephone," she entreated.

"Bugger the telephone, stand still," he ordered.

"It might be important," she begged.

"I said let it ring," he retorted, though she knew the spell was broken. Capshaw hated to be interrupted and his unsatisfied lust would probably now give way to anger. She was right. Malcolm Capshaw removed his hand from Charlotte's heat, ran it down her leg until her skirt dropped back into place, and snapped at his secretary: "Answer the damned thing," he growled. "And it had better be bloody important!"

Charlotte hurried from Capshaw's office as fast as her high heels could carry her, and closed the door behind her. Passing through the second door that led back to her own office she breathed a sigh of relief as she walked to her desk and pushed the 'answer' button on the desk telephone.

"Mr. Capshaw's office," she spoke into the receiver in her most professional voice.

"It's Maitland, put me through," the voice at the other end of the line demanded.

"Right away, Mr. Maitland, just a moment."

Charlotte buzzed her employer who answered immediately. She could almost feel the heat of his anger through the telephone.

"Well, who the bloody hell is it?" he snarled.

"It's Mr. Boris Maitland, sir," she replied. "He sounds as if he's in a hurry."

"He's always in a bloody hurry. Alright, put him through."

Charlotte flicked a button on the desk phone. "Putting you through now, Mr. Maitland," and closed the connection from her end, allowing Capshaw and Maitland to speak in private. Charlotte would never dare listen in on any of Capshaw's conversations and certainly not one with Boris Maitland.

If Charlotte was sometimes afraid of her employer, she was absolutely terrified of Boris Maitland. To her mind the man was a thug; a designer suited and well-spoken one it was true, but a thug nonetheless. He'd been to the office on at least half a dozen occasions in the past and Charlotte could never get over the cold, hard, penetrating look in his eyes. It was as if he could see straight into her soul, and that unnerved her greatly. Everything about Maitland made her uneasy and it had reached a point where just being in the same room as the man made her flesh creep. She knew that Malcolm Capshaw occasionally had dealings with certain people who were not entirely on the right side of the law, but how he'd got himself mixed up with a thug like Maitland was entirely beyond her understanding. From her own enquiries she'd learned that Boris Maitland and his brother Karl were suspected by the police to be the leaders of a notorious and murderous crime syndicate based in the heart of London. Between them the brothers were suspected of being responsible for at least a dozen murders. It appeared that if anyone got in the way of the Maitland brothers, they were apt to disappear from the face of the world for a time, only to be found at some later date, dead and hideously mutilated, perhaps by the propeller of a river boat, or churned up in the blades of a hotel rooftop air conditioning unit, that kind of thing.

Charlotte would have been very surprised to learn that Boris Maitland and Malcolm Capshaw were in fact very old friends, and that the two of them had been at the same school many years earlier. For now however she was simply very frightened at the mere mention of Maitland's name, and if she searched deep into her subconscious she might have been able to admit that her biggest fear was that Capshaw might at some future date order her to sleep with Maitland or his brother, perhaps as some kind of perverted favour.

"Well?" asked Maitland. "Have they made any progress?"

"Give them time, Boris. They've only been at it for a few days and it was raining solid for three of them."

"Fuck the rain, and fuck you," Maitland snapped. "I want the bloody job done, Malcolm old chap. We have to find it, and find it soon. I want results, and I thought you said you'd got good people working on it."

"Bloody hell, Boris," Capshaw replied, "It's been in the ground long enough, a few more days won't hurt. Graves is the best at what he does, and Cutler and his team are legit and reliable. If anyone can find it they can, believe me."

"Listen, old boy," said Maitland in his most cultured voice, "I've bankrolled this operation because the rewards are so high, but if anyone finds out what we're looking for and sticks their nose into our business the whole thing could blow up in our faces, you do know that don't you, old son."

"No-one will find out. Trust me for God's sake, and stop getting so bloody worked up about the whole thing. We've invested a lot of money between us, so success is just as important to me as it is to you, you remember that, my old friend."

"Yeah, right, well you just keep me posted, old son, you got that?"

"Course I will, Boris. Now for pity's sake get off my back and leave my people to get on with their jobs. When there's something to report I'll let you know, alright?"

"Right, well, I've got things to do. You mind what I said. While we're talking, how's that sexy little secretary of yours? She never sounds too pleased to hear my voice on the phone."

"Charlotte's fine, thanks, Boris, and I'm sure you're imagining things when you talk to her. She's the most efficient secretary I've found in years, so hands off, d'you hear?"

"Efficient? Yeah, and the rest I'll bet, you old lecher. Don't you worry, Malcolm old boy, I won't play with your little toy, at least, not yet. Maybe one day you'll get tired of her, and then me and little Charlotte might have a little fun together."

"Fuck off, Boris," snarled Capshaw.

"You, too, Malcolm," Maitland growled back, and then laughed. "See you soon, old boy. Don't do anything I wouldn't do."

The phone went dead in Capshaw's hand. Furious that his fun with Charlotte had been interrupted by his impatient and at times grisly business partner he pressed the 'call' button on his phone. Charlotte answered efficiently in two seconds.

"Charlotte. Get back in here now," he ordered. "And don't bother with a notepad!"

Chapter 15

"Put your back into it, girl!"

"I am putting my back into it you great lummox," Sally grinned in response to Winston's jovial urging. "Try doing the same yourself. You're twice my size."

Between them, the two, with help from Cutler, had dug a large trench-like hole in the spot indicated by the radar. They were working in a pair, with each taking rest breaks so that they didn't all tire at the same time. In two hours they'd dug to a depth of about one and a half metres, watched by Walter Graves who as usual had taken up his watchful stance in his camping chair. Never once had the historian offered his help as they toiled under the increasing glare of the sun as it rose higher in the sky.

"You sure ain't doing badly for a girl, that's for sure," Winston admitted as he wiped the beads of sweat from his brow.

"I'm pleased to hear it I'm sure," Sally replied, and then paused to throw a spadeful of earth in the direction of her fellow digger.

"Whoa," shouted Winston as the soil splattered across his chest.

"Give over you two," Cutler called from his place of rest on the grass a few metres away. "Come on, Sally, your turn for a break. Give me that spade."

Sally gladly stepped out of the hole and handed the spade to Cutler as he stepped down to take her place. She looked down at Winston and added as a parting shot, "Keep sweating, big man. Hope you don't get too hot down there."

Winston merely looked up, grinned at her and drove his spade deeper into the soft earth. His hands suddenly felt the resounding thud as the spade struck something hard and unyielding.

"Boss," he uttered breathlessly. "There's something here."

Cutler quickly joined Fortune in digging out the remaining earth that covered whatever it was that Winston's spade had struck. Sally joined them, quickly abandoning her break, grasping the small hand shovel and doing her best to help uncover the hidden object.

"Sounded wooden, boss," Winston said as the sweat continued to pour from his brow.

"I think you're right, Winston."

"What is it?" asked the voice of Walter Graves, who had suddenly appeared at the top of the hole.

"We'll let you know when we've uncovered the thing," Cutler replied.

"A bit of help wouldn't go amiss," Sally rasped in the direction of Graves.

"That's really not my department at all, Miss Corbett," was Graves's answer. "Advice, guidance and consultation, that's my remit on this job, as you well know."

"Course it is," said Winston. "We're just the donkeys remember, Sally girl?"

"Come on you two, we're almost there," urged Joe Cutler as the last remnants of the earth covering the find were removed and the shape of a large and lengthy wooden box was gradually revealed.

"You said it would be in something resembling a grave, Mr. Graves," Cutler said to the watching historian. "Could this be it, d'you think?"

"We won't know until you've uncovered enough of the thing to let us open the lid, if it has one."

Ten minutes later, the three surveyors had dug down around the sides of what appeared to be an old wooden chest, or perhaps a coffin. There were metal hinges on the box, well rusted and decomposed, but still in place where they'd been bolted many years before. To those who'd unearthed it, it certainly looked like the type of container described in Gareth's Chronicle. Could this really be the hiding place of Excalibur? Had they really found the legendary sword of King Arthur, and so soon into their search?

"Here goes then," said Cutler as he pried the lid of the box open a minute later. There was an ominous cracking as the aged wood began to splinter under the pressure of his crowbar, brought for the specific purpose of opening any stubbornly difficult containers they might find.

"Wait," Graves shouted as he heard the sound of splintering wood. "Let me." They were amazed to hear those words. Was Walter Graves at last going to get his hands dirty and join them in some good honest toil?

"Please, all of you step out of the hole," he ordered. "I have something better to use than your rather cumbersome tool, Mr. Cutler. Far better I think to try to remove the hinges than to shatter the lid and possibly damage the contents."

Cutler couldn't think how removing the lid could possibly damage a sword forged from steel if that was indeed what lay in the box, but when he saw Graves begin to reach into his inside pocket he quickly realised what the man may be reaching for.

"Quick, everyone, out," he demanded, and he led the way out of the hole they'd spent so long excavating, followed by Winston, who then gave Sally Corbett a hand up and out of the grave-like hole.

As the three of them stood on the rim of the hole, Graves removed his hand from his pocket and revealed not the handgun that Cutler had half expected, but a screwdriver, a screwdriver with a pistol grip!

"I usually carry this with me when I'm in the field," said Graves as he dropped down into the hole. "It comes in handy for all sorts of things. You never know when a good screwdriver will be useful."

Cutler felt pretty foolish at that point. Little did he know that the day before, when he'd seen the other man's jacket swing open to reveal the handgrip that he'd taken to be a gun, Graves's intuition and professional training had told him that Cutler had seen the weapon, long enough to make it out for what it was. Graves knew he had to diffuse any suspicions that Cutler might have had as a result of his small but crucial slip-up and had spent some time in a local hardware shop that morning selecting the pistol-gripped screwdriver he now brandished in his hand for all to see. He hadn't thought that he'd get the chance to show it off quite so soon; the discovery of the box had come at a highly opportune moment and now he had the chance to assuage the fears of Cutler and the others, as he assumed that Joe would have confided his fears to them.

As Graves twisted the first of the screws holding the hinges on the lid of the box, Winston Fortune moved close to Cutler and whispered very softly into his employer's right ear: "A gun, huh, boss?"

"Alright, Winston. We can all make a mistake, can't we?" he whispered in return. "Sorry if I worried you, Sally," he carried on by leaning towards Sally who was well aware of what they were discussing.

"Everything okay up there?" Graves shouted cheerily from the bottom of the hole, knowing only too well what they were probably discussing.

"Yes, Mr. Graves, everything's fine," Sally shouted down to him. "We were just saying that we're a little surprised to see you down there doing manual labour to tell the truth."

Impressed at Sally Corbett's quick thinking in giving an instant reply to his question, Graves smiled, looking up. "Ah, but you see, Miss Corbett, if this is really what we're looking for then it becomes my responsibility to verify the sword's existence and ensure its safety. As the specialist on-site so to speak, any actual removal of historical artefacts from their place of internment rests solely on my shoulders, I'm sure you understand."

"Yes, of course we understand."

It was Joe Cutler who replied to Graves's slightly unbelievable statement. Having made a fool of himself already, he wasn't prepared to question Graves's slightly preposterous illogical reasoning. Instead, he urged the historian on in his quest.

"Please carry on, Mr. Graves. I'm sure we're all anxious to see if we've succeeded in what we set out to do. Let's see what's in the box."

"Thank you, Mr. Cutler. That's what I intend to do if you'll allow me to get on."

Five minutes later the last of the screws yielded to the urgings of the screwdriver and the lid was effectively free of the framework of the box.

"May I ask you to give me a hand, Mr. Fortune?" Graves asked, and Winston dropped down to join the historian in the hole. Together, they slowly lifted the lid from the box, moving it up and to the side as best they could in the narrow confines of the excavation.

As the lid finally fell to the side of the box to reveal the interior a layer of material was all they could see. Once white, the cloth was now a dirty grey, and showed a marked deterioration. It appeared to adhere to whatever it covered, and Graves took a deep breath as he slowly attempted to peel the shroud-like membrane from whatever lay beneath.

It took only seconds for Graves to reveal enough of the contents of the box for them to realise they had not found Excalibur, or anything remotely resembling it.

"Bloody Hell," was the exclamation that broke from Winston Fortune's mouth as his eyes took in what Graves had seen a mere millisecond after the historian viewed it.

"Shit," said Cutler.

"Oh my God, no." was Sally Corbett's reaction to the sight of the aged and grinning skull that looked up at them from its last resting place. Far from discovering the whereabouts of King Arthur's Excalibur, they'd managed to find and unearth a grave, and the skeleton that inhabited that long-forgotten unmarked burial site now presented them with a new and complex problem, one that would take all of Walter Graves's ingenuity to solve if the search was to continue.

Chapter 16

The leering grin of the skull seemed to penetrate deep into the soul of young Sally Corbett as she tried with all her will to steer her gaze away from what was now all too apparently a grave. She'd never been close to the aftermath of death before, despite losing her twin sister she had certainly never come into the close proximity of a real skeleton before. The fixed stare of the sightless sockets unnerved Sally, as though even lacking the presence of the eyes that once sat within them, they were still capable of projecting a death-stare in her direction, a stare that came close to causing her to run and flee from the graveside.

Worse still, and she later realised that it was probably her imagination that caused the feeling, she felt as though a cloud rose from within the grave, a cloud that carried the acrid stench of death, and as it rose to engulf her and Joe Cutler as they stood looking down at the remains within the grave, it was all she could do to hold on to whatever remained of her breakfast within her stomach. Much to her credit, Sally held on, the urge to retch passed, and she looked away from the skeletal remains long enough to inhale a deep breath of fresh air.

Sensing her feelings, Joe took a gentle reassuring hold of Sally's right arm and said quietly in her ear so as not to embarrass her in front of Graves: "You alright, Sally?"

"I'll be fine, Joe," she replied. "Just came as a bit of a shock, that's all."

"Yes, same for all of us I think. It certainly wasn't what we expected to find."

"Who do you think it is?" she asked.

"It's unlikely we'll ever know the answer to that question, Miss Corbett," said Graves from his position beside the casket. "I fear that this poor devil has been down here for a very long time."

Winston Fortune pulled himself out of the grave and stood beside the others. He'd had enough of his close proximity to the remains in the coffin, and needed to be up in the fresh air of the field.

"It smells bad down there, man," he said in disgust. "I s'pose we'd better call the police, let them know what we've found."

"That won't be necessary at this point," Graves said very quickly. His mind had been racing to find a solution to the problem presented by the very suggestion that Winston had just put forward. No way could he allow the police to be involved. That would ruin the operation for good and Capshaw's wrath would be unforgiving.

"I think we'll find that this poor wretch has been down here for at least a hundred years or more. It's quite possible that this is a plague burial. There were numerous small sporadic outbreaks of the Black Death in this area towards the end of the nineteenth and beginning of the twentieth centuries. It may be that this poor devil lived in a settlement or a farm in the area, perhaps now long gone, and the body brought here to be buried away from the residences of others. That was usual with such cases at one time."

"I thought they burned the remains of plague victims," said Cutler, displaying a little of his own historical knowledge.

"You're quite right, they usually did, Mr Cutler, but in this part of the country it was still held to be something of a sacrilege to cremate the dead, and unless there was a local epidemic, if, for example, this was a sole victim, then it's probable that permission was given for the body to be buried here, as I said, away from any living inhabitants of the area, thus negating any chance of contamination among the local population. It may even have been that the spouse of this poor wretch buried the body without the knowledge of anyone else. They may have been hermits, travellers or whatever, we may never know."

Graves paused for breath, impressed by is own ingenuity and improvisation in concocting this possible version of events. He hoped he'd sounded sufficiently plausible to sway the others' opinions in his direction.

"Even if that's the case," Cutler continued, "Surely we still have a duty to inform the police of the discovery. It is a body after all."

"I agree with you of course, Mr. Cutler. However, I'm sure you're aware that if we call the police now they'll probably cordon off the area and begin a search for other remains perhaps. They'll want to dig up the ground all around the burial site. Local historians could well become involved, and anything we hope to achieve here could be irretrievably lost. For all we know, Excalibur could be buried in this very field, and we've only scanned the first two grid lines so far. Do you really think the police will allow us to merrily go on working while they investigate what is in fact an old and irrelevant skeletal find? I don't think so. No, all I would ask of you, Mr. Cutler, and you two also, Mr. Fortune and Miss Corbett, is five days. Five days to try and find what we came here to look for. All we have to do is rebury the coffin for now, and once we've completed what we're here for, we simply open it up again and make the call to the local police. That way we get the chance to finish the job without interruption. Surely you can see that it won't make an ounce of difference to this poor wretch in the box?"

Cutler and the others looked at each other as though waiting for one or another to speak. At first it appeared that no-one wanted to be the first to voice their opinions. Graves wondered if he'd said enough to convince them. Finding the body had been an unexpected development and he hadn't exactly had long to come up with a convincing story. In the end it was Joe Cutler who spoke first.

"Speaking for myself, Mr. Graves, I have to say that I'm a little uneasy with this whole thing, but you're right. If we involve the police at this point in time we'll lose the privacy we currently have to get the search completed without interference. On the other hand, this poor sod in the box should be given a proper burial in consecrated ground. If the others agree, I'll go along with you for the five days you've asked for. After that, we unearth the box again and call the police, agreed?"

"You have my word on it," Graves replied. "Now, Mr. Fortune, Miss Corbett, how do you stand on the matter?"

Winston and Sally were equally hesitant but eventually agreed that they would go along with his request. Graves and Cutler agreed that they should now fill in the grave and leave as little trace as they could of the day's excavations. It took an hour and a half of hard labour before they finished, and though the end result wasn't as perfect as they might have hoped, it was unlikely that anyone would suspect what may lie beneath the freshly disturbed earth, especially as the surveyors were known to be searching and digging for artefacts relating to Joseph of Arimithea.

The rest of that day's search was uneventful, the remainder of the field revealing nothing more to the radar. Cutler called a halt to the day's work just after five p.m. and the team quickly packed away their equipment. Graves made a hasty departure, heading back to his room at Meare Manor to make what he said were a few important phone calls.

Joe, Winston and Sally stowed away the last of their equipment and climbed wearily into the van. As Winston started the engine and engaged first gear he looked across at Joe Cutler who was sitting by the passenger window, Sally between the two of them.

"You've got something on your mind, Winston."

"Well, boss, it's not much really, but, well, you know when I was down in the hole with Graves? When we found the skeleton and pulled the shroud back, he seemed a bit reluctant to uncover the whole of the body. He pulled it back just enough though."

"Enough for what, Winston?"

"Enough for me to disagree with his 'diagnosis' that the stiff was a plague victim from over a hundred years ago."

"How come?" asked Sally, intrigued by Winston's statement.

"Easy," said Winston, and his next sentence brought the conversation to a sudden and shattering conclusion, such was the shock that reverberated around the cab of Cutler's van. "How many nineteenth or early twentieth century plague victims would you expect to find buried in box in a field, wearing a Timex wristwatch?"

Chapter 17

"You're sure it was a wristwatch?" Sally asked as they sat around a low coffee table in The Rowan Tree's residents lounge a short while later. "No chance you could have been mistaken?"

"Hey, Sally girl," he replied indignantly. "I know a bloody wristwatch when I see one, and that's what that skeleton had draped around its wrist bones. Like I said I saw enough of it to read the name on the dial, so don't ask me if I was mistaken."

"Okay, Winston, don't get your knickers in a twist, I was only checking, that's all."

"Listen," Joe said, "we've got to think this through. We've just gone along with what I expect is a highly suspect, if not downright illegal arrangement with Graves. If we succeed in finding the sword and report the body to the police then okay, but something is beginning to smell with this job. I'm not sure yet what it is but it's not a good smell, that's for certain."

"What I want to know," said Winston "is why Graves would lie about the skeleton? If he really is a historian then it's certain he knows that the skeleton isn't a plague victim from a century ago. He moved so quick to stop me seeing the whole of the remains, it was as if he was trying to cover something up, or rather, not let something be revealed. If I hadn't had my eyes exactly on the spot where the wristwatch was revealed I could easily have missed it, man. It was only in sight for a couple of seconds. I'm wondering if there might have been something else there that he didn't want us to see."

"I hope you realise what you've just said, Winston," Cutler replied, as worry lines appeared from nowhere to crease his brow. "If Graves knew what was in that grave then he probably also knew *who* that poor sod was, and if that's the case and the body was buried quite recently, then we have to assume that something very fishy is happening here."

"There's something else, as well," Winston continued, getting into the flow now that he had everyone's full attention. "That shroud the body was wrapped in was no piece of nineteenth century linen. At one time it was a blanket, old, but not that old. I recognised the ticking on the edge of the blanket."

"Ticking?"

"Ah. Well before your time, young Sally girl," Winston replied to her query.

"He means the stitched edging along the blanket," Cutler added.

"Ah, I see, I think," said Sally, "and the significance of this ticking is…?"

"Sally girl, you know I was in the army once?"

She nodded in the affirmative.

"Well, let me tell you, girl, you never forget an army blanket. They haven't changed in years, and that thing in the grave was an army blanket, I'll stake my life on it. It was an old one for sure, maybe fifty years or more old, but an army blanket nonetheless."

"That puts it well and truly in the modern age Winston," Cutler commented.

"Oh yes, boss, too modern to have anything to do with Excalibur or King Arthur or Sir Pelleas or…"

"*Okay* Winston. I think you've made your point," said Cutler.

"Listen, you two are getting me really worried now," said Sally. "You're really saying that Mr. Graves isn't a historian, that he knows who's buried in the grave, and that we're not actually searching for Excalibur, despite what we've been told?"

"You catch on quick Sally," Winston answered.

"Joe, this is starting to scare me," she continued, looking almost imploringly at Cutler, as if he could take away the fear that had suddenly gripped her in a vice-like grip.

"I'm sorry, Sally." Cutler tried to calm her. "I'm sure we'll get it all sorted out. But if Graves isn't on the level, then we have to assume that neither is Malcolm Capshaw. We may have been hired to find something of a more modern ilk than Arthur's sword, and that they don't trust us enough to tell us what it is."

"You mean the whole thing is probably criminally connected," Winston butted in," and they daren't tell us what it's really about, 'cause if they did they know we'd go running straight to the police."

"Which we should have done straight away when we found that poor man in the grave today," Sally added, a slight quiver appearing in her voice for the first time.

"In retrospect I think you're right. We should have done just that," Cutler agreed, "regardless of what Graves said."

"And the gun?" asked Winston. "He made you look a fool there didn't he boss?"

"I still think he has a gun, Winston," Cutler said thoughtfully. "He probably caught me looking the other day, and thought up the pistol-grip screwdriver ploy to drive me away from the scent."

"That makes him a very clever and very devious man," Winston Fortune concluded.

"And the police? Why don't we call them now?" asked Sally.

"Look, I know you might think me a fool, and I'm sure Capshaw and Graves think me one, but I want to know what this is all about Sally. If we go to the police now, what do we actually have to report? A skeleton in a field with no known connection to Graves, as far as we know? He'd get round that one with his historical search ploy, no problem. A gun that only I've seen, and that was only a quick view of what I thought was the handgrip of a pistol. He'd show them the screwdriver. I don't think he'd have the gun where they could find it easily, knowing I've seen it he probably won't have it on his person any more while we're doing the job. They need real evidence for a search warrant, which they'd need to go searching in his room or his belongings, and I don't think we've got enough to give them at the moment. At the very worst he'd say we're in it together and we'd all end up being considered complicit in unearthing and then concealing a grave of someone who died a long time ago."

"How do we know it was a long time ago? Winston said it was a fairly modern watch and blanket."

"I said about fifty years old, I think," said Winston, "and that's just a guess."

"But it's certainly not ancient," she went on.

"No, Sally," Cutler continued, "but we need more before we can go to the police. Come on, be honest, don't you both want to know what's really going on here, because I do? I hate anyone trying to make a fool out of me."

"I'm with you, boss," said Winston Fortune, making his decision. "Let's go along with Graves until we find out what's going on and then if we confirm that he's up to no good we go to the cops with a cut and dried case against the creep."

"And you, Sally? Are you with us?" asked Cutler.

Sally Corbett went quiet, and appeared lost in thought for a good thirty seconds. She was afraid of what they might unearth if they went on with this mad scheme, but she couldn't help but be intrigued by the mystery that had grown around Walter Graves and the strange and possibly false nature of the search in which they'd become involved.

"Sally?" Cutler broke into her thoughts. "Well?"

"Call me a bloody fool as well then," she said, taking a deep breath and forcing out a smile that betrayed only a hint of false bravado. "I'm with you, boss. Just promise me please, that if things start to look too dangerous or we do find out that Graves is involved is some sort of criminal activity we go straight to the police, without hesitation."

"My word on it." said Cutler, and rightly or wrongly, for better or worse, the three of them had made the decision to stick with the search, to try to outwit a man they barely knew, and who may or may not have been highly dangerous. For one of the three members of the Strata Survey team seated at that table that evening, the danger presented by Walter Graves would soon become all too evident, but for now, they were determined in their resolve to solve the mystery, and to find out who or what lay beneath the earth somewhere nearby that had caused Malcolm Capshaw to pay so much money and devise what appeared to be an elaborate deception in order to unearth it.

The decision made, they all seemed to relax a little, and soon all three rose from the table and made their way to their respective rooms to shower and change. Sally was also determined to try to contact Professor Doberman to try to ascertain what, if anything, he'd learned from the copy of the chronicle she'd e-mailed him that morning.

The answer, which she relayed to the others when they met in the bar a short while later before dinner, wasn't particularly encouraging.

"I spoke to Lucius from my room," she informed the two men as they enjoyed a pre-dinner bottle of wine between them.

"Oh, it's 'Lucius' now is it? said Winston, grinning that cheeky lascivious grin he used when in a tormenting mood. "What happened to Professor Doberman?"

"The professor asked me to call him Lucius," said Sally indignantly. "I'm not a student any more as he said, and he prefers to be known by his given name to anyone other than those studying at the university. Anyway, are you interested in what he had to say or not?"

"Hey, sorry. I'm just pulling your leg, you know that."

"Shut up, Winston," Cutler ordered. "Please tell us, Sally. Was he able to enlighten you at all?"

"Well, as he said to begin with, it isn't easy to work with a copy such as I was able to send him. For a start he wasn't able to verify the age of the document, only the original would suffice for that purpose, so he's tried to concentrate on the wording of the document."

"And?" Cutler prodded.

"He can't be sure, it's as simple as that I'm afraid. He says that the wording and writing style is typical of the era we're investigating, but the other difficulty is that he can't see the actual ink it was written with, which would apparently have given him a clue to the age of the chronicle. He did say, though, that there were one or two small anomalies in the text, almost as if the writer were 'hesitating', as Lucius put it when writing certain letters, particularly some of the upper case letters at the beginning of various sections of the chronicle."

"Like maybe he was looking at something he was trying to copy?" asked Winston. "As if he was a modern writer referring to an old text for the way to form those letters?"

"That's exactly the way Lucius put it!" she exclaimed.

"So, basically, your professor is saying that he thinks it's a fake?" asked Cutler.

"He's not saying that exactly, but he's recommending caution, that's all. He says that the information in the chronicle is interestingly tantalising, but is certainly like nothing he's ever seen or heard of before. He thinks it strange that such a document could have existed for so many years without anyone having even a hint of its existence, or of the information it contains. His own personal view and he stressed that it is only his own view, is that the whole thing may be a carefully contrived hoax. He said that there are always unscrupulous people who are prepared to perpetrate massive hoaxes and make money from 'gullible fools' as he described them, who think they can be the one to find the Holy Grail, or a long-lost DaVinci, or a new Biblical writing or some such thing. If, and again he stressed the word 'if', this is a hoax, it may be that Capshaw has been taken in by someone out to make money from him by use of a fake Arthurian Chronicle. His final word was that he personally doesn't believe that the Arthurian legend is anything more than just that, a legend, and that we should be very careful about believing in a document which is wholly unsubstantiated by any known historical fact or point of reference."

"Sounds to me as if the professor is stating his case quite unequivocally, Sally," Cutler said thoughtfully as she finished her narrative of her conversation with Doberman. "The whole Chronicle of Gareth is a fake, that's what he's saying. I know you keep saying 'in his opinion' but that's precisely why you contacted him wasn't it? To get his opinion?"

"I didn't want to be too discouraging, Joe," she said quietly.

"Hell no, Sally. You and your professor have done a great job if you ask my opinion," Winston added to the conversation. "What you say, boss?"

"I agree with Winston, Sally. I think that from now on we have to assume that the document and the map are bogus, and we should proceed with great caution."

"Do you think that Graves is part of a plot to make money from Capshaw then, Joe?" Sally queried.

"I'm not sure what part Graves plays in all of this," Cutler replied. "We have to remember that he's being paid by Capshaw, just as we are. Not only that, but he reports to Capshaw every day as far as I know, which in my book means the two of them are a lot closer than we might think. If he was part of a plot to make money out of Capshaw I don't think he'd be quite so 'in' with him. No, I think that Capshaw is all part of bigger picture, a conspiracy of some kind that excludes us from the real nature of what's going on. We're the only dupes in this affair, Graves knows exactly what's going on, you mark my words."

"So what do we do, boss?" asked Winston gravely.

"What do we do, Winston? Why, we have a damn good dinner, that's what we do. Then tomorrow, we go along with our friend Mr. Graves in his search for Excalibur, and while we're doing it, we try to find out exactly what the hell's going on and why someone thinks they can make bloody fools of the three of us!"

Chapter 18

Walter Graves sat in the bar of Meare Manor, his brow etched with a frown that showed no sign of disappearing. He was sipping his second large brandy of the evening somewhat absent-mindedly, as though the warming liquid in the glass were nothing more than a prop to sustain his presence in the comfortable surroundings of the bar. His mind was obviously elsewhere as he appeared oblivious to the various comings and goings around him as other guests entered or left the bar, even managing to avoid the cheery 'Good evening' launched in his direction from an elderly, slightly rotund gentleman of the old school, complete with handlebar moustache and navy blue blazer sporting the badge of the Royal Air Force. Had he looked up and acknowledged the man, Graves would have made the instant assessment that he was being spoken to by a retired Wing Commander, or group Captain or other such high ranking officer. His people-watching skills, usually one of his greatest assets and skills in the performance of his work had taken the evening off.

The skeleton had been a surprise, and an unwelcome one at that. Though he knew there'd been a chance that they'd unearth the remains of the man in the grave, he'd considered the chance to be a small one and he certainly hadn't expected it to happen quite so soon in the search. Added to that was the fact that he'd had to lie on his feet, concocting a rapid explanation for the purposes of directing Cutler and the others away from the truth. He was clever, and well used to improvising and manipulating a situation when necessary, but this whole thing was getting a little too complicated for his liking.

Whether he'd managed to convince Cutler, Fortune and Corbett with his 'plague victim' scenario was now the single-most important problem which beset his mind. He'd tried hard to prevent Fortune from seeing too much of the skeleton, making sure that he kept the majority of the remains covered by the blanket that had acted as a burial shroud, but had he done enough? He knew that Winston Fortune was no idiot; he was ex-Special Forces for God's sake, a trained observer with a quick eye. Not only that, but he couldn't be certain that the ruse with the screwdriver had been enough to deflect Cutler from the presence of the Ruger in his pocket. Again, Cutler was no fool, and Walter Graves was beginning to think that what had seemed a fairly simple job at the outset might just begin to turn a little messy before much more time had elapsed. Even Sally Corbett who he'd originally thought would be the one most likely to hang on his every word had appeared to be growing sceptical and more than a little cynical towards his historical knowledge, and his interpretation of the document.

He'd been putting off the call he knew he'd have to make sooner or later that evening, and as he glanced at his watch he knew that Malcolm Capshaw would have left his office at least an hour ago. He'd be at home by now, which was where Graves wanted him to be when he made the call. Better for Capshaw to be in the more relaxed surroundings of his own luxury home when Graves passed on the less than satisfactory news of the day's developments; or at least, that was theory. Walter Graves drained the last of the

Napoleon Brandy from his glass, hardly appreciating the fine liquor as it slipped down his throat. He then made his way up to his room to make the call.

"You found *what*?" Malcolm Capshaw exploded at the end of the telephone line as Graves relayed the information about the discovery of the skeleton.

"Like I said, we found Hogan, or at least, what's left of him."

"How can you be sure it was Hogan?"

"Come on," said Graves. "How many bodies do you think are going to be lying around waiting to be discovered so close to what we're looking for? The age of the skeleton looked about right, certainly the blanket he was covered with was from the correct era, and the box they'd put him in was exactly like those described by your friend Maitland."

"And Cutler and the others? What did they do?"

"They wanted to go running straight to the police, but I think I managed to convince them that the body was much older, probably a turn-of-the-century plague victim, carried away and buried away from the village or farm or wherever they lived in the hope of keeping infection at bay."

"You *think*?" stormed Capshaw, so loudly that Graves held the phone away from his ear. "I'm paying you a great deal of money for your skills and expertise, to make this job run nice and smoothly and you hit a little problem and the whole thing is jeopardised. Do you realise how much time and money I invested in setting up the fake Excalibur documents just so you'd be able to keep those bloody surveyors nice and sweet and away from the real object of the search? Fucking hell, Graves! You're acting like a moron when I'm paying you to be a professional. If Cutler and his idiots learn what we're really after do you think for one minute that they'll

Brian L. Porter

125

keep quiet and just go along with it? They'll be running to the law as fast as their feet'll carry them."

"Everything's under control. I can manage Cutler and his people. Don't worry about them."

"It's not them I'm worried about. It's whether I've hired the right man for the job that worries me right now. Hogan disappeared over sixty years ago, and he was supposed to stay buried for ever. If the police ever find him we'll have next to no chance of finding what we're after. You'd better get things under better control than they are right now, Graves, and if Cutler and his people start to become a serious problem or a risk to the project then you'll have to arrange a little accident for our poor unfortunate surveyors. Do you understand what I'm getting at?"

"Of course I understand, but I assure you that things aren't as bad as you seem to believe them to be. Leave Cutler to me. I've promised them that if we don't find what we're looking for in five days then I'll go to the police with them and report the finding of the skeleton."

"You've promised *what*?"

"Look, it doesn't matter either way, does it? If we do find what we're after then Cutler and his crew will have served their purpose anyway and they'll quietly disappear forever as arranged. If we don't find it in that time then we'll still have to say goodbye to Strata Survey Systems. Either way, they'll have no chance to voice their worries to the law. As long as I can keep them believing in Excalibur, they'll keep working and we'll have more chance of success than if we dump them now and try to find replacements."

"I just hope for your sake that they do believe you, Graves. You'd better be bloody convincing in your role as a professor of history, that's all I can say."

"You seem to forget," said Graves solemnly into the telephone, "that I *am* a professor of history."

"As well as everything else," Capshaw replied menacingly. "Don't you ever forget, *Mister* Graves, that I know exactly who you are and what you do. That's why you work for me, remember?"

"As if you'd ever let me forget," said Graves resignedly, and wishing that he'd never set eyes on the man on the other end of the phone line.

"Now, now, Mr. Graves, let's be fair about this. You might think I exploit your talents to my advantage, which I do of course, but you are also extremely handsomely rewarded for your efforts. Now please, just get on with what I'm paying you for, and find what you're being paid to find."

"I'll find it, don't worry," said Graves, but the line was already dead.

Malcolm Capshaw had made his point and hung up on the historian. It was clear to Graves that he had little choice other than to try to play out the Excalibur scenario as long as he could. He still had his trump card to play of course. If Cutler looked like getting too close to the truth, Graves would take and use Sally Corbett as leverage to convince Cutler and Fortune to go on with the search. In fact he almost wished that Cutler would force him into that particular option. Walter Graves decided that he would quite appreciate getting up close and personal with Miss Sally Corbett.

For now, though, it was time to eat, enjoy a couple more brandies, and then to get some much needed sleep. Graves anticipated a busy and interesting few days ahead of him, he needed as much sleep as he could get. He wanted to be bright and alert for any sign of suspicion from Cutler and his people. Duck in a redcurrant sauce formed the basis of the meal he enjoyed that evening in the dining room at Meare Manor. He was quite enjoying his stay at the old guest house; despite the trials and tribulations of the days this was a first-rate place to spend his evenings. A few more drinks after dinner and Walter Graves had relaxed to the extent that when he returned to his room and undressed and climbed into bed, he was asleep within seconds.

The sound of the back of Malcolm Capshaw's right hand connecting with the side of Charlotte Raeburn's face shattered what was left of the peace in his bedroom in Stratford.

"Get out," he shouted at the unfortunate girl, the only one he could vent his feelings on now that he'd hung up on Walter Graves. Charlotte reeled from the blow, her face burning where his hand had made painful and firm contact.

"But, Mr Capshaw, what have I done?"

"Don't argue with me you ungrateful bitch, just get the hell out. I'll see you in the office in the morning."

Charlotte rose tearfully from the bed, still naked, and crossed the room to where her clothes lay draped over the back of one of the two armchairs which adorned Capshaw's bedroom. She dressed quickly, and turned to face her employer once more.

"Mr. Capshaw?"

"What, are you still here?" he asked sardonically.

"Don't you remember, sir? I came with you in your car. You wanted me to stay tonight and go into the office with you tomorrow. My car's still in the car park at work. How will I get home?"

"Why should I care?" He asked quite brutally, then hesitated before reaching into a drawer beside the bed and pulling out a wallet stuffed with twenty pound notes, two of which he threw haphazardly into the air, where they floated gently to the floor and lay on the think pile carpet.

"Pick it up," he ordered, and as a shamefaced Charlotte complied he added: "Go downstairs and phone for a taxi, and leave me in peace. And don't be late in the bloody morning!"

Feeling more of a whore than she ever had in her entire life Charlotte left the bedroom as fast as her feet would take her, ran down the stairs and phoned the first taxi firm whose number she could find in the local directory. Ten minutes later the cab arrived and she let herself out of the mansion clutching the forty pounds. It would cost only half that for the taxi ride home, the rest was obviously her compensation for her 'services' for the evening. As the cab carried her towards her own home her hand reached up to touch the flesh where Capshaw had slapped her. Her skin was hot to the touch, and she worried about a bruise showing by morning. Strangely, Charlotte felt more hatred and disgust for herself than she did for the man who was so quick to use and abuse her. After all, he did it because he paid her for the privilege of doing so, in Charlotte's case she couldn't even begin to figure out why she allowed herself to be used in that way, and that, more than anything was the reason for her self-loathing at that moment.

As the taxi sped through the dark through the streets of Shakespeare's hometown Charlotte Raeburn decided she had to escape the clutches of Malcolm Capshaw. It was a good job, there was no doubting that, but the price of earning the right to be the highly paid personal secretary of the brutal and sadistic millionaire was beginning to seem a little too high for Charlotte.

Chapter 19

Dazzling fingers of sunlight streamed through the window of Joe Cutler's room as he sat with his feet up on the bed the following morning. He'd pulled one of the curtains halfway across the window to prevent the sun from shining directly into his eyes and now he checked the time on his watch for the third time in as many minutes. Breakfast for Joe had been a hurried affair, and he'd left Winston and Sally to finish their third cup of coffee together as he needed to make a very important phone call from the privacy of his room.

As soon as his watch read eight-thirty Joe dialled his own office number. The ever reliable Mavis Hightower answered on the second ring.

"Mavis, hello. How are you?" he enquired.

"Fine as ever, Mr. Cutler, thank you for asking."

Another minute of pleasantries had passed amiably between them before Cutler directed the conversation to the business at hand.

"So tell me, Mavis, how's the amateur sleuthing been going?"

"We'll have less of the 'amateur' if you don't mind, Mr. Cutler. I'll have you know I've been very busy on your behalf, and I think I may have come up with one or two little surprises for you."

"No insult intended, Mavis. I know you never do things by halves. Now don't keep me in suspense. What have you got for me?"

"Well now. Let's take your Mr. Malcolm Capshaw for starters. On the surface he's everything your original cursory checks indicated."

Cutler winced at Mavis's use of the word 'cursory', the word becoming a fierce accusation on the lips of his trusted employee.

"Millionaire businessman, financier and international trader in stocks, shares, and in short, almost anything that poses as a saleable commodity. He's well known as a backer of various archaeological and historical projects around the world and his name is mentioned on the plaques adorning more than a few exhibits on display in many of the world's great museums. It's what's behind the public façade that should interest you though, Mr. Cutler."

Mavis paused for effect. It worked.

"Come on, Mavis, what is it?"

"Malcolm Capshaw seems to have another, less well publicised side to his business, and indeed to his personality. Very few people are aware that he was born and went to school in the old East End of London, not far from the old stomping grounds of Jack the Ripper himself. His closest friend at school, and I might add one with whom he is still in close contact, was none other than a certain Mr. Boris Maitland."

"Maitland? You don't mean...?"

"Oh yes I do mean," said Mavis triumphantly. "Your Mr Capshaw is closely allied with Boris and his brother Karl, and one of the biggest criminal fraternities in the whole of London. Though the police have so far failed to pin anything serious on the brothers, they are known to be responsible for dozens of major crimes committed in the last few years. They've just been very clever, always managing to keep one step ahead of the law. It's suspected that Capshaw's millions have helped them more than once in their efforts to evade justice, not to mention that he may be up to his eyes in whatever criminal activity they're involved in."

"Bloody hell, Mavis! You didn't get that little lot from an internet web page. Where on earth have you been digging?"

"Ah, well, there you are you see. You should never underestimate little grey haired old ladies, now should you, Mr. Cutler?

"Anyway, I did tell you once, though I imagine you've forgotten, that my nephew Eric is a detective inspector with the Metropolitan Police. When I called him and told him that you'd accepted a contract with Malcolm Capshaw and that I was worried that you might be in a bit of trouble and had he heard of him, it was hard to shut him up. The Met have a file on Capshaw an inch thick, and growing, as Eric put it, and it's not only in business that he has a reputation for playing dirty. He's also known to have some, how shall we say, less than savoury appetites of a sexual nature. In other words, he likes it rough, Mr. Cutler, and any woman who gets involved with Capshaw had better watch out. Apparently, his money was the only thing that managed to keep him out of court when one of his previous secretaries reported him to the police for rape. Two days after she made the allegation she suddenly withdrew it, and though the police couldn't prove it they were sure that Capshaw had bought her silence. Put it this way, she left a very small one roomed apartment and moved into a beautiful detached house in the country not long after she dropped the charges, so you just have to make up your own mind."

A mental picture of Capshaw's current secretary leaped into Cutler's mind, that apparently cold and hard nosed girl in the smart business suit who'd shepherded him in and out of Capshaw's office a couple of weeks ago. Suddenly, he didn't despise the girl quite so much. Perhaps behind that cold exterior she was simply hiding a fear of her employer, though Cutler knew there was little he could do to prove or disprove that particular theory. He did know, however, that he was beginning to like Malcolm Capshaw less and less with each word that came to him over the telephone from the mouth of Mavis Hightower. With that dislike came more than a growing suspicion that he, Winston and Sally might be in over their heads in something far bigger than he could have imagined. His attention returned to Mavis who was far from finished.

"Apparently, the poor girl was covered in bruises when she staggered into the police station, so it must have cost him an arm and leg to buy her silence after something like that. Eric says the report stated she was in a bad way, Mr. Cutler. It must have been his money and her fear of the man that made her drop the charges, nothing else makes sense. You must be careful with that man, really you must."

"I'll be careful, no doubt about it, Mavis, you can count on it. Now, what about Graves? I don't suppose you have another nephew squirreled away in the Department of Education or whatever the governing body is for history professors?"

"I did even better than that, Mr. Cutler, much better than that in fact. You told me that Walter Graves served in the army before taking his doctorate so I started at the only logical place."

"Which was?"

"Why, Betty Hunter of course."

"Betty Hunter, Mavis? I can't wait to hear this one, go on."

"Well, Betty is a great friend of mine, lives two doors away from me, and she works at G.C.H.Q."

"Spy Central," Cutler interrupted.

"Yes, well, when I told Betty of your little predicament with the man, she phoned a friend of hers at the Ministry of Defence and, Bob's your uncle, she came back to me with all I needed to know."

"Er, Mavis, isn't your friend bound by the Official Secrets Act or something like that? Should she have been telling you all this? She might get into trouble."

"Oh no, Mr. Cutler, it's quite all right. We're *friends* after all."

Mavis said this as if it excused any possible breach of national security committed by her friend in revealing details about Walter Graves to her. It couldn't possibly be wrong if they were friends, could it?

"Oh well, that's alright then, Mavis. Please, go on."

"Anyway, she didn't actually tell me anything at all. She just sort of dropped subtle hints, and I filled in the gaps with intuitive guesses and when I was on the button so to speak, Betty just gave me an affirmative response. So there you are, everything is quite alright, I assure you."

Amazed, astounded and delighted at his office manager's depth of duplicity and talent for covert undercover investigation, Cutler waited for Mavis to get to the point.

"So, where were we? Oh yes, Walter Graves. Mr. Graves was indeed a soldier, and a highly well-thought of one at that. He was highly decorated and fought in the Falklands campaign and was at the Battle for Goose Green and took part in the liberation of Port Stanley. He held the rank of Major and was respected and admired by all those who served under him, and also by his superiors. Unfortunately, there was a hint of some minor scandal surrounding an action he was involved in while in the Falklands, something to do with the treatment of prisoners of war. It never became public knowledge and Graves was allowed to resign his commission and return to the UK without a stain in his character. Whatever happened in the Falklands was quietly covered up and forgotten, not because of any loyalty to Graves himself, but the mission he was on was apparently of a highly sensitive nature and it was deemed 'not in the public interest' for the specifics of the mission to be revealed.

"Anyway, Graves soon gained a place at Oxford, where he graduated with honours and began his new career as a historian. He discovered he had a talent for the 'Indiana Jones' type of adventure and it was his penchant for becoming involved in all manner of overseas expeditions that probably brought him to the attention of Capshaw. Five years ago he was offered the professorship at his college, which he accepted on condition he was allowed to pursue his exterior researches. The college agreed and he's still there today."

"Is that all, Mavis?" asked Cutler, sensing more to come.

"Oh no, Mr. Cutler, that most certainly is not all. They're only rumours, of course, but it seems that trouble and tragedy seem to follow Mr. Graves around. On more than one occasion, people with whom he's been in competition in order to discover or unearth certain historical artefacts have met with unfortunate 'accidents'. Over the last three years those accidents have resulted in at least three fatalities, though as I said, they can only be connected to Walter Graves by virtue of rumour and innuendo. In short, if Malcolm Capshaw is to be considered corrupt and criminally inclined, I would say that Walter Graves should be considered highly dangerous and the man should be avoided if at all possible."

Mavis fell silent, and Cutler took a deep breath before replying to her report.

"Mavis, you should have been in MI5, or some such branch of the intelligence services. You're quiet amazing, d'you know that?"

"Why, thank you," she replied gracefully.

"I can't tell you how much all that information helps. At least we know to some extent who and what we're dealing with now, thanks to you and your nephew, and Mrs. Hunter, of course. Please thank them both for me, won't you?"

"Oh I will, when the time is right," Mavis went on. "It wouldn't do to let them know I was passing on all this secret information to you now, would it?"

Cutler laughed.

"Mavis Hightower, you're incorrigible, but I don't know what we'd do without you. Thank you, really, you've discovered far more than I thought you would in such a short space of time."

"You're welcome, Mr. Cutler," she replied. "Oh, there was one more thing that Eric mentioned about the Maitlands."

"Oh yes, what was that Mavis?"

"Well, their father Albert was never as big a fish in the criminal pond as their grandfather Samuel. Albert was a bit of a wimp by London Gangland standards and he was killed by a rival gang in an execution style shooting when the boys were only five and seven. Samuel brought the boys up himself and it's rumoured that he always told them that one day they'd reap the biggest legacy they could imagine. All they had to do was find it. This came from his ex-wife Moira who died in suspicious circumstances some time after she'd told the story to her own mother, and well, you know how old ladies talk and rumours begin?"

"Oh yes, Mavis, I know just what you mean." Cutler laughed softly into the phone.

"I just wondered if this so-called 'legacy' might have something to do with why you're all in Glastonbury."

"Hmmm, we'll have to wait and see, won't we, Mavis? Now, thanks again, but I have to go. I'm going to have to go to work. I'll keep checking in with you. If you learn any more..."

"Don't you worry, Mr. Cutler; I'll let you know as soon as I find anything out."

The two said their goodbyes, and Joe Cutler made his way out of his room, along the corridor and down the stairs to the foyer of the guest house where Winston and Sally waited. He'd have to fill them in on Mavis's report as they drove to meet Graves.

As they walked out onto the street outside the Rowan tree, the sun that had been shining so brightly a little earlier disappeared behind a large bank of cumulus that hung like a shroud over the town. The grey cloudy atmosphere that replaced the earlier warmth seemed to suit Cutler's mood entirely. Any flippancy he may have felt about the task ahead of them, any thoughts he'd harboured that it would be easy to outwit Graves and in doing so solve the mystery of their presence in Glastonbury now hung by a thread in Joe Cutler's mind. As Winston Fortune turned the ignition key and the van's engine kicked itself into life, Cutler wondered just how to tell Winston and Sally of what he'd just learned. He'd try hard not to show it, not to let them know how bad things might be, but in truth, Joe Cutler was a very worried man.

Chapter 20

Joe Cutler wasn't the only one to feel a sense of trepidation that morning. Malcolm Capshaw hated leaving his home in Stratford except to travel to work or to one of his favourite night-time drinking haunts. He'd moved to the beautiful and peaceful birthplace of William Shakespeare five years earlier, after the unfortunate incident with that stupid girl Maggie. He'd made it plain to her exactly what was expected of her when he gave her the job as his secretary, (or at least he thought he'd made it clear), and then she cried rape the first time he imposed his sexual desires on her. He'd paid the bitch a tidy sum of money to drop the charges and move out of London, but he also felt that the time had come when he should also seek new pastures.

He'd decided on Stratford-upon-Avon after much deliberation. The price of both commercial and private property was well within his means. Something about Stratford seemed to suggest an air of respectability and stability. Capshaw was keen to get out of London and it took less than a month for him to locate suitable office premises and a further two weeks to decide upon the palatial house that he now called home.

London soon became less substance and more memory in his mind as his business expanded and he found it less and less necessary to visit the city. Only his connection with the Maitlands tied him to London. Most of the time his business with them was conducted by phone or e-mail, with the brothers occasionally travelling to Stratford to deal face-to-face with Capshaw when the need arose. Only rarely did Boris Maitland insist upon Capshaw's presence in the Capital, and after Capshaw had relayed the latest information from Glastonbury to him the night before Maitland had made it clear that this was to be one of those occasions.

As his driver sped along towards London, Malcolm Capshaw did his best to switch his mind off from the coming meeting with the Maitland brothers. He tried to focus on the view from the car window, the green fields, the trees, the villages and towns they passed along the way, but all the time the thought that he'd soon be back in London, and facing the possible displeasure of the Maitlands returned. As hard and corrupt as Capshaw himself might be, Boris and Karl Maitland still had the power to instil fear in the millionaire businessman. They were perhaps the only people in the world who possessed that ability. Ever since their days at school together Boris in particular had wielded a certain level of influence over Malcolm Capshaw. They'd been friends, that was true, but Maitland had always been the dominant partner in their friendship, able to manipulate and control Capshaw, to bend him to accept the Maitland way of thinking and doing things, and so it had continued into adulthood.

At first, Capshaw had derived a sense of satisfaction from his close connection with such a notorious family as the Maitlands, but as time went on and Capshaw's own wealth and influence had grown he became less dependent on the relationship with the brothers. Boris and Karl, however, had seen things a different way. With Capshaw's wealth and seemingly legitimate business connections they found a new outlet for their own criminal activities. Capshaw was able to provide a legitimate front for some of their less than savoury dealings, and it wasn't long before he had become an integral cog in the wheel that represented their world of crime and wrongdoing. By making sure Capshaw was deeply embroiled in a host of illegal transactions they had made sure he would remain loyal to their cause. The chances of Malcolm Capshaw ever betraying the Maitlands had been reduced to zero.

Now, as the green of the countryside began to give way to the grey of the city, and the leaves of the treetops replaced by the rooftops of the suburbs of London, Malcolm Capshaw wondered just what the day would bring. He knew Boris Maitland was unhappy with the fact that the survey team had unearthed the body of Hogan, though how he could have indemnified against that possibility was anyone's guess. Knowing that the prize they sought had to be in quite close proximity to Hogan's burial place must have meant there was a strong possibility that the body would have been found first. It was plain bad luck that Cutler's team had blundered upon the grave first; it could so easily have been the other way around. Capshaw knew that either way, Cutler and his team would have to be 'dispensed with' at some point in the operation. Finding Hogan meant that Walter Graves would have his work cut out keeping a lid on the discovery of the body until Cutler had served his purpose. That was the problem he knew the Maitlands wanted to discuss with him that day.

Baines the driver suddenly broke into his thoughts.

"We're almost there, Mr. Capshaw."

Capshaw abandoned his thoughts and turned to look out of the window. Sure enough, the entrance to the Maitland's home was coming up on the right. Baines slowed the car and turned into the entrance gates to the mansion. He brought the car to a standstill at the closed wrought iron gates and pressed a button on the intercom panel attached to one of the gate's two supporting pillars. After announcing their arrival, a camera atop the left hand gate swung to take in the view of the car and its occupants, and the gates swung open, allowing them entry. Gravel scrunched beneath the wheels of Capshaw's Bentley as Baines drove along the long sweeping tree-lined drive that led up to the Maitland's home. Built originally in the nineteenth century as a sanatorium for the wealthy, complete with lake and boathouse, Dangerfield Hall had been the home of the Maitland family since old Samuel Maitland had bought it as a ruin soon after the end of the Second World War. He'd invested much of the ill-gotten gains of his criminal enterprises into renovating and improving the old sanatorium until it had assumed the imposing proportions of a neo-gothic mansion. Even today, his grandsons were perpetually adding to and improving the various wings of the twenty-five bedroom hall.

As the Bentley drew nearer to the hall itself, the driveway opened up, becoming wider and ascending a gentle incline. Beautifully kept gardens swept outwards from the verges of the drive, the grass a deep emerald green and cut as short as a bowling green. Occasional trees broke up the view, giving the observer the impression of being far from the city, deep in the English countryside as opposed to the reality of being only fifteen miles from the centre of the city. A pair of peacocks was strutting across the grass to the left of the car as the Bentley swung in a wide arc at the end of the drive to pull up in front of the steps that led up to the main entrance of Dangerfield Hall. Baines applied the brakes and the car came to a graceful halt, the tires quietly crunching the gravel beneath them. Capshaw's driver was out of the car as soon as the engine died, and opened the door for his employer to exit the vehicle.

Capshaw stepped out into the fresh air, breathing in deeply as he stretched his arms and legs after the long journey from his own sanctuary in the country. Compared to this place, however, even he was forced to admit that his own home in Stratford was small by comparison. Nevertheless, he preferred it to what he thought of as a rambling old pile of masonry from a bygone era. Stratford had class after all!

Baines had no need to ring the doorbell on Capshaw's behalf. As the two men ascended the steps that led to the imposing double doors fashioned in oak, the doors swung open to reveal the person of Howard Mallory. Employed by the Maitlands for as long as Capshaw could remember, Mallory had at one time been the chief enforcer for the criminal family. Anyone who had ever fallen foul of the family's temper would have had good reason to fear Howard Mallory. An ex-professional boxer, he'd left the ring under a cloud when a scandal broke in respect of the alleged 'fixing' of certain bouts. "Mr. Boris and Mr. Karl are expecting you Mr. Capshaw," he announced as Capshaw crossed the threshold of the hall. "They're in the library."

"I know my way thank you, Howard," Capshaw replied. "Perhaps you could take Baines here to the kitchen and fix him up with a drink and a sandwich."

"My pleasure, Mr. Capshaw," Mallory replied, motioning to Baines to follow him. As the two men disappeared through a door at the far end of the entrance hall Capshaw took a deep breath and headed in the opposite direction. The door to the library stood off to the left of the hall. His footsteps echoed, announcing his progress as he walked across the highly polished stone floor.

As he approached the door to the library a voice from within said, "Come in, Malcolm, we've been waiting for you."

Capshaw pushed the heavy library door open and walked tentatively into the vast room that lay beyond. He'd never failed to be impressed by the Maitland's library. Row after row of books, many leather-bound antiques of great value stood side by side with more modern tomes, reflecting the family's eclectic taste when it came to literature. The brothers were well-read, highly educated, and could hold an intelligent discourse on almost any subject one could name. Criminally minded they might be, illiterate they most definitely were not.

Boris was leaning against the beautifully restored Edwardian fireplace. In colder weather a log fire would have been burning in the grate, today was warm, and no flames welcomed Malcolm Capshaw as he walked into a decidedly chilly atmosphere.

"Hello, Malcy" announced the voice of Boris's younger brother Karl, who sat cross-legged in a luxuriously padded leather armchair at the far side of the library, a goblet of brandy warming in the palm of his hand. Despite the hour, it was no surprise to see Karl with alcohol in close attendance. His alcoholism was an open secret between those who knew the family well.

Malcolm Capshaw hated the familiarity of the name that Karl addressed him by; even Boris always used his full given name. Not wanting to antagonise Karl however, he let it pass without comment.

"Morning, Boris, Karl." He spoke as confidently and cheerfully as he could.

"Come and sit down, Malcy," Karl ordered. "I think we've got a problem."

"A problem?" asked Capshaw. "I've no idea what you mean, Karl."

"Oh, but I think you do, Malcolm, my old friend," said Boris, slowly and with a hint of menace in his voice that Capshaw had only heard once or twice before in his life, and never delivered in his direction. "Now be a good boy and do as Karl asked you. *Sit!*"

Like an obedient dog under orders from his master, Malcolm Capshaw sat in the chair facing him, opposite Karl Maitland, and waited for the anticipated interrogation to begin.

Chapter 21

"So, Malcy boy," Karl Maitland sneered. "You still fucking that neat little whore of a secretary of yours?"

"I thought we were here to talk business, Karl, not discuss my sex life," Capshaw retorted.

"You know Karl always gets down to the important things in life first," Boris laughed. "Anyway, it was your sex life that nearly got you into big trouble in the first place wasn't it, Malcolm, and who supplied the lawyer who handled the negotiations with that last little whore and got you off the hook?"

"Look, I know you helped me back then, and I'm grateful for that, Boris, you know I am, but what I get up to with Charlotte is my business and mine alone, do you understand?"

"Of course it is, Malcy," Karl interjected with a sneer on his face. "I just wondered what it would be like to spend an hour or two in close company with your Charlotte. Nice tight little body, great figure, good tits. How about you fix us up for an evening's entertainment? Me and Boris wouldn't mind a piece of that, would we, brother?"

"You bastard," Capshaw shouted at Karl. "Charlotte may be a whore, but she's my whore and a bloody good secretary as well, and I'm not sharing her with you and your brother, is that clear?"

"Well, well now. Do I detect an ounce of feeling there, brother? Can it be possible that Malcy here actually likes little Charlotte a bit more than his usual tarts?"

"I've told you, Karl, Charlotte's not for sale, so let's drop it and get down to whatever you asked me to come all this way for, shall we?" said Capshaw, trying to deflect the conversation away from the uncomfortable subject of Charlotte and his sexual relationship with her. He knew that if the brothers applied enough pressure, he'd probably be forced to try to convince Charlotte to sleep with them. He was well aware that he wielded sufficient power and influence over his secretary that if he insisted, she would grudgingly go along with any such arrangement, but would resent him for forcing her into such a position. Charlotte knew far too much about the hidden side of Capshaw's business enterprises for him to risk any such resentment that might lead to a betrayal of confidence. Charlotte might be good in bed and subservient to his will in that department, but she was intelligent, and he couldn't take the risk of doing anything that might destroy the employer/employee bond that existed between them. Not only that, but Malcolm Capshaw couldn't bear the thought of Boris and Karl pawing and enjoying the body of the girl who he thought of as his own personal property.

"Hey, calm down, Malcy," urged Karl. "I'm only joking."

Capshaw didn't believe him for a moment.

"That's enough," said Boris Maitland, his voice changing to a brisk and businesslike tone. "Forget what Karl said. We can get any girl we want, any time we want, so why should we want your leftovers, eh? You keep your Charlotte to yourself old chap. Karl, shut up about it, we need to be together about we're doing. I will not tolerate any petty squabbles, is that understood?"

Karl Maitland simply shrugged and nodded in the direction of his elder brother. Malcolm Capshaw nodded to Boris who now left his

position by the fireplace and took a seat at the highly polished an-
tique Italian walnut table in the centre of the library and motioned
for the others to join him.

"Listen, Malcolm. We've waited a bloody long time to get our
hands on what is rightfully ours. Granddad went to a lot of trouble
to make sure that it was well hidden, and what came afterwards
was just bloody bad luck. How was anyone to expect that they'd
all end up like they did? If he'd lived, Dad would have done just
what we're doing. It's ours, and we're damn well going to have it,
just you remember that. You and Graves are being paid a fucking
fortune to carry out this little treasure hunt, and nothing, I repeat,
nothing had better go wrong. Is that clear?"

Capshaw had nodded, his mouth dry, unable to speak.

"If anything does go wrong and we lose it, then I'll hold you and
Graves personally responsible Malcolm, do you understand?" Boris
said.

Another nod from Capshaw signified his understanding. He
didn't dare make a sound, knowing that his voice would betray
his fear.

"Hogan died over sixty years ago. I agree that it's unlikely that
he'd be identified quickly if the cops did become involved, but I
can't take that chance. At the first sign of Graves losing control, or
of these fucking surveyors screwing the operation then we get rid
of the lot of them straight away, Graves as well if necessary. I've
nothing else to say to you, Malcolm, except *is that all quite clear?*"

Capshaw gulped and nodded, still not yet confident that his voice
wouldn't betray his fear.

"Will you answer the man for God's sake?" Karl snapped. "Or
have you lost your tongue, lover boy?"

"Yes, Boris, it's quite clear. I know what has to be done," Capshaw
suddenly blurted out, his voice returning in one splendid moment

of bravado as he directed his answer to the elder Maitland, ignoring Karl's sneering. "Now, if there's nothing else I'd like to get back to Stratford as soon as I can."

An hour later the three men emerged from the library. Capshaw's brow was coated in the residue of the sweat that the conversation had induced in him. His armpits were damp; his shirt felt as though it were stuck to his back. The two Maitlands had managed to make Capshaw feel more uncomfortable than he could ever remember feeling. Most of the conversation had centred on the discovery of Hogan's body. Boris was concerned that Graves might be losing control of the situation in Glastonbury; that Cutler and his people might discover the truth or go running to the police, or both. As he'd pointed out, if Hogan's remains were to be exhumed and identified then the whole enterprise would be placed in jeopardy.

Karl had joined in by suggesting that the time had come for Cutler and his people to be eliminated. They were already a liability and why should Graves be trusted when he said that Cutler would keep silent for five days? All of them knew that the survey team would have to disappear at some time, so why not sooner rather than later?

Capshaw had reiterated his faith in Graves and his abilities, and urged the brothers to be patient. Plans had been laid by Graves that would make the eventual demise of the Strata Survey Team appear to be no more than a tragic accident. They still needed the team and their ground penetrating radar, and moving too soon to eliminate them would be counter-productive. He urged the Maitlands to trust Graves; he was an expert after all, that's why they were paying him so much.

So the meeting ended, and Boris Maitland had summoned Mallory with instructions to order Baines to bring Mr. Capshaw's car to the door. Ten minutes later a much relieved Malcolm Capshaw sat back in the plush leather rear seat of the Bentley and allowed himself a large sigh of relief. The morning had been bad, but not as bad as he supposed it might have been.

The car swished out of the Maitland's driveway, the tires kicking up a small amount of gravel before they took a firm grip on the tarmac of the main road outside, and Baines pointed the Bentley back in the direction they'd approached from. Capshaw relaxed a little, knowing that he'd soon be back in Stratford, in an environment where he was the master, though as the wheels ate up the miles beneath him, the last mocking words spoken by Karl as he'd pulled away from the front of Dangerfield Hall echoed in his head.

"Say hello to that little whore Charlotte for me, Malcy boy, and next time you put your hands on that tight little body, give her one for me!"

Somehow, Capshaw knew that he hadn't heard the last of the younger Maitland's lust for Charlotte Raeburn, and that, more than the worries about what was happening in Glastonbury, gave him greater cause to be anxious. After all, Glastonbury was business, but Charlotte was personal!

Chapter 22

"Sounds to me like our Mavis chose the wrong profession, eh, Boss?" quipped Winston as he drove towards their rendezvous with Graves. "The old dear should have been a private eye, she's a veritable Miss Marple, don't you think?"

"Don't let Mavis hear you referring to her as an 'old dear'. She'll kill you," Cutler joked in reply.

"Hey, man, I think she's great to have found out all that info in a short time," Winston went on.

"Seriously though, Joe, aren't you a bit worried by what she told you?" asked Sally, who felt a little unnerved herself after Cutler had brought them up to date with Mavis's findings.

"I'd be a liar if I said no, Sally," he replied. "It looks as if by taking the job from Capshaw I may have signed us all up to a whole load of trouble. If I have then I apologise right now, and if either one of you wants to quit and get back to Cheltenham that'll be fine with me."

"I ain't goin' anywhere, boss man," was Winston's instant reply. "What you gonna do without me if you go gettin' yourself into trouble now, you answer me that?"

"And you, Sally," asked Cutler. "I'd understand if you wanted to go home and sit this one out. Mavis could use the company in the office."

"Are you kidding, boss?" she came back at Cutler without hesitation. "Do you think just because I'm a woman I've got no sense of adventure? This could be big, bigger than any of us can imagine. Okay, so there might be an element of danger in it somewhere, but I'm not going to run away and leave you two to face Graves and Capshaw's machinations on your own."

"Good for you, Sally girl," said Winston, taking one hand from the steering wheel long enough to drape it around Sally's shoulder and give her a one-handed hug.

"You're sure this is what you want to do?" asked Cutler seeking a final reassurance from Sally. "You're not just doing this out of some weird sense of loyalty or bravado, or feminist empowerment?"

"Oh come on, Joe," Sally retorted. "Since when have I been a member of the feminist lobby?"

"True," said Winston thoughtfully. "Must be somethin' to do with that nice pair of legs you flash at us now and then when you come down to the bar or for dinner."

Sally playfully punched Winston on the arm, careful not to do anything that might upset his driving.

"Winston Fortune, if you weren't driving this van I'd slap your face," she said.

"Are you saying that you wouldn't open a door for me if I turned up in my muddy jeans and sweatshirt? It's just my legs that do it for you, is it?"

"Ha, ha," he laughed. "Now you should know me better than that, Sally girl."

"Yes, well, you just watch it, Winston, that's all," she went on, jokingly scolding him once more before the conversation turned serious again.

"Honestly, Joe," she said, turning to Cutler, "Wild horses wouldn't keep me away from this one. I'm with you and Winston all the way, whatever happens."

"Well, I guess we're all in it together then," said Cutler as Winston Fortune turned off the main road and onto a rough track rutted with the tracks of passing tractors. A wooden sign that had obviously seen better days hung from a pole as they made the turn.

"Here we are then, boss, Maiden's Farm," Winston announced.

"Remember what I said to both of you," Cutler said with a serious note in his voice. "If Graves thinks for one minute that we're on to him it could prove more than a bit dangerous and I don't want any of us getting hurt. We've a good idea that the Excalibur search is just a blind to cover up the search for something else, but until we know what that something else is we can't do much. If we're to stand a chance of finding out what it is we're going to have to go along with Graves and act as though nothing's changed."

"Don't you worry, boss, we know the score," said Winston.

"Yes, Joe, we're ready, Graves won't suspect a thing," Sally added. "Just one thing though. What about the body?"

"We keep quiet as we agreed, Sally, at least for now. When we're ready, when we know what's going on, then we can report it to the police and I'm sure they'll be pleased to have a word or two with our friend Mr. Walter Graves."

"Speaking of the great man, there he is," said Winston as they turned off the track into a rather muddy farm yard where Graves stood beside his gleaming BMW, still unnervingly free of dirt, a mobile phone pressed to his ear.

Winston circled the van until it was facing the same direction as the BMW and revved the engine twice, just to annoy Graves, before switching the ignition off. The engine juddered in protest as its fuel supply ceased and the yard fell silent. The three surveyors dropped from the cab of the van to be greeted by Graves, as usual displaying that cheerful smile and displaying a body language that could have seen him being taken for a gentleman farmer rather than a professor of history and a... a what? That was the big question. Could he really be a killer as Mavis had hinted at in her conversation with Joe Cutler?

Winston Fortune smiled at Graves as he walked towards him, holding his hand out and shaking Graves's in greeting. Behind that smile, however, Fortune's old Special Forces training had clicked into gear and from now on Winston would make very sure that Mr. Walter Graves was watched very closely indeed, and his every word would be carefully screened and scrutinised by the big Jamaican, who now considered himself to be on a kind of active duty once again. Joe Cutler was his boss, his employer, and a clever man as well, and Sally was a brave and plucky girl, but if things were about to turn nasty in the wilds of Somerset Winston knew that he was the man with the ability to extricate them from a potentially life-threatening situation. He hoped, of course, that it would never come to that.

"Gentlemen, Miss Corbett, welcome to Maiden's Farm," Graves called out as they drew nearer to him. "I've already spoken to Mr. Garforth the farmer. He's quite happy for us to carry out part of our search for artefacts connected with Joseph of Arimathaea on his land."

"Oh good, yes of course," said Joe, remembering the cover story under which the search team was operating when dealing with the public.

"He says we can come and go as we please," Graves continued. "He's busy up in one of the fields to the east of the farm. Luckily, our search area is in the opposite direction."

"Lucky for us," said Sally, feeling that she should say something.

"Most certainly," Graves replied. "Now, I've got the grid marked out on this plan of the farm so I suggest we get the equipment out and make a start."

As usual Graves's 'we' seemed to exclude himself from any kind of physical work, and the three Strata Survey people were left to unload their equipment from the van and haul it to the field where they were to set up the first search area of the day. Graves seemed content to carry the weight of his mobile phone, animatedly involved in conversation with some unknown associate. Cutler would have loved to get closer to try to ascertain what Graves was discussing and who he was talking to but judged it prudent to stay back and not appear too inquisitive. For now, he'd play it coy, keep up the charade of the search as he knew Graves expected him to, and bide his time until he knew more. Patience and observation would be far more important.

The rest of the day passed in almost boring fashion. They marked out the search grid, inserted the posts and markers, took turns to walk the lines with the hand-held radar unit, and found absolutely nothing, apart from one small moment of excitement when they'd detected a ground disturbance and dug down only to discover an old tractor radiator obviously buried years previously. Farmers did that sort of thing all the time Winston told Sally. Why waste time and fuel trekking to such places when it was just as easy to dispose of old equipment beneath the earth on their own land?

It was a very frustrated team of surveyors who eventually packed up their equipment for the day and drove back to their temporary home in town at five o'clock. Sally was upset that Joe and

Winston had both decried her idea of using her feminine wiles on Graves. They were both too protective of her so she thought, but she couldn't get them to alter their opinions and Joe had been determined in his resolution not to invite Graves to share their table for dinner that night. Winston had tried to lighten things a little when he quipped: "That don't mean you can't dress up for me and the boss though, Sally girl. I'd just love to see those pretty legs of yours again."

"Pervert!" she'd snapped back at Winston with a grin on her face and it was clear that his tactics had worked. The tension had lifted.

Graves had sped off in his BMW before they'd even packed up the equipment into the rear of the van. Joe Cutler was more than frustrated as he wanted to know more about what Graves got up to in the hours they were separated from him. Perhaps he should have allowed Sally to invite him to dinner. As quickly as the thought entered his mind he dismissed it. Whatever Graves was up to, he would obviously suspend any out of hours work until after any meeting with Joe and the others. No, there had to be a better way to get close to Graves, Joe just wished he could think of it. Maybe a long talk with Winston and Sally over dinner would throw up some ideas.

As things turned out, it was good that Joe had decided not to invite the historian to dine with them that evening. As they arrived back at the Rowan Tree, Winston parked the van while Joe and Sally went indoors. Cutler was surprised when, as they walked into the foyer of the guest house, a tall well-built man with a shock of black hair, combed back from is forehead rose from one of the armchairs in Mrs. Cleveley's reception area and moved straight towards him and Sally.

"Sally, so good to see you," the man growled in a voice that reminded Cutler of Christopher Lee in one of his Dracula roles.

"Lucius! What on earth are you doing here?" Sally gasped as the man threw his arms around her and almost crushed her in a bear hug of monumental proportions.

"I thought you might need some help with this little project of yours, and as I had some time to spare, and a friend of mine gave me a spot of information I thought you'd be interested in, I thought I'd take a break from the stuffy old halls of learning and enjoy a weekend in the country. Now, who's your friend?"

The man released Sally from the hug and stood back, offering his large paw of a right hand to Joe.

"Yes, of course," Sally hesitated as Winston walked in through the front door. She beckoned him to join them. "Er, Joe Cutler, Winston Fortune, please, may I introduce you to Professor Lucius Doberman?"

Joe Cutler gave way to Winston who pumped the hand of the learned professor in a warm welcome. Winston also saw Doberman's likeness to the actor.

"Well now, ain't this a turn up for the books?" said Winston as he stepped back to look at the tall and unexpected visitor.

Joe Cutler turned to the professor and his next words confirmed his gratitude to the man for having travelled all this way to offer his help to their cause.

"Professor Doberman, I can't thank you enough for coming. You may not realise it yet, but your arrival couldn't have come at a better time. Sally, it looks like you'll have the chance to dress for dinner after all!"

Chapter 23

Lucius Doberman swept into the bar room of The Rowan Tree just after seven p.m. If Winston and Joe had thought the professor bore a strange resemblance to the famed cinematic portrayer of Count Dracula that thought was reinforced by the entrance made by Doberman as he arrived to join them for a drink prior to dinner. The man was taller than they'd at first realised, being at least six feet four or five, and he walked with a particularly upright bearing that gave him the appearance of being a man of great strength as well as one of supreme self-confidence. He wore a black Edwardian style jacket with a high and wide collar that wouldn't have looked out of place on the vampirical count himself, with equally black trousers, and a white shirt with a slight ruff at the collar. On anyone else it might have looked slightly effeminate, but on Doberman the whole ensemble simply reeked class, and shouted out to the world that here was a man perfectly at peace with himself and who cared little for the everyday conventions of ordinary men. 'University professor' could have been stamped across his forehead. It was that obvious who and what the great man was to almost anyone with a modicum of intelligence.

Doberman shook hands with the men and bent forwards to give Sally a kiss on the cheek. Joe Cutler could see the man had a genuine affection for Sally, but he could also see why Sally hadn't been interested in the professor's advances at the university. The man just wasn't her type! He wasn't as old as, say, Walter Graves, but the fact that he was a professor of history, his lack of modern style and dress sense, and his overall appearance was something that Joe couldn't see as being particularly attractive to women in general, let alone one as young as Sally had been when she'd first known him.

"Well, now, isn't this nice?" said Doberman as he sat between Sally and Winston, with Joe directly opposite him at the circular bar table. "I never thought to hear from you again in such a mysterious manner Sally. Your call was intriguing to say the least."

"We're very grateful to you for the information you gave to Sally, Professor," said Cutler, anticipating Sally's response.

"Oh please, call me Lucius Mr. Cutler, 'Professor' sounds so stuffy and formal don't you think?"

"Then I'm Joe, and this is Winston," said Joe, nodding in Winston's direction, "and Sally of course needs no introduction."

"Good that's settled then," said Doberman. "Er, Winston old chap, might I suggest that you're staring?"

The professor had caught Winston Fortune staring at him as he spoke and it was obvious from his reaction that the man was used to plain speaking.

"Oh man, I'm sorry profess...er, Lucius. I didn't mean to. It's just that you remind me of..."

"Ha," Doberman laughed. "I know, don't worry old chap. You're not the first to see the resemblance. I'm quite used to it, and the 'Dracula' nickname that I'm sure Sally was well aware of when she was on campus."

"Oh, Lucius," Sally began, but the professor cut her off.

"Oh come now, Sally, we know it's true, and I'm also well aware that for the most part, the name is used in an affectionate sense, so there's no need to feel uncomfortable about it. I certainly don't. I suppose my slightly eccentric mode of dress doesn't exactly help to dispel the use of the name, and anyway, I've grown accustomed to it, and I actually quite like it."

"Right, well I'm glad that's all cleared up," said Cutler, reaching across to pour a glass of wine for Doberman. "I presume an Australian Chardonnay is acceptable, Lucius?" he asked as he poured.

"Oh yes, quite admirable, Joseph, old chap. The old colonies have become quite accomplished in the art of producing half-decent wine these days. Pour away."

It was rapidly becoming apparent that Lucius Doberman spoke as he dressed. There was an old-world flamboyance and affectation about the way he talked, and it was plain to Joe and Winston that 'old chap' was about to become the usual means of his addressing them. Joe wasn't sure if he could stand the continual use of his full Christian name, but for now he'd let it ride.

"So tell me, Lucius, what on earth brought you all this way? Couldn't whatever you've discovered have been passed to Sally over the telephone?" Winston asked.

"Ah, let me tell you, when I discovered what I have to tell you all, I judged it best to come down in person, for I fear that what I have to tell you will serve merely to further muddy the murky waters you all seem to have dipped your feet into at the moment. Also, I'm intrigued by this whole scenario. I can't believe that someone may have gone to a lot of time and expense to perpetrate a massive hoax without there being a very lucrative and devious resolution lurking in the background. Then, when Marcus told me what he knew, well my dear boy, I simply couldn't *not* come!"

"Marcus?" the three surveyors chorused at the same time.

"Ah yes, didn't I mention Marcus before? Oh well, maybe not, but anyway, Professor Sir Marcus Farthingwood is a fellow don at the university. The old boy is eighty five if he's a day and possesses more degrees than I could mention. He's officially retired, of course, but still lives in rooms at the college and many of the students still visit him and call upon his vast knowledge of the world and myriad subjects in seeking solutions to many of their academic and, at times, personal problems. Anyway, on top of all that, Marcus is considered by some to be one of the world's leading authorities on all things trivial and otherwise not classified by subject. In short, if this little case of yours were a Sherlock Holmes type mystery, and I were to describe myself as taking the part of the great detective, then Marcus would be Mycroft to my Homes"

"Er, I'm afraid you've lost me, man," said Winston quizzically.

"Ah, Winston old chap, allow me to explain. Sherlock Holmes as created by Sir Arthur Conan Doyle was indeed a wonderful and varied character, capable of solving many mysteries, but, at times, even he was at a loss to deduce certain facts from the clues available. In such circumstances Holmes would seek the advice of his brother Mycroft, who seemed to spend his entire life in a strange private establishment known as the Diogenes Club. Being totally averse to any sort of physical exertion Mycroft would sit in his chair and deliberate upon all manner of world affairs and criminal matters and Sherlock apparently admitted to Doctor Watson that Mycroft was, in fact, his intellectual superior and that he could solve a case purely by assessing the evidence placed in front of him, and was thus a source of great help to his more energetic and famous brother."

"Hmm, I think I see," said Winston, still patently unsure what Lucius was talking about.

Sally grew impatient to know exactly what Lucius had discovered that he considered it so important to warrant a trip to Glastonbury and a stay in Mrs. Cleveley's homely establishment.

"Please, Lucius, won't you tell us what it is you've discovered? Winston might need the lesson in English Literature but I'm sure we'd all rather hear what you've discovered."

The men nodded in agreement with Sally, but Lucius Doberman simply smiled enigmatically at them. "All in good time, young Sally. All in good time. What I have to tell you will wait a little while you all tell me what you've up to down here. That might help me put some of Marcus's information into better context before I reveal it to you. Now, I'm famished! Let's all eat and you can fill me in."

Frustrated, the three of them had no choice but to acquiesce to Doberman's request. They made their way from the bar into the dining room, where, over dinner, they brought Doberman up to date with everything that had happened since Joe Cutler had accepted the commission from Capshaw, leaving nothing out, even the possibility that Walter Graves possessed a firearm. Lucius Doberman sat quietly and proved to be a good listener, only interrupting the flow of the conversation with queries here and there when he felt he needed to know more. The discovery of the skeleton of the unknown man in the field caused him to raise an eyebrow, as if he saw some great significance in the find.

As Claire Cleveley cleared away the plates and cutlery from the table, their appetites sated, the four of them made their way back to the bar and found a quiet table in the corner, away from any other guests who might wish to listen in to their conversation. As they settled down to enjoy brandies in the men's case and a gin and tonic in Sally's, Lucius sat back, and cleared his throat. "Now, people, I suppose it's my turn."

"Come on, Professor," said Cutler, "You've kept us in suspense long enough."

"Yeah, man, spill the beans," Winston added, lapsing once again into his best homeland accent.

Sally sipped from her glass and joined in the chorus of anticipation.

"Lucius, please!"

"Okay everyone, I hope you're all listening carefully."

Lucius Doberman took a deep breath and solemnly placed his brandy glass on the table in a gesture that was purely theatrical, and began his story.

"After I'd spoken to you the other day, Sally, I admit that I was more than a little intrigued by the whole scenario you'd presented to me. At first I thought that you'd found yourselves involved in some kind of historical or archaeological practical joke, such things are known, of course. On reflection, however, I could see no logical reason for anyone to devise such an elaborate plot unless it was intended to disguise another purpose. The more I thought about it the more I concluded that this was a hoax, for the Arthurian legend can be no more than that, a legend. It's true that little is known of life in Britain during the Dark Ages, and it's possible that Arthur did exist, not as king of all Britain as the legend tells, but more likely as a warlord or minor ruler of one of the many small kingdoms that existed within what was in fact a very divided nation in those days. Even Cornwall and Northumberland for example were independent Kingdoms, as were many of today's counties and regions. Anyway, Camelot, Avalon, Merlin, Excalibur and the Knights of the Round Table could really be no more than stories passed on around camp fires, perhaps by poets or lyricists of the day, and somehow those stories become interwoven with fact to produce what we now know as the Arthurian legend. That's putting it in a nutshell, of course, but that's the gist of what both I and Marcus Farthingwood believe. You must all realise surely that if the Arthurian tales bore any semblance to truth and reality then someone would have found some supporting archaeological evidence at some time in the last fifteen hundred years. It's a fantasy, no more and no less. It has to be. The more I looked at the copy of the document you sent me, Sally, the more I knew that it was *not* the supporting evidence required to prove the existence of Arthur or his sword."

Doberman paused for breath, held up his empty glass in an imploring gesture towards the bar and Claire Cleveley obligingly saw the gesticulation, nodded in return and instantly came across to the table with another goblet of warming liquid for the professor. He thanked the girl and then returned to his narrative.

"Where was I? Oh yes. Now, when I showed the copy of the document to Marcus, he took his time in reading and studying the wording very carefully. We sat and discussed it at length, and as I've said he concurred with my opinion regarding its authenticity. The one thing that seemed to catch his attention was the use of the name 'Livara' in the document. He swore that he'd heard the name somewhere before but he couldn't quite remember in what context. He was sure, however, that it had nothing to do with the story of King Arthur, or a place name in Somerset. Suddenly, his eyes lit up and he sent me scurrying across to one of the innumerable bookshelves that adorn his rooms at the college. Marcus is an expert on many things as I've told you, but one of his most fervent areas of study is the war at sea during World War Two. His own father was the commander of a naval destroyer in those days so I suppose in some ways the sea is in his blood, though Marcus himself could never have been a sailor. He gets terribly seasick apparently. Anyway, I did as he bade me and brought a particular volume from the shelf he'd indicated. I admit I thought the old boy had lost his marbles at that point as the book concerned itself with the history of convoys from 1939-45. I could see no connection whatsoever between merchant shipping and the legend of Arthur or with what you people were doing here.

It took Marcus less than two minutes to find what he was looking for and he simply held the book out toward me without saying a word. I told you he was an absolute master at the art of the trivial. He'd have had to be to have remembered the one short entry in the book which he passed to me. Sure enough it was there, in black and white and Marcus sat and watched me reading the page with a knowing grin on his face, a look of triumph almost as if to say, 'There! Aren't I a clever old chap then?'

My friends, in April of 1940 a convoy set sail from Bristol, bound for Canada. There were thirty two merchant ships in total, escorted by two destroyers and two corvettes. Three days out from Bristol the convoy was attacked at night by a waiting pack of u-boats, one of Admiral Doenitz's famous wolf-packs. In the space of that one night twelve merchant ships, one corvette and a destroyer were sunk, it was a veritable slaughter of the innocents by all accounts. The convoy pressed on and lost four more ships the next night, and only the decision of the escort commander in the one remaining destroyer to scatter the convoy saved them from even greater losses. In the event, only five merchantmen made eventual landfall in Nova Scotia. To get to the point of all this history, one of the ships sunk on that terrible first night of u-boat attacks was a small and insignificant grain carrier, apparently unladen and sailing to Canada in order to pick up a cargo of life-sustaining wheat from our colonial brothers. She went down in less than two minutes, with all hands, and probably still lies rotting hundreds of feet below the Atlantic. She is listed in Lloyds register as having been lost that night and it is doubtful if anyone would ever have heard of her again if you hadn't sent me that document, Sally.

You see, that grain carrier was none other than the *S.S. Livara*, uniquely named using the initials of the owner's children, and I'd be grateful if any of you could tell me what the hell a ship sunk by a German u-boat over sixty years ago in mid-Atlantic has got to do with your Mr. Capshaw's supposed search for King Arthur's Excalibur?"

Chapter 24

Lucius Doberman sat back in his chair, picked up his brandy goblet and waited for a response from his companions. At first, nothing but a palpable silence greeted the end of his revelation. Joe Cutler was the first to break the silence.

"A ship? A bloody ship? Like you say, what has a ship to do with all this? Glastonbury's nowhere near the coast as it is, so where's the connection?"

"You tell me, old chap," said the professor. "I told you my news would only serve to muddy the waters further."

"But couldn't Livara still have been the name of a long forgotten village or settlement, and the ship's owners came up with that name by coincidence?" asked Sally.

"Barely a chance in a million, Sally," Doberman went on. "Marcus and I looked it up, and the Livara was one of two ships owned by the grandly named Blandford Shipping Lines. In fact, the owner was a gentleman by the name of Harry Blandford, himself an ex-ship's captain. The other was the aptly named *Blandford Star*, another freighter, and she was also sunk by a u-boat about six months after the *Livara*. Our ship was named as I told you, after his children, *Linda*, *Valerie* and *Raymond*. Believe me, Sally, there was never a place in this country by the name of Livara, it was simply an old sea dog's concocted name to pay tribute to his children."

"And you say she was sailing empty? Wasn't that a bit unusual for convoy traffic during the war?" asked Winston.

"Apparently it could happen," said Doberman. "It's true that they would normally carry export cargo one way and war essentials the other, but it wasn't unheard of for some ships to sail in ballast on the outward voyage and pick up a cargo on the return leg."

"Even so, it don't sound right to me, man," Winston went on, unwilling to let the subject of the *Livara's* cargo (or lack of it), drop.

"Winston, Lucius has explained that the ship was unladen and why, and that's all there is to it. What can we gain by wondering why she was empty?" Joe Cutler tried to bring the subject to a close.

"Actually, Joe, there might be something in what Winston is getting at," Doberman continued. "The *Livara* wasn't a large ship by any means, and was typical of the small freighters that plied the oceans in those days. She normally carried a crew of twelve to sixteen men and yet on the night she was torpedoed she was listed as having sunk with the loss of all *thirty eight* souls on board! Why on earth should an empty freighter sent across the Atlantic to pick up a cargo of wheat need to be carrying more than double her normal crew compliment? The official records give no indication of why those extra men were on board; in fact they give no further details of the ship at all. As far as the official story goes, she sailed, she was sunk, and that was it, end of story."

"What a shame there were no survivors," said Sally.

"Indeed," Lucius went on. "Marcus and I tried everything, but records for those days are quite scant anyway. I'm afraid the *Livara* is just another enigma to add to your strange series of events here in Glastonbury, as I suggested it would be."

"There is another way of looking at it," said Joe, who'd been thinking hard and taking in every word that Lucius Doberman had spoken.

"Go on, Joe," said the professor.

"This is just a theory, okay? Now, suppose Capshaw knows, or knew, someone who knew something about the ship. Maybe it was being used for a special purpose, or maybe it wasn't the ship itself, but someone who'd sailed on her. I'm not quite sure what I'm getting at, but we know that Capshaw is connected to the Maitland family, and they go back a long way in London's criminal underworld. I've no doubt that Boris and Karl Maitland's grandfather would have been very active during the war. Even criminals didn't give up their nefarious ways just because of the hostilities. It's quite possible that old man Maitland had something to do with the ship. He could have been a friend or acquaintance of the ship's owner, and maybe even had a share in the *Livara* and whatever she was up to."

"Hey boss, you know, you just said a lot, and also a whole lot of nothing," Winston grinned. "Half of that was barely in English, man."

"That's rich, coming from you," said Joe laughingly. "Look, I know I was babbling a bit, but I think you know what I was getting at."

"Of course we do Joe, don't we Winston, Lucius?" Sally jumped in defensively.

"Yes, I rather think we do," said Lucius, "and, if I'm not mistaken, you people have already touched on one potentially vital clue in the puzzle."

"The skeleton!" Sally exclaimed triumphantly.

"Exactly! Good girl," said Doberman. "Now, if we could find out who the poor unfortunate chap was who now lies beneath the earth in that field we might be some way along the road towards solving this little mystery."

The rest of the evening was spent with the four of them trying to work out methods of finding out who the skeleton in the field belonged to in life, without arousing official suspicion of course. Between them they hit brick wall after brick wall in their theorising and suggestions. Short of kidnapping Walter Graves, tying him to a chair and beating him into submission with a rubber hose, (Winston's suggestion), they could think of no way to coerce the man into giving away the secret of the skeleton's identity, if indeed he was aware of it. They knew that there had to be a chance that Capshaw was keeping Graves in the dark about certain aspects of whatever they were involved in.

Tiredness began to creep into their conversation, it had been a long day for everyone concerned, not least Lucius Doberman who had made the long journey to join them in Glastonbury, to everyone's surprise and as it now seemed, their delight. He had rapidly become accepted as an honorary member of the Strata Survey team, and Doberman himself seemed as excited as a child with a new toy at the prospect of becoming involved in a real-life mystery as opposed to the ones from the pages of history he was more accustomed to studying.

As the hands on the clock moved inexorably toward the midnight hour, they decided to retire for the night, with Lucius Doberman promising to contact Sir Marcus Farthingwood again the next day to see if he could offer any helpful suggestions that didn't involve kidnapping and rubber hoses.

As Joe Cutler laid his head on his pillow a short time later, he reflected that although Lucius Doberman had merely added to the confusion surrounding their presence in Glastonbury, his arrival might just provide them with the extra knowledge and intelligence they needed to outwit Capshaw, Graves and whoever else might be lurking in the background as they searched for...what?

Chapter 25

Spectral fingers of moonlight crept through the gently swaying bedroom curtains as Charlotte Raeburn reached out unsuccessfully for the welcoming arms of sleep. She wished she could keep her eyes closed and just drift into a deep slumber that would carry her through to the morning, but she kept opening her eyes watching the curtains, seeing the beams of moonlight as they danced around the darkened room, playing upon the silhouetted forms of the bedroom furniture. She wished she could rise from the bed and close the window Capshaw always left open at night, but she knew that he would most likely awake if the room became too warm and airless, and she couldn't bear to face his anger in the middle of the night.

Capshaw's 'lovemaking' had been particularly brutal and demanding that night and Charlotte had been glad when he'd finally drifted off to sleep, his sexual appetite sated at last. She'd waited until he was deeply asleep before she'd slowly slid from under the duvet and made her way to the en-suite bathroom where she'd bathed herself to eliminate the signs of Capshaw's desires. She felt bruised and sore between her legs, and her breasts ached from the rough handling to which they'd been subjected. Charlotte was sure that something bad had taken place during his visit to the Maitland's mansion, but Malcolm Capshaw was not one to share everything with his secretary/mistress, and it was more than she dared do to ask him about it. She'd returned to his bed as there was nothing to be gained by leaving and going home, that would only serve to fuel his anger when he woke up alone and she would have to face him at the office in the morning.

As she lay next to the sleeping figure of her employer Charlotte tried to think of ways to leave her job without creating any animosity in her boss's manner towards her. Capshaw could be violent and vindictive, of that she was only too aware, and she feared his reaction if he thought that she wanted to leave him, and to seek alternative employment. She would have to think of a plan that would allow her to leave without Capshaw seeking some form of revenge on her for 'betraying' him, as he would surely see it if she were to resign.

There was also the tricky problem of Charlotte's inside knowledge of many of Capshaw's less than legitimate business dealings. She knew that he trusted her, and under normal circumstances she would have taken such trust as a compliment, but now it acted as a double-edged sword and could be brought to bear against her. He had in effect tied her to him by allowing her the knowledge that she now possessed, and she knew that the hold he had over her would not be an easy one to break.

She tossed and turned, hour after interminable hour through the night and found no solution to her problem. Sleep continued to evade her until, as the first grey streaks of dawn began to force a way through the crack in the bedroom curtains, she finally drifted into a sort of half sleep, neither one thing nor another, but at least for a short time she seemed to be resting.

Her rest was short lived however. As the grey of dawn gave way to the pale early sunlight of the day, she felt Capshaw beginning to stir beside her. His hand reached out across the bed and found her nakedness. He moved closer and pulled her to him, his hand moving abruptly to that space between her legs that still felt bruised and sore from the treatment she'd received the night before. Charlotte tried to pretend she was asleep, but to no avail. She felt powerless to stop him as Capshaw rolled over, climbed on top of her and used his knees to force her legs apart.

"Please, not now," she begged, but Capshaw simply ignored her plea with a brusque, "Yes, now," and she had no choice other than to lie compliantly as he forced himself inside her and began thrusting until he grunted in satisfaction as he spurted within her.

Luckily, he was quick and the whole act was over in less than five minutes. Capshaw rolled off and, relieved of his weight upon her, Charlotte allowed herself to breathe again. Capshaw exited the bed without a word and made his way to the shower. Pulling on a pink silk robe that Capshaw had bought her recently, Charlotte made her way down the stairs to the kitchen where she made coffee and croissant for herself, and waited ten minutes before beginning preparations of her employer's early morning meal.

As she removed the bacon from the grill and the eggs from the pan Capshaw walked into the kitchen as though on cue. Charlotte smiled and served his breakfast, then left him in solitude as he preferred her to do while he ate. She made her way back upstairs and tried to shower away the bruises and the pain that he'd imposed upon her last night and that morning. She dressed quickly and, now the epitome of a smartly dressed efficient and polite businessman's secretary, Charlotte tried to blot out the thoughts of what another day and night in the employment of Malcolm Capshaw might bring.

Chapter 26

The same sun that brought light to the day in Stratford-on-Avon broke through the curtains that had held back the night in Joe's room, some eighty-three miles, or 134 kilometres distance from Capshaw's mansion. The room felt warmer than it had for the last few days, and Joe himself felt a cheerfulness that came from a good night's sleep. The previous evening's conversation and the brandy had helped, but somehow Joe knew the presence of Lucius Doberman had made a difference to his overall mood. He wasn't sure exactly how the learned professor was going to make a difference to their quest in solving the riddle posed by Capshaw and Graves; he just instinctively knew that he would.

Therein, however, lay Joe's next problem. His plan for the day was relatively simple: breakfast, check in with Mavis back at the office, meet with Graves and continue the search and try to prise some kind of sense from the puzzle they were faced with. That just left the professor. What was Lucius to do all day while they toiled in the Somerset countryside? He'd be virtually worthless as an addition to the search team, knowing next to nothing about the equipment and its operation, aside from Joe having to explain his presence to the sinister Walter Graves.

It was Doberman himself who provided the answer to Joe's quandary as he sat enjoying one of Mrs Cleveley's hearty English breakfasts with Cutler and the others. Winston asked the question that had been burning in Joe's mind.

"So, Professor, sorry, *Lucius*, what's your plan of action while we're out in the field, man? I don't suppose you plan on joining us out there and meeting our friend Mr. Graves and comparing historical notes?"

"Oh no, of course not," Doberman replied. "They have a rather adequate library in town which I scouted out yesterday before we met, complete with computers for public use. While you're out continuing your search for whatever it is you're searching for, I shall make use of one of those computers to make contact with Marcus. I'm sure that I will be better occupied in trying to discover more information that might be of help to us through the internet and e-mail than I would by joining you in some muddy field somewhere and being able to do little more than help to carry your equipment around. As for Professor Graves, to give him his correct title, Marcus and I will attempt to dig a little deeper into his background. If he's an academic, then there will always be a contact of Marcus's somewhere that can provide us with information. As to meeting the man, I think that would better arranged to look like an accidental meeting at some point. Perhaps you could invite him to dine one evening and then introduce me as a friend of Sally's who just happens to be here on holiday or some such concocted tale. I'm not particularly adept at scheming and intrigue but I'm sure we can think of something between us."

"Do you know, Lucius?" said Sally, "I really do think that you could be quite devious if you put your mind to it. Perhaps you and I could put our heads together to devise a ruse that would seem plausible. I do think that the sooner you meet Graves then the sooner you'll have a chance to weigh the man up and see what we're up against."

"A jolly good idea, Sally," said Doberman, "But I think your companions might wish to have a say in whatever plan we formulate."

"Well said, Lucius, I think we should all get our heads together over a drink in the bar this evening and put a plan together. Meantime, you never know, we might actually find something today."

"All I can say to that, Joe, is please don't be too optimistic or too thorough in your search. I also have a feeling that if you locate whatever Graves has been commissioned to find, you might find yourselves in a difficult predicament. After all, if the object of Capshaw's desire is in some way illegal or the result of criminal activity then I don't think that he and Graves are just going to let you, Winston and Sally walk away armed with information that could put the two of them behind bars, if you see what I mean?"

A silence that could be cut with a knife greeted the professor's last words. Not one of the Strata team had previously thought the whole scenario through sufficiently enough to realise that Lucius Doberman was quite right. Suddenly, though it all became clear to the three of them. If they found what Graves was looking for then their own lives could be in considerable jeopardy. The thought that Capshaw and Graves might be willing to stoop to murder had never until now crossed any of their minds. Now, however, the stark realisation that such a thing could happen became a reality that was hard to ignore.

"Bloody hell, Lucius!" Joe exclaimed. "Do you really think that they'd go that far?"

"Why not?" asked Doberman. "After all, you have no idea what it is that they're really searching for. It could be the proceeds of a bank robbery, hidden jewels, I really don't know, but they obviously don't intend to take you into their confidence. If you were in their place and you found whatever it is they're looking for, ask yourself what you would do in such circumstances."

"You make a very good point," said Winston, "even though it does scare the shit out of me"

"Me, too," added Sally.

"It doesn't do a lot for my peace of mind either I must admit," said Cutler gravely, "but I have to admit you're probably right, Lucius. I think it's just become imperative that we find out exactly what these characters are after."

"And in the meantime, you must not under *any* circumstances admit to finding anything," said Doberman, "even if your instruments indicate a find of some sort. Simply log any finds in your memories and let Graves think that you're still searching. Marcus and I will do our best to help from this end, but in the meantime you'll have to play for time, my friends."

The warmth of the day seemed to have developed a cold edge as Joe and the others climbed into the van and set off for the day's rendezvous with Graves. As they drove away from the guest house Winston looked in his rear view mirror and saw the tall and imposing figure of Lucius Doberman standing on the pavement outside The Rowan Tree waving as they drew further from his sight. He was still waving as Winston made a right turn at the next junction, almost, thought Winston, as if he knew he wouldn't be seeing them again.

As soon as the van disappeared from sight Lucius returned to his room, gathered up whatever papers he deemed necessary for his days work and set off at a determined pace for the library. Sally Corbett and his new friends required his help, of that there was no doubt in his mind, and together with Sir Marcus Farthingwood he intended to give them every bit of assistance he could.

Five minutes after arriving at the library and establishing his credentials, (he didn't of course have a library card for this particular library), Lucius sat at one of the computers provided by the library service for its customers. As soon as he was connected to the internet he fired off an e-mail to Sir Marcus, and two others to a couple of associates who he thought could be of help, and then began to trawl through various websites searching for anything that might give him a clue as to the connection between the *SS Livara* and the ancient town of Glastonbury. He was certain that somewhere there was a connection between the two, and he was determined to find it. It could after all be the only way to help his new friends not only to find out what was really going on, but to stay alive! He was a simple historian, a mild mannered and usually sedentary person, but today Lucius Doberman felt as though he'd been galvanized into action in a way that he'd never been before. There was not only a historical mystery, but lives were now at stake, of that he was sure, but for the life of him he couldn't think why Sally and her two friends hadn't realised the danger earlier.

Within ten minutes of his sending his e-mails, the first reply came through and as he read the words that appeared on the screen before him Lucius nodded and said to himself; "Mmm, interesting, very interesting."

He quickly typed in a response to the sender and began his own days' work which, like that of Joe, Winston and Sally would involve a great deal of patient searching.

Chapter 27

"Lucky thing for us your professor friend turning up like that, Sally girl," said Winston as he drove towards Maiden's Farm, where they would continue the search in a different area to the day before.

"To be honest, I really can't get over him just turning up out of the blue," she replied. "I would never have thought of Lucius Doberman as the impetuous or impulsive type."

"Maybe he still fancies you," Cutler volunteered.

"Oh, I doubt that, Joe. He might have done at one time, but I made it plain that I wasn't interested, and he's enough of a gentleman to take no to mean no. I really think he genuinely believes there's something sinister behind all this and it wouldn't surprise me at all if he and Sir Marcus had a theory already, but that they daren't share it with us yet."

"Did you ever meet this Marcus Farthingwood character when you were at the university?"

"No, I didn't. In fact, very few of the students got to meet him. He was regarded as a sort of demi-god by the faculty and the students, sometimes thought of as a court of last resort in cases of academic disputes. He *is* a genius without a doubt, and there's every chance that he and Lucius can come up with something to help us. After all, look how quickly he cottoned on to the Livara thing."

"Yeah, but look how quickly he scared the shit out of us as well," said Winston, his eyes never leaving the road as he spoke.

"You have to admit he had a point though, Winston." Joe Cutler spoke in a hushed tone, almost as though he were afraid of being overheard. "After all, if what he said last night is true, and I've no reason to believe it isn't, then Capshaw and Graves are using us as innocent dupes to locate something they want very badly, and if we do find it, then we are likely to become a liability to them. I told you Graves had a bloody gun, and now we sort of know who he intends to use the damn thing on. I wish I'd never got you two involved in this whole affair. I could have said 'No' when I went to meet with fucking Malcolm Capshaw."

"Don't be silly, Joe," said Sally. "In the first place, you didn't know that there was anything suspicious about Capshaw or the job. Secondly, you'd have been a fool to yourself and the business to turn down what appeared to be a lucrative contract that would keep the company in the black for years. And finally, Joe Cutler, don't you forget that Winston and I are both over twenty-one and know perfectly well what we're doing. You gave us the chance to back out and we both said we were with you all the way. I don't see that anything's happened to change that, so for God's sake stop apologising and let's prove to ourselves that we can come out of this on top, alright?"

"Amen to that, Sally girl!" Winston Fortune grinned from ear to ear. "I think that's put you in your place, boss man. You sure ain't gonna get rid of us that easily."

"But what about the contract, the money? If Lucius is right then we can't really expect that we're going to make anything at all out of this. The retainer I got from Capshaw is all very well, but if he expects us to pop our clogs if we find his treasure, whatever it is, then I don't think he's likely to pay the rest of the fee into the company account, do you? In effect, we're working for nothing, and we still have to earn a living after all."

"Oh, come on, boss, where's your sense of adventure?" Winston went on. "And anyway, I doubt that Capshaw will just allow us to walk away without finishing the job, do you? I mean, what you gonna say to the man? 'Look Mr. Capshaw, sir, we think you're a crooked murdering bastard and we don't want to work for you any more?' Try that one and he'll probably have Graves put us all out of our misery there and then. Whatever happens, boss, we've got to see this thing through to the end, and hope we can outwit the bad guys."

"Winston's right, Joe," Sally added. "We don't seem to have many options, other than to go along with the charade until we can work it out."

"Listen, when I was a kid growing up in Kingston there were lots of Capshaws and Graveses around. They exploited a whole load of youngsters, almost a whole generation, man. Drugs, prostitution, rape, robbery and murder, you name it, they were bastards then and they're still bastards today, but you know what? There were people in Jamaica then and now who stood up to those evil bastards and every so often one of them ends up in court or with a police bullet in the brain, and very slowly, the good guys are starting to take control again. What I'm trying to say, Joe, my friend, my dear boss, is that we're the good guys, and if we stand up to these crooks and think smarter and faster than them, then we can bring them down just like those gang bosses back home."

"But this isn't Jamaica, Winston," said Cutler.

"No, boss, it sure ain't. This is fucking England, man, and this is s'posed to be a peaceful and civilised country. But you know the thing 'bout civilisation, boss? It only works if the people refuse to accept the lawbreakers and maintain the rule of law. If the Capshaws of this world think they can get away with whatever they want then there'll be no peace, no civilised society, and the bad guys win, you know what I mean?"

Cutler was silent for a minute. He knew that Winston was an intelligent and learned man, but he was surprised to hear him be quite so fierce in his condemnation of the ills in modern society. Perhaps he'd have been less surprised if he knew that, as he spoke, Winston was remembering his younger brother Gladstone, accidentally caught in the crossfire during a turf war between rival gangs many years previously. The bullets that tore five year old Gladstone apart had narrowly missed the eight year old Winston, who was walking just a few yards ahead of his little brother. Winston and his family had lived with the grief of that day for the rest of their lives, and it was the sound of the gunfire, and the short and swiftly extinguished screams of his brother as he fell to the ground that haunted the powerful Jamaican as he laid his head on the pillow each night. He'd never forget the sight of his little brother lying there, his blood seeping into the ground as Winston cradled his head in his arms, unable to move or speak, until a policeman had gently pulled him from his brother and they'd loaded his shattered body into an ambulance. That was the sight that returned to haunt him in his dreams every night, even after all these years.

Winston had never told Joe about Gladstone, he rarely spoke of what had happened to anyone, and when he did it was only to mention that he'd had a brother who died young, so Joe Cutler and Sally Corbett knew none of this as they approached the entrance to Maiden's Farm once more.

Cutler simply responded to Winston's apparent moral indignation by replying to the big Jamaican: "Wow, Winston, powerful words my friend. You're right of course. We have to stand up and be counted sometime or let anarchy rule. I guess for the three of us it's time to stand up."

"Let the counting begin, boss man," Winston said in a deep and resonating voice that instilled confidence by the sheer determination in its tone.

"We'll beat them at their own game, Joe, we really will," said Sally, sounding just as positive as Winston.

"One more thing," said Joe as they pulled into the parking area at the farm, "When I spoke to Mavis this morning before we left she had nothing to report from home, but she did say that her nephew who's the policeman in London called her to say that Malcolm Capshaw was seen leaving the Maitland's mansion yesterday in his Bentley. He thought we might be interested; it seems the police have got their eye on the Maitlands for some reason and Capshaw just sort of 'popped up' in the course of their surveillance."

"So at least that confirms the connection between the Maitlands and Capshaw," said Sally.

"Yeah, man," added Winston, "but it also raises the spectre of whether the Maitlands and Capshaw are involved in this thing together, and if they are, then the 'scared shitless' factor of this affair just went up by at least ten points."

Before they could continue the conversation Winston brought the van to a halt, and they were met by the smiling face of Walter Graves who waited for them less than ten yards from the stationary van, leaning on his BMW, gleaming annoyingly as usual.

Graves raised an arm in a welcome gesture, and as they readied themselves to step out of the van, Winston couldn't resist making the comment, "Come into my parlour, said the spider to the fly."

Not quite sure who was now fooling who, and whether Winston saw their small team as the hunters or the hunted, Joe Cutler added to his friends words: "Yes, but which of us is the bloody spider?"

Chapter 28

Walter Graves had spent a sleepless night before meeting up once more with Cutler and his team at Maiden's Farm. He'd put his mind to work on trying to figure out exactly when things had started to go wrong with the plan. Was it the discovery of the skeleton, or was it much earlier? True, there had always been a chance that they'd stumble upon Hogan's remains, but from the information Capshaw had supplied to Graves, he'd been certain that the body was buried at least a mile to the west of where they'd found it. That just went to prove how inaccurate Capshaw's information had been. If they hadn't found the skeleton the search would have continued with Cutler and his people happily going about their jobs in the belief that Excalibur lay beneath the ground somewhere under their feet. Now, an air of suspicion emanated from every member of the survey team and it had taken all of Graves's powers of improvisation and persuasion to stop them from running to the police as soon as the body was unearthed.

Even then Graves was sure that the whole thing had started to go pear shaped earlier, much earlier in fact. When he'd first met Cutler and his team there was still an air of scepticism about them, as though they didn't fully believe in the Excalibur story. In other words Capshaw hadn't done his job properly. The 'historical docu-ment' and the map were okay, and Graves knew that Capshaw must have paid a lot of money for such convincing fakes, so the fault had to lie purely at the door of Malcolm Capshaw. He obviously hadn't sold the concept well enough to Joe Cutler. If Cutler had been a hundred percent convinced he would have been able to swing his team around into enthusiastically carrying out the search. As it was, Graves knew that Winston Fortune was still dubious about the project and even Sally Corbett was beginning to have her doubts, that was clear.

Now, suspicion was growing amongst the surveyors, he could feel it more and more the longer he spent with them. He knew that he had some hard work ahead of him if he were to keep them on board without those suspicions growing so much that they became an early liability. He had no doubts about the course of action he'd have to take if that were to occur, but for now, he needed them and their expertise, as long as he could continue to keep them believing in the legend of Excalibur.

He hoped he wouldn't have to carry out an early termination of the Strata team, his carefully laid plans for their final disappearance in the case of a successful search had been meticulously put in place and it would be a massive complication to have to bring things for-ward. If all went according to plan there would be nothing to link Graves with the 'accident' that would lead to the disappearance of Cutler, Fortune, and Corbett, but that depended on them finding what they searched for. A premature end to the mission was of no use to him or to Capshaw. Only if they failed in their search within the time limit of Cutler's agreement with Capshaw would the sur-vey team walk away in one piece. Then, another team would have to be hired to continue the search, which at least was a clever move on Capshaw's part. By limiting the time the searchers spent on the project there was theoretically less chance of them discovering the true nature of the search, and there was no danger to Capshaw if Cutler and his team were to come up empty handed. Simply hire another team, and if they failed, yet another, until sooner or later someone succeeded. Unfortunately, it seemed as if Capshaw had underestimated the intelligence of Joe Cutler and those who worked for him. If Walter Graves wasn't very, very careful they would work it out and cause him a monumental problem.

"Good morning everyone," he called to the two men and the young woman who alighted from the van a few yards away. "I hope we're all ready for another day in our quest."

"Oh yes, *we* are," Sally replied a little sarcastically, knowing how little the word 'we' seemed to mean to Graves.

"I've been doing a little more research overnight," he went on, "using some of the books I brought with me, searching for tiny clues here and there."

"Oh, that's good, man" said Winston, "and have you found out where the sword is buried from this research of yours?"

"Of course not Winston," Graves replied, "but thanks to an obscure monk by the name of Talbert, I think I may have discovered a clue to the location of Livara."

At the mention of the name Livara Cutler and Fortune exchanged a quick knowing look. They could hardly wait to hear what Graves was about to come up with.

"Oh, do tell us what you've found out, Mr. Graves," Sally exclaimed excitedly, leading Winston to think that the girl would have made an excellent actress.

"Yes, please do," added Cutler.

"Well," said Graves, "As you know the name Livara has kept us all guessing as it doesn't appear in any of the texts which have survived from the Dark Ages,"

I wonder why? thought Cutler.

"Anyway, whilst I was reading an account of the everyday lives of the monks who inhabited the abbey all those years ago, written by this Brother Talbert I came across a reference to a hill known as *Lyncarran*, which was used as grazing land by the monks for some of the many sheep they kept for their wool and meat."

"*Lyncarran* doesn't sound too much like *Livara* to me," said Winston, playing along with what he was sure was a ploy by Graves to keep them interested in the job.

"But don't you see my friends?" Graves went on. "Gareth wrote his chronicle and drew the map in such a way as to confuse Arthur's enemies. It was surely intended that some day Arthur's heir would be led to the site where Excalibur lay perhaps to retrieve the sword and bring about the rebirth of a golden age for the people of Britain. He therefore wrote the chronicle in such a way that his fellow monks would be able to decipher the locations, but the chronicle was lost and disappeared for centuries so no-one in the modern age would have a clue what it was all about."

"I still don't see the connection, man," said Winston, growing impatient.

"It's simple really," said Graves. "In the section of the chronicle where he tells of the sword being buried at Livara, Gareth goes on to say that 'the lamb' will live and be blessed in this place for ever. At first I thought that 'the lamb' was a biblical reference to Jesus Christ, meaning that the sword was blessed and would be kept forever safe by the spirit of Christ who lives in this place for it is, or was Holy Ground at the time. I now believe that he actually meant 'the lamb' to mean just that, the sheep that graze on the hill. That's where the sword is buried, and that's not all. When you look at the ancient writings of the scribes in the time of Arthur, there was a diversity in the way they wrote certain letters, and one word could often be mistaken for another unless the reader were familiar with the lettering of the particular writer. In other words, Gareth couched his words in such a way that someone familiar with his writing, the monks from his own abbey for instance, would be able to decipher the directions he'd indicated. We don't know how or why the chronicle disappeared for so many centuries, but I'm sure if the monks of Glastonbury had had it in their possession all those years ago, then Excalibur would have been raised from the ground a long time ago."

God, the man was good. At least that was the thought that ran through the mind of Joe Cutler as he listened to Graves's new version of the story of Livara. Joe wondered how long Graves had stayed awake to concoct this latest fairy tale, as Cutler was certain it was. To anyone who didn't have the benefit of the information that he and his team were privy to, it might even be believable, but now it simply served to tell Joe that Graves was as crooked as they'd thought, and that they would have to be very careful from now on.

"But how does knowing this help us to locate the sword," asked Sally, seeming to hang on Graves's words like a puppy following its master.

"*She's damned good,*" thought Joe, knowing that Sally was putting on a superb performance for Graves's benefit.

"Well, you see, Sally, the good news is that though *Livara* is mentioned nowhere in the contemporary maps and texts of the time, we do have an approximate location for *Lyncarran*."

"And that is?" asked Winston.

"Right here," Graves exclaimed, spreading his arms out as if to enfold the land on which they stood. "Well, not exactly here, but certainly within a two mile radius of where we're standing. The hill that was once the home of the sheep has disappeared over the centuries and is now probably one of the rolling strands of countryside we see all around us, maybe just a gentle slope, a bump in the ground, I can't say for sure, but what I can say for sure is that we are on the threshold of finding what we came to look for. All I can ask is that you redouble your efforts and we may find what we came for well before the five days you granted me in your deadline, Mr. Cutler."

Graves ended his presentation of the new 'facts' at that point and stood back as though to allow his words to sink into the minds of his audience.

"Well! What do you have to say to that then, Winston?" said Joe Cutler effusively.

"Man, that's some story," said the big Jamaican. "So what you're saying" he addressed Graves, "is that we don't have far to go and we're all gonna be rich, yeah?"

"Quite possibly, Mr Fortune, quite possibly," replied Graves.

"How exciting!" Sally exclaimed, managing to continue her Oscar winning performance. Joe almost wished she'd tone her enthusiasm down a bit, in case Graves got suspicious at her sudden display of exuberance.

"I think, Mr. Cutler, that you'll agree it's in our best interests to 'get the show on the road', as they say," Graves went on.

"It's time to get to work, people," said Joe, and the three surveyors moved to extricate their equipment from the van as Graves lingered by the side of his BMW.

"That was the biggest load of bullshit I've ever heard," Winston whispered to Joe as they unloaded the radar and various markers and poles from the back of the van.

"Amen to that, Winston," Joe replied.

"Does he think we're stupid enough to believe all that?" asked Sally.

"He thinks that we think that we're searching for Excalibur, remember that, Sally," Joe replied.

"You don't think he knows we're on to him then, boss?" asked Winston.

"Why should he? He might think we're a little sceptical about the whole thing, but then who wouldn't be? Anyway, he must think we believe in it to some extent otherwise we wouldn't be here conducting the search, would we?"

"I hope you're right, Joe, I really do," said Sally, now back to herself after dropping her act.

Their whispered conversation was ended by the sound of Walter Graves's voice calling to them from his position by the car.

"You fellows make a start laying out the grid," called Graves as he took his phone from his pocket. "I've just got a couple of calls to make then I'll join you."

The three surveyors began transferring their equipment from the van to the field where the search would begin, leaving Graves holding one of his many mysterious telephone conversations. As soon as they were out of sight, however, Graves quickly snapped the clamshell phone shut and moved across to the van. No-one saw him dip his right hand into his jacket pocket from where he removed a small packet containing what appeared on first sight to be a small microchip or transistor, something that might have come from the inner workings of a modern personal computer perhaps. Still no-one saw him as he snapped the packet open, bent down as though to scrape some mud off the surface of his shoe, and quickly placed the microchip under the arch of the nearside rear wheel of the van, quickly rising to his full height, peering around to make sure he was alone.

Walter Graves knew that his story leaked credibility as a sieve leaks water, but it was the best he'd been able to devise in the space of one night and morning. He was sure that the Strata Survey team suspected that all was not as it should be with the search for Excalibur. The small radio transmitter he'd just placed under the wheel arch of their van might go some way to confirming that thought when they finally left for the day. If he'd suspected that they were becoming a liability sooner he might have placed the bug on the van much earlier and saved himself some time, but now at least, he had an ear in the enemy camp.

The rest of the day proved frustrating for Graves as the survey team seemed to be incapable of detecting anything whatsoever, not even a buried rusting old bicycle revealed itself to the radar. He wasn't to know of course, that Joe and Winston were being very careful not to admit to any soundings they did receive from the radar, though in truth, the day did in fact reveal absolutely nothing to their scanners.

At 5 p.m. Cutler and the others packed away their equipment and bid Graves farewell for the night as he lounged against the BMW. They had decided that this was not the night for Graves to be introduced to Lucius, though the conversation that took place in the van as they drove back to town did serve to confuse Walter Graves as he sat in his car and switched on the portable receiving unit he'd kept hidden in the glove compartment until now.

Chapter 29

"What a waste of a day," Winston said dejectedly as the van bumped off the rough surface of the track that led away from the farm and onto the smooth blacktop surface of the road back to town.

"I can't disagree with that," Joe agreed.

"Did either of you actually pick anything up on the radar?" asked Sally as she tried to remove the dust that had accumulated in her hair with a fine comb.

"I got six readings," said Winston, but none of them were big enough to be the box we're supposedly searching for, if indeed it is a box. Anyway, the readings were no larger than tree holes, probably where the farmer or his predecessors cleared the land before turning it over to fields. How about you, boss?"

"Much the same, a couple of tree holes and nothing else. At least Graves kept out of our way and let us get on with the job."

"Didn't you find that a bit strange?" asked Sally. "I mean, you'd have thought he'd have been on our backs wanting us to find the thing as soon as we could, wouldn't you?"

"He trusts us to report to him if we find anything, that's what it is, Sally," said Joe. "Remember, he thinks we're still convinced we're looking for Excalibur."

"Speaking of Excalibur, what did you think of that tale of his this morning?" Winston asked the question, his eyes never leaving the road as he drove at a steady thirty miles an hour.

"You know, until he came up with that ridiculous fairy tale about Livara I might still have been prepared to believe that Graves at least was on the level," said Joe. "At least now we know that whatever this is really about, he's up to his neck in it as much as Capshaw. I also know why they picked us as opposed to real archaeologists or students to carry out the search."

"Do tell, boss man."

"It's simple really. We're surveyors, not historians. Our knowledge of the subject is so sparse that neither Capshaw nor Graves would have thought us capable of working out that we're on a wild goose chase. Graves is a professional historian, as well as whatever else he does, and Capshaw obviously thought that he'd be able to keep us fed with enough pseudo-historical information to keep us believing in the quest for Excalibur. Their plan might just have worked if I hadn't seen the gun in Graves's pocket and become suspicious. That screwdriver ploy didn't fool me for a minute. A gun is a bloody gun, I'm not that stupid. I just hope they don't know we're on to them, or things could get very uncomfortable for all of us."

"Don't you think my sucking up to him this morning was convincing enough then?" Sally asked. "Surely that should have convinced him that we believe in him."

"Hell, Sally girl, I almost believed that you believed in him" Winston quipped, grinning from ear to ear.

"Yes, your Oscar's in the post," Cutler joked.

"Very funny," she said haughtily. "At least I did my best to make him think that we were hanging on his every word."

"And a very good job you did, Sally, no joking, really you did," said Joe.

"Anyway," said Winston, changing the subject, "I wonder what Lucius and his friend Marcus have discovered while we've been chasing shadows around the fields of Somerset."

"Hmm, I've been wondering that, too," said Joe. "It should be an interesting evening, assuming of course that he has something to tell us."

"We're nearly there, folks," said Winston. "So we'll find out soon enough."

Lucius Doberman wasn't at the Rowan Tree when they arrived, however. Mrs. Cleveley informed them that he'd arrived back at the guesthouse just after eleven that morning and had left soon afterwards. He'd asked her to tell Joe that he'd be back later that evening, and that he'd meet them in the bar at about seven thirty, if they'd be so kind as to be there when he returned.

"Well, there's not much we can do until he comes back, so I propose we all get changed and meet in the bar at seven," Joe suggested.

The others raised no arguments, a hot shower and a change of clothes were just what they needed to raise their spirits after the day spent in pretending to be searching for the mythical sword of King Arthur. They each went up to their separate rooms, and allowed the hot water from their respective showers to wash away the dust and grime of the day.Lucius, Marcus? What the hell were they talking about? Walter Graves had been concerned, though not overly surprised to hear the first half of the conversation in the van after the Strata team had left him. He'd suspected that they were more than sceptical about the whole affair, now they'd simply confirmed it. What did worry him though, was that they were only too aware that they weren't searching for Excalibur. He'd failed singularly in his attempts to keep them believing in that one. That being the case, why were they going on with the search? It could only mean that Cutler knew exactly what they were looking for, (which he found highly unbelievable), or they were naïve enough to believe that they find out the truth behind the search and either keep the secret for themselves, or turn him and Capshaw over to the police. Knowing Cutler as he did from the last few days, Graves was prepared to bet on the third option. Cutler, Corbett and Fortune were all boringly law-abiding, and they would have no qualms about calling in the police if they knew what was really going on. Now there was the added mystery of Lucius and Marcus. It sounded as if the surveyors had called in a couple of members of Caesar's legions to help them, but what exactly were these cohorts doing for the Strata Survey Systems people? In what way could they also pose a threat to Graves, and thus to Capshaw?

It was obvious that Cutler and his people were up to something, and Graves knew that Capshaw would lay any blame squarely at his (Graves) feet if anything were to go awry with his carefully laid plan. Walter Graves needed to investigate these newcomers, find out who and what they were, but he'd have to do it without Cutler's knowledge. He could always drop in to the hotel and see if these newcomers were there with Cutler, but that would be too obvious, and could also prove counter-productive. He'd be playing his hand too soon, letting the opposition know he was on to them, and that wouldn't help him one little bit. No, he'd have to be clever, make his enquiries in a way that wouldn't raise Cutler's suspicions, and Walter Graves suddenly hit on just the means of checking out the mysterious Lucius and Marcus; Mrs. Annette Cleveley. He knew that he'd charmed Cutler's landlady on their first meeting and that she'd been impressed by his being a history professor, so Graves planned to make some excuse to leave the search area the next morning, drive back to Glastonbury, and carefully question the proprietor of the Rowan Tree. As long as he was cautious with his words, she'd never know that she was being interrogated.

"Damn them," he thought aloud. He was frustrated that their conversation had ended where it did. The bug in the van had become useless to him the second they'd exited the vehicle and disappeared into their guest house for the evening. He'd get nothing more from that source until the morning, and he wished that he could find a way to plant a similar device in Cutler's room perhaps, or at their regular table in the bar of the Rowan Tree, but there was too high a chance of being discovered that way. Walter Graves wished that he could be a fly on the wall of the Rowan Tree's bar that evening when the surveyors met up for a couple of drinks before dinner as he knew they always did.

Meanwhile, though, he had to find a way to relate the latest news to Malcolm Capshaw in such a way as not to antagonise the millionaire too much. Graves didn't want to become the fall guy if this all went wrong, and whichever way he put it to the man, he knew that Capshaw would be very unhappy with the latest developments., even if, as Graves believed, it was Capshaw's poor preparation and planning with respect to his choice of Cutler and his team that had directly led to this situation developing.

Had Walter Graves been that previously mentioned fly on the wall of the Rowan Tree's bar, the conversation that took place between Cutler and his team, not long after he emerged from his own room at Meare Manor to savour a pre-dinner brandy would most certainly have given him cause for concern.

Chapter 30

Lucius Doberman swept through the door to the bar of the Rowan Tree, his aura almost preceding his body into the room. Such was the presence of the man that Joe and the others seemed to sense his arrival even as his tall frame burst through the door, his long black coat flapping in his slipstream, revealing the rich red silken lining. Their heads turned in perfect synchronisation as the smiling professor of history held his arms out in greeting as though to encompass them all in a single hypothetical bear hug.

"My friends, my very good friends, please forgive me for not having been here upon your return, but I have indeed been busy on our behalf, and my news will, I'm sure, be a pleasant surprise to you all."

Joe Cutler thought that almost everything to do with this quite remarkable man was surprising. From his fortuitous arrival the night before to his overall persona, this man was truly unlike anyone Joe had met before. Far from being the archetypal stuffy university type Joe would have imagined, Lucius Doberman exuded confidence, and that confidence seemed to rub off on those around him. His looks, his manner his speech all gave him a larger than life personality that helped Joe realise that this was indeed a man who would be an asset, a true friend to those he chose to bestow his own care upon.

"Come and sit down, Lucius, and tell us all about it," said Joe, rising from his chair long enough to shake Doberman's outstretched hand. "Claire, a large whisky for the professor, please," he called to the landlady's daughter who nodded, smiled, and rushed across with a drink for Doberman. Winston pulled a chair out for him and sat down, stretching his long legs out in front of him, underneath the table.

"Forgive me," Doberman said breathlessly, "I rushed back as quickly as I could. I knew you'd all wonder where I'd disappeared to and I didn't want to keep you in suspense too long. I don't think I've ever driven as fast as I have to get back to Glastonbury tonight."

"Back from where, Lucius? What on earth have you been up to all day?" asked Sally.

"Ah, Sally, the impetuousness of youth as always, eh? A moment please, whilst I sample this excellent example of the produce of our Scottish cousins."

Lucius downed the large scotch in one gulp and signalled to Claire to bring him another. She arrived with his drink in seconds and he ordered a refill for his companions before continuing.

As he settled down with his whisky clutched like a theatrical prop in one hand, Lucius began to relate the story of his first full day in Glastonbury.

"Now then, where was I?" he began. "Ah, yes, I suppose I should start with this morning. When I'd seen you off to work, which you must tell me about soon I might add, I went to the library. I was able to obtain the use of one of their computers where I conversed via email with Marcus and a couple of other friends who I thought might be able to help me with my research into your very strange case.

I'd decided, you see, to apply a spot of lateral thinking to what seems to a most perplexing little problem. You know that you're searching for something, but you don't know what. The man you're working for does know, but is unlikely to tell you, and he also has a spy on-site to keep him apprised of your progress. For some reason, he has produced a bogus document to mislead you into believing his silly story about Excalibur, and whether for reasons of showman-ship or some other stupidity, he has incorporated an unwitting clue into said document by mentioning the name *Livara*. Now, as we know, the Livara was a ship, not a place, so the logical conclusion must be that your Mr. Capshaw knows that and therefore the search upon which you are engaged has something to do with that ship, do you all agree?"

Three heads nodded and the professor went on.

"So, why include the name of the ship in his fake document? He knows of course that you are highly unlikely to find any connection between the ship and your visit to Glastonbury, for the reason I out-lined, so his ego allowed him to put the name quite clearly before you. Of course, he felt quite safe in doing so, as, if Sally had not tele-phoned me, and I hadn't spoken to Marcus, and then come here to inform you of my findings, you would not have discovered the link. After all, if his deception had succeeded why on earth should you?"

"Professor, I mean, Lucius," Winston butted in. "You're beginning to lose me, man."

"I'm sorry, Winston, please, bear with me. Going back to this morning, I thought that my search should take a completely dif-ferent direction to yours, so I decided to concentrate on the ship."

"But she sank over sixty years ago," said Winston.

"Ah yes, but, and it is a very big but," Doberman went on, "What if she didn't sink, or what if she didn't sail empty as the original manifest claimed, why did she carry double the normal crew com-pliment and who were the additional men who went down with her if she did indeed sink?"

"Bloody hell, Lucius. When you say lateral thinking, you damned well mean it, don't you?" Joe asked, breaking his silence at last. He was enthralled by the professor's words and wanted to hear the rest of what Lucius had to say.

"Thank you, Joe," Lucius said gracefully, and then continued with his report on his day. "You see, I realised that as the ship was lost with all hands, and officially there were no survivors, and the original owner must have died years ago, then my search could only begin in one place."

"Like I said, you've lost me, man" said Winston.

"The word *Livara* was invented by the ship's owner to honour his children. If I couldn't find Harry Blandford, then perhaps there was still a chance that Linda, Valerie or Raymond might still be alive, or maybe they had children?"

"Of course," said Joe, as realisation dawned on him, "you went looking for the children, the only ones who might have known something about the truth surrounding their father's ship?"

"Exactly, dear boy," Lucius said triumphantly. "I received a reply to one of my e-mails quite quickly. I have a friend who works for the Admiralty and he was happy to provide me with the information I requested, me being a historian and all. Anyway, Paul, that's his name, Paul Davies, he told me that there's a bit of conflicting information surrounding the *SS Livara*. He had no trouble finding the initial report of the sinking and of the rest of the detail surrounding the convoy she sailed in, but that the numbers didn't add up, as he put it. He promised to investigate further and get back to me, which he did an hour later. As we already know, the *Livara* was carrying a larger than normal crew, and according to the usual maritime practice of the time the crew's wages would have stopped at the precise moment of the sinking. Even though all hands were lost, the records show that the only names listed were those of the ship's original crew. There's no mention of the additional souls who were listed as having gone down with the ship, so who, I asked Paul, could they be? In the hour he'd kept me waiting he unearthed something very interesting. You might remember that I told you a destroyer was also sunk on the same night as the *Livara*. Well, *H.M.S. Firefly* appears to have been listed as carrying a crew of 280.

In the official records it appears that someone had got their sums wrong. There were 68 survivors from the *Firefly*, which should have meant that 212 crew members were lost. The official record, however, states that 234 souls were lost, an increase of twenty two on what it should have been. The Royal Navy's records were, of course, separate from those of the Merchant Marine, so it's unlikely that anyone at the time would have made the connection that Paul and I made today, though no-one in 1940 would have had reason to be suspicious of casualty figures when so many lives were being lost at sea on a daily basis."

Cutler and the others were still enthralled by the professor's words, though none of them were quite sure where his story was heading. After pausing for breath and taking another sip of his drink Doberman continued.

"Don't you see?" he asked, and went on. "The twenty two additional lives listed as lost when the *Firefly* went down matches the twenty two extra crew members supposedly on board the *Livara*, assuming her to be carrying her normal crew compliment of sixteen, which tallies with the named casualty figures by the way. For some reason, rather than list them as being lost on board the Livara, the Royal Navy placed them on board the *Firefly*, which to Paul and I could only mean one thing. The extra personnel on the *Livara* were Royal Naval personnel, not merchant marine, and they could only have been assigned to the freighter if she were involved in some operation of importance, under the auspices of the military, and perhaps carrying a cargo of value to the nation."

At last Cutler found his voice again, long enough to ask, "You're leading up to something, Lucius, I know you are. Come on, out with it, you've teased us long enough."

"Patience, dear boy, patience. I beg you. Now, it's evident that someone somewhere made an administrative error all those years ago, otherwise, we wouldn't be having this discussion now. Wires got crossed somewhere between the military and civilian authorities and they left us this tantalising clue, though what it leads to we're still in the dark about. Now, this is where things got really interesting. My second contact this morning was with Margery Forbes, who is a leading genealogist. I simply asked her to trace the progeny of Harry Blandford, the owner of the *SS Livara* and it didn't take her long to reply to my inquiry. Tragedy made the job easy you see. You'll recall that Blandford named his ship after his children Linda, Valerie and Raymond. Well, Raymond was killed in 1944 serving with the Fleet Air Arm as a naval pilot. His aircraft was shot down while attacking a Japanese battle squadron in the Pacific. Valerie was killed when a V1, the German's flying bomb, scored a direct hit on the house she shared with her husband in London in 1945. They had no children, so that left only Linda, who did survive the war, married and had one daughter, Doris, born in 1949. Doris died of cancer in 1980, but her own daughter Angela, who was born in 1976 is still alive and well and living in mild luxury in a quite beautiful country house in Wiltshire, which of course is not exactly another world in distance from where we now sit."

"You've been to see her?" Sally exclaimed.

"That's where I went haring off to this morning, of course," said Lucius, "and a very warm welcome I received I can tell you. Angela Trent, that's her married name of course, was delighted to meet someone who was so eager to talk about her grandfather, who it seems is something of a hero figure to Angela."

"You clever old professor," said Winston, beginning to comprehend exactly how hard Lucius had worked on their behalf during just one day in Glastonbury.

"Thank you, Winston," said Lucius, before going on with his tale.

"She was happy to discuss many things about old Harry Blandford, but most of it was purely family stuff, and not of great interest to my investigation. I was polite and didn't interrupt, of course, thinking that if she did have anything significant to divulge it would come out in the natural course of her story. Eventually, she told me something that made my ears prick up, figuratively speaking. Harry Blandford was a retired sea captain as we know, but when he first started his shipping company, he needed capital in order to make his first ship *The Blandford Star* fully seaworthy. It seems that old Harry lived in a part of London also inhabited by a man whose name we've come across already, a man who was known to the local population of the time as a source of money for those requiring loans, what today I believe we would refer to as a loan shark. Harry Blandford went to and received a sizeable loan from that man, and was able to get his ship operational, and his small success story grew from there. He soon acquired a second ship the *Livara*, and as far as Angela is aware, Harry was able to repay the loan to his financial benefactor before the outbreak of war. Now, can anyone guess the name of the man who loaned Harry Blandford his start-up cash?"

"Bloody hell, Lucius!" Joe Cutler exclaimed loudly, "He borrowed the money from old Sam Maitland, didn't he?"

"You've got it in one, old chap" Lucius replied. "Now all we have to do is figure out what Maitland had to do with the *Livara's* last voyage and we may be close to unravelling this strange tangled web that you've got yourselves caught up in. Now, my friends, I know there is still much to discuss and you must have many questions, but I implore you, as a man who has worked extremely hard all day, as I'm sure you have as well, can we eat now please?"

The others reluctantly agreed. They wanted Lucius to go on with his revelation, but he assured them that there was nothing else of great importance to relate, and what there was could wait until after dinner. Dinner itself was a thoughtful affair, the conversation quite muted as Cutler and the others allowed the news that Lucius had brought them to sink in. Once or twice questions were asked, but Lucius deflected them, saying that he would rather talk after dinner. He was famished, and he soon devoured his meal of steak and kidney pie with mashed potatoes and a medley of green vegetables.

As they returned to the bar Joe and the others couldn't wait to take up where they'd left off before Lucius's stomach had taken command of the evening.

Chapter 31

"What the hell d'you mean, 'they're on to us?'" Capshaw screamed down the telephone. Such was the volume of his anger and the venom with which he delivered his tirade that Graves held the receiver of his own phone a good two inches from his ear, and still the voice of his employer seemed to reverberate in every cell of his brain. "Speak you bloody fool. Tell me I wasn't a total numbskull to hire you to keep an eye on the 'sharp end' of the job."

As Capshaw's vociferous harangue came to a close Graves tried to explain the situation to the millionaire businessman in simple terms.

"When I say 'on to us' I mean that they know they're not searching for Excalibur. Having said that they don't know exactly what we're looking for. I planted a bug in their van because I suspected that they were thinking along those lines, and their conversation after today's search proved me correct. It might have helped if you hadn't told Santorini to place the name Livara in the document. That's what led them to become suspicious and I've been working my rocks off trying to keep them believing in the whole ruddy story. What on earth made you do that any way?"

"That's got nothing to do with you, Graves, just remember that. If I chose to put the name of the fucking ship in there, then it's no business of yours or anyone else's."

Despite his anger and chiding of Graves, Capshaw knew that he'd made an error, allowing his own pompous vanity to let him include the name of the *Livara* in his bogus document. What had possessed him to do it? Of course he thought that no-one involved in the operation would ever question the so-called Chronicle of Gareth and he'd allowed himself the luxury of a little private joke on Cutler and his team. He hoped now that his decision wasn't about to rear up and bite him where it would hurt, in his wallet. Added to that was the reaction of the Maitland brothers if they were to find out that his stupidity had put the search in jeopardy. Now that was a thought that didn't bear consideration. He returned to his conversation with Graves.

"I think the time has come to get a little 'forceful' with Mr. Cutler and his people, Graves. I'm sure you know what I mean."

"I know exactly what you mean," Graves replied then added: "But there is something else, what you might call an added complication."

"Dear God, Graves, don't tell me you've fucked up somewhere else in all this. What sort of added complication?"

Graves went on to relate the strange appearance on the scene of the two characters he knew only as Lucius and Marcus. By the time he'd finished Capshaw's fury had grown once again, and was now on a par with an Atlantic gale blowing from the coldest reaches of the Arctic.

"Find out who they are, and what they've got to do with anything," he yelled down the phone at Graves. "I don't care what you have to do to achieve success with this job, Graves, just bloody well get on with it, and don't, I repeat, *don't* leave any loose ends, even if that includes these bloody strangers who're poking their noses in where it doesn't concern them. Do I make myself clear?"

"Abundantly clear, sir," Graves replied as respectfully as he could in an attempt to assuage Capshaw's anger. "Leave it to me, I have a plan."

"I just hope it's better than the one you've been adhering to so far, that's all I can say. I'm sure I don't have to tell you what's at stake, or the price of failure."

The implied threat wasn't lost on Walter Graves, who well knew the reputation of the Maitlands and their connection with the search. He might be good, and he might have wriggled clear of some tricky situations in the past, but taking on the entire criminal fraternity of East London had never been in Graves's plans.

"I've told you, it's all under control. Cutler will do anything I want him to by the time I've finished with him, as will that Jamaican sidekick of his."

"And the girl, Corbett? Will she do what we want as well, Mr. Graves?"

"Oh yes, sir," Graves replied with a hint of real menace in his voice. "Little Miss Corbett will not only do as I say, but she's the key to my plan. Thanks to her, Cutler and Fortune will be falling over themselves to do as I ask."

"Ha, I think I get your drift, Graves. I don't want to know the details, just let me know when your plan bears fruit, and I'm warning you, it had better do just that."

Capshaw hung up on the historian, as he had a penchant for doing to people when he considered a conversation over and done with. Graves breathed a sigh of relief. Capshaw had really shaken him, and that wasn't an easy thing to do, or something that happened to Walter Graves very often. Few people had the power to instil fear in him, but Capshaw, thanks to his millions and his connections to the Maitland family was one of those who had that ability.

Now that he was left alone and in peace in his room at Meare Manor, Walter Graves began to mentally put the finishing touches to his plan to coerce Cutler and Fortune to continue the search. The plan would unfortunately involve a level of fear and discomfort for Sally Corbett, but then that was the price she would have to pay for her and her colleagues' suspicions and meddling in Graves's nicely laid plans. Graves would spend the next day doing his best to lull the Strata Survey team into a false sense of security before making his move the following day. From then onwards the ball, and therefore full control, would be firmly back in his court!

"So you see," Lucius Doberman said to the others as they sat around their usual table in the bar, "my visit to see Angela Trent threw up the odd clue or two, and gives us a little more information to work with. Oh yes," he suddenly announced quite theatrically, as he seemed to like to do when metaphorically pulling a rabbit out of his hat. "There was one more thing she told me which might be of some significance to us, though I'm not sure quite what bearing it has on the case."

"Hey, Professor Lucius, I knew you'd been holding out on us man." Winston was grinning again as he spoke, as if he knew that Lucius had saved the best until the end, and appreciated the fact that this strange man had suddenly appeared as if from nowhere and was pulling out all the stops to help them.

"Yes, Lucius, come on, put us all out of our misery," Sally implored.

Cutler simply sat resting his chin on his hands, waiting to hear what else Lucius had discovered.

"Well," said the professor, "it seems, according to Angela Trent, that there was some small mystery involving the last voyage of the

SS Livara. She was captained as she had been all her voyages by Captain David Scott, a man who her grandfather trusted implicitly she was quick to point out. He'd been a seafaring man all his life and had served on board ship with Harry Blandford in their younger days. When Blandford bought his own ships he asked his old friend to join him in the enterprise, and Scott commanded the *Livara* on every voyage she made under the flag of Blandford Shipping. The ship's regular first officer, an Irishman by the name of Seamus O'Rourke was unable to sail on the ships two voyages prior to the fatal convoy sailing as he'd broken a leg in a bar-room brawl, and was in a plaster cast. His place on the bridge had been taken by a man named James Hogan, who Scott took a dislike to. When he asked Blandford to find him a different replacement for the reliable O'Rourke he was surprised when Angela's grandfather told him that Hogan would stay with the ship until the Irishman returned to duty. It was unlike her grandfather to go against the wishes of his captains when it came to operational matters and the affair was said to have left a bad taste in Scott's mouth. This story was relayed to Angela Trent by her mother by the way, as she related the family history to her daughter as she lay dying from the cancer which killed her. Anyway, Scott's pessimism regarding Hogan was apparently well-founded as the man simply disappeared the night before the Livara was due to sail on her last voyage. There was no message, no nothing; he just failed to arrive back on board after leaving her earlier in the day to conduct some 'personal business' in the city of Bristol, so he'd said.

"The *SS Livara* sailed on her fateful voyage without a first officer. Scott simply hadn't had the time to find a replacement before she sailed. Captain Scott went down with his ship, of course, but Hogan's no-show was reported by the Captain to Blandford in an 'I told you so' telephone call the night before the convoy departed from Bristol. Strangely, my friends, the man known as James Hogan was never seen or heard of again, and Angela Trent could be of no help in suggesting where he'd disappeared to or what had happened to him."

Doberman leaned back in that typical way of his that implied he'd finished, and he reached out to take up the brandy from the table. Cutler and the others took a few seconds to allow his latest words to sink in, and then Cutler himself broke the silence.

"I think, Lucius, that we might have a good idea what happened to Mr. Hogan to prevent him joining his ship that night, don't we, folks?"

Winston and Sally both nodded gravely in agreement with their boss, and it was Winston who voiced the thought they were all thinking.

"James Hogan couldn't join his ship, Lucius, because he was dead, and lying buried in a shallow grave near Glastonbury. He's the bloody skeleton in the field, man, I'll bet my life on it."

"I was kind of hoping that you'd deduce that," said the professor, "as that's exactly the way my own thoughts have been leaning."

As the gravity of this latest twist in their strange quest sunk in to the minds of the small survey team, Sally Corbett probably spoke for all of them when she said:

"Lucius, Joe, will you please tell me what the hell we've got ourselves into here?"

It was Joe Cutler who provided her with an answer, not that it did her much good or served to allay her fears.

"That, Sally, is something that only time, and perhaps our Mr. Graves, is going to reveal."

Joe Cutler didn't know it at the time, but his reference to Walter Graves and his part in revealing the truth of their situation was to prove highly prophetic.

Chapter 32

Charlotte Raeburn slipped out of the bed as Malcolm Capshaw lay sleeping beside her. Making her way to the bathroom, she could feel the metallic taste of her own blood in her mouth where Capshaw had lashed out at her. Using a damp tissue she wiped the dried blood from the corner of her mouth, sat on the toilet seat, and sobbed quietly.

Whatever Graves had said to Capshaw had infuriated him to the point of violence, and Charlotte had borne the brunt of that anger. Not only that, she had overheard the Maitlands being mentioned in connection with the Glastonbury project, confirming that they were deeply involved with Capshaw in the enterprise. Her fear of the Maitlands coupled with Capshaw's beating had convinced her more than ever that she had to escape the clutches of her employer.

As soon as he'd hung up on Graves her ordeal had begun. Capshaw's sexual demands had been brutal and painful. When he'd reached down the side of the bed and produced a whip that Charlotte hadn't seen before, things begun to get out of hand. She twisted and tried to see the marks that she knew he'd left on her back. She could feel the wheals where his blows had landed, and could make out the raised red stripes that showed the track of the whip as it stung into her flesh. When she'd protested to Capshaw he'd swung his hand in a vicious arc and connected squarely with Charlotte's mouth, drawing blood instantly. The beating seemed to turn him on, and after giving her a moment to catch her breath, he'd jumped on her once more, gratifying himself before leaving her feeling utterly used and dejected. Soon afterwards he'd made her lie down beside him and had fallen into a deep sleep.

Charlotte made a decision. She would leave, not in the morning, but now. Being as quiet as she could she returned to the bedroom, gathered up her clothes and went out onto the landing where she hurriedly dressed. Five minutes later, Charlotte was in her car, driving into the night, her first priority being to put as many miles between her and Malcolm Capshaw as she could. She drove home and swiftly threw a few clothes and personal items into a holdall before hitting the road once more. She had to get as far away from Capshaw as she could. His fury would be unabated when he found out that she'd disappeared, and Charlotte couldn't be sure how far his tentacles of revenge would reach. At least she wouldn't be missed until he arrived at his office in the morning. Sure, he'd be mad to find her gone when he woke alone in his bed but he'd probably put that down to her own anger at being used so badly the night before. He'd drive to the office ready to vent yet more anger on her, and would only realise that she wasn't coming in to work when she failed to arrive on time, as she always did. He'd be ringing her home trying to bully her into going in to work and when he got no answer Charlotte's troubles would really start. He'd probably do everything he could to find her, and, as she drove through the night Charlotte began to have the first pangs of doubt as to whether running away from Malcolm Capshaw was the wisest decision she could have made.

Eventually, she decided that it was too late to turn back. She tried to formulate a plan as she drove, having left Capshaw's mansion with no real idea where she was going. Her cousin Jenny lived in a small village not far from Hereford, well within range of a night's driving, and Charlotte decided to visit her cousin, Jenny, and maybe stay for day or two while she figured out where to go next. Charlotte had enough money in the bank thanks to Capshaw to live for quite some time without finding gainful employment, so she'd have plenty of opportunity to find a new town and a place to settle into.

As she drove a light rain began to fall, and the windscreen wipers beat a steady rhythm as the car ate up the miles, the headlights picking out the curtain of raindrops that fell incessantly in the darkness. The further she drove away from Stratford, and away from Capshaw the more Charlotte allowed herself to relax a little. Soon, she began to feel slightly proud of herself for having the courage to make the break from the man. After all, what right did he have to use her the way he had? She wasn't his property even though he may have treated her as such. Charlotte could still feel the pain from the whiplashes on her back as she pressed against the back of the car seat, and her mouth still carried the taste of blood, and those combined sensations helped to convince her that she'd made the right move. Let Capshaw rant and rave as much as he liked. Charlotte was gone, and she sure as hell wasn't going back!

By the time she arrived on the outskirts of Hereford, the rain had stopped and the morning sun had begun to burn off the dew that had formed overnight. Where traces of that dew still clung to the bushes and plants that made up the hedgerows she drove past, it was as if nature had deposited a haul of tiny diamonds amongst the green that lined the roads. Charlotte drove slowly along the country roads, now and then spying the beautiful creation of the jewel that was a spider's web, also littered with miniscule dew-diamonds. Her mood lifted with every mile she drove, and shortly found herself entering the quaintly named village of Stretton Sugwas, where her cousin had made her home some years before.

Jenny was an artist, and had moved to Hereford because she admired the countryside of the area, and because it afforded her a useful base for exploring some of the most unspoilt countryside in Britain. From here she could reach the Cotswolds, the Brecon Beacons in Wales, the Forest of Dean, and other notable locations that displayed the beauty she so loved to record on canvas. She was far from wealthy, but at least she made enough to live on, and to pay the rent on the beautiful stone cottage she'd lived in for the last five years.

Charlotte pulled up outside the cottage which she'd visited only twice before. She and Jenny weren't particularly close but had always been friendly, and she was sure Jenny wouldn't turn her away. Charlotte thought it strange that the thought of not being made welcome by her cousin hadn't entered her mind until now. But it was a little late to turn back now. Besides, Charlotte knew she had no other alternatives.

She needn't have worried. Jenny was delighted to see her cousin, and didn't appear at all surprised to find her standing on her doorstep at just before eight in the morning. She wrapped her arms around Charlotte in a warm embrace, released her, and led her into the tiny kitchen where the kettle was about to boil, and the smell of frying bacon filled the air. Charlotte suddenly realised how hungry she was, and took little persuading to join Jenny for breakfast.

Once breakfast and dishes were cleared, Jenny finally asked her cousin a question. "Who hit you, Charlotte?"

There was no, "has someone hit you?" or "what happened to you?" Jenny spoke as though she knew exactly what had happened, and Charlotte answered her honestly.

"The bastard," said Jenny, after Charlotte had related her story of the treatment she'd received at the hands of Malcolm Capshaw. "Why did you let him treat you like that? For God's sake, girl, you should have had more respect for yourself, and got out of there at the first sign of him showing any ugly sexual tendencies. You've let him turn you into a virtual slave by the sounds of it."

"I know I've been a fool, Jenny, but, well, the money was just so good, and the job wasn't too hard, and he seemed alright at first, you know, very generous and so on. He used to take me to the theatre and to expensive restaurants and…"

"And you let him think he'd bought you. Honestly, Charlotte, you've been a bloody fool, but at least you've shown some sense now in getting away from the brute. You're welcome to stay as long as you want as long as you don't mind me coming and going with my work. Just make yourself at home."

Charlotte sniffed, once again on the edge of tears. She managed to get a hold of herself. "Thanks, Jenny, you've no idea how much this means to me. I won't stay long, just a day or two until I decide where to head for next. I have to start a new life as far away from Capshaw as possible. I just hope he doesn't trace me here and cause trouble. I'd hate to bring anything like that on you."

"Ha, I doubt that he'd do that, Charlotte. My experience with bullies is that once you've stood up to them or given them their marching orders, they will soon forget you and move on to some other poor soul. Do you really think a wealthy man like Capshaw will give up important money-making time to go searching for his missing secretary, who, I might add, has a very good case for calling the police and reporting the bastard for assault, both sexual and physical?"

"I don't want the police involved, Jenny, really I don't. I feel enough of an idiot already without making myself look even more foolish. Anyway, Capshaw would probably say that I was a willing participant, and I suppose in a way he's right. I never actually did much to try to stop him."

"Well, as long as you're sure."

"I'm sure. I'm just glad to be away from there, believe me."

"Right, no more lectures from me then, that's a promise," said Jenny, adding, "You just forget about Mr. Malcolm bloody Capshaw. I doubt you'll ever see or hear from that bullying shit again, you mark my words."

Charlotte wished she could share her cousin's optimism, but she omitted to tell her one or two things about Capshaw. Charlotte thought that what her cousin didn't know couldn't harm her, and hoped to herself that she'd be well away from Hereford before Capshaw came after her, or worse still, sent someone else to find her. For some reason Charlotte suddenly realised she might have to spend the rest of her life looking over her shoulder and that was not a prospect that endeared itself to her.

Jenny had to go into town that morning to buy various materials she needed for her work and left Charlotte to rest and settle in the cottage. The cottage was eerily silent after Jenny had driven off in her old battered Range Rover. Tiredness suddenly overwhelmed Charlotte and she made her way on slightly groggy legs to the spare bedroom, where she stretched out on the bed, pulled the duvet over herself, and fell into a deep sleep asleep in seconds.

Chapter 33

Breakfast at the Rowan Tree was a somewhat subdued affair. Despite Lucius's revelations of the night before, they were still no nearer to discovering exactly what Capshaw and Graves were searching for. All of the Strata Survey team were now aware that their lives might be in considerable danger from Walter Graves, but how and when he might strike against them was still an unanswered question. Lucius informed them he thought it unlikely anything would happen while there was a chance they might yet find whatever Graves was looking for. Cutler agreed, but only as long as they could convince Graves that they hadn't caught on to his Excalibur charade. If Graves thought for just one minute they were on the verge of discovering the truth, Joe felt that the man would have no hesitation in taking punitive action against all of them. Lucius Doberman and his contacts remained Joe's ace in the hole. As long as Graves had no inkling that Cutler was receiving outside help in attempting to solve the mystery then they still had a chance of thwarting whatever evil he and Capshaw were perpetrating in the heart of the English countryside.

"So," said Lucius, mopping up the juice from a grilled tomato with a slice of heavily buttered bread, "today I shall try to carry my investigation a little further. I must tell you that amongst other things, yesterday I asked Marcus to look into the background and credentials of our friend Graves. I know your worthy Mrs. Hightower did her best, Joe, but when it comes to digging the dirt on members of the academic fraternity, I can assure you that no-one is more adept at the art than Marcus. Also, I forgot to add that he is a close personal friend of the Dean of St. Aidens College, where I believe Graves is employed?"

"You sly old fox," said Joe. "You kept that one quiet, didn't you?"

"Purely because as yet I have had no reply from Marcus on the subject. However, I felt it only fair to inform you at this point so that you may have something to look forward to when we meet this evening. I fully expect Marcus to have spoken to the Dean by sometime this morning, and I'm sure he'll have some news for me before you return from the field."

Sally clapped Lucius on the back. Winston grinned his infectious ear to ear grin. Joe spoke once again.

"You know, if I didn't know better, I'd say that you were thoroughly enjoying this Sherlock Holmes role, Lucius."

"Well, I must say, it's certainly exercising parts of my brain that perhaps haven't been utilised to their fullest capacity for a while," the professor replied. "Now, please, don't let me delay you all any longer. You must go and keep our friend Graves amused and bamboozled for another day whilst I try to discover further intellectual weapons with which we may yet defeat him and his dastardly employer."

"Man, don't you just love the way the man talks," said Winston.

"Very flowery at times I must say," said Joe

"I'm afraid that's the academic in me, old chap," said Lucius. "Just can't help myself I'm afraid."

"Well, I think you're just wonderful. Thank you so much for coming to help us."

Sally planted an affectionate kiss on the cheek of Lucius Doberman, who actually blushed as she did so.

"Hmm, yes, well, like I said, off to work with the lot of you," he repeated, and without further delay they said their goodbyes, and left the professor to his academic intrigues while they set off for another day in the company of their potential Nemesis.

At around the time that Cutler and the others were leaving to begin their day's work with Walter Graves, Malcolm Capshaw was arriving at his office in the centre of Stratford. The beauty of the day, the warmth of the sunshine and the singing of the birds were totally lost on the millionaire who was in the foulest of moods. He'd been incensed to find Charlotte missing when he'd woken up at six-thirty. He'd rung her home, expecting to give the little trollop a piece of his mind only to be met by the mechanical voice of her answering service. Thinking that she'd be at her desk at the office when he arrived, he was stunned to walk into a deathly quiet room, devoid of any sound. Charlotte was nowhere to be seen, and there was no sign that she'd even been in the office that morning, no chance that she'd just popped out to the shop for cigarettes or a newspaper.

Capshaw believed she was still mad with him for being a little heavy handed with her after Graves's call the previous night, but, what the hell? He paid her enough, didn't he?

The morning wore on, however, and still no sign of Charlotte. Capshaw realized she may have walked out on him without saying a word. Stupid bitch! Didn't she realise what trouble she'd be in if she'd done something so stupid? Surely she must know that he wouldn't let her get away with such a thing, besides which, Charlotte knew too much about Capshaw and his illegitimate dealings to be allowed to walk around like a loose cannon. As lunchtime approached with still no word from his secretary Capshaw began to accept that he'd gone too far the night before and Charlotte had, indeed, 'done a runner'. His problem was going to be in finding her, bringing her back if necessary and making sure that she realised the error of her ways. The prospect of 'disciplining' Charlotte before forcing her back to work made Capshaw hard all over again. Now, all he had to do was trace the stupid little harlot.

As he was about to lock up the office and leave for lunch the telephone rang. Capshaw reluctantly answered the infernal machine, not really wanting to talk to anyone, but thinking that it might be Charlotte ringing him with some flimsy excuse for not being there.

"Hello, Malcolm. How come that juicy little secretary of yours isn't answering the phone. You given her the day off?"

The unmistakeable voice of Boris Maitland boomed down the telephone line, and Capshaw felt as though his knees had turned to mush.

"Er, hello, Boris. No, Charlotte isn't here, she's..."

"Something's wrong, isn't it, Malcolm? I can tell by the way you're hedging, old friend. Tell me, come on, do we have a problem?"

"It's just that Graves phoned me last night and I lost my temper with him and afterwards I was a little rough with Charlotte, and when I woke up this morning she was gone and I haven't seen or heard from her."

"You fucking idiot, Malcolm. That blasted dick of yours has got you into trouble before, now it looks like you've done it again. What was it; you beat her up while you were fucking her?"

The silence that greeted his question merely served to confirm Maitland's hypothesis.

"I'm asking you a question, Malcolm. Have you gone and put us in trouble again because of your nasty little appetites?"

"I just don't know where she is. Maybe she'll come back tomorrow."

"And then again maybe she won't. How much does the bitch know about Glastonbury?"

"Er…"

"I said, *how much, Malcolm?*"

"Almost everything."

"Oh, that's bloody good isn't it, Malcolm? That's just bloody fantastic, you fucking idiot! Where can she have gone? Think man, you must have some ideas. Has she got a mother or someone she'd run to?"

"I don't know, Boris, honestly. Wait a minute. When she came to work for me I had her fill out a next of kin form in case of emergencies. It must be filed somewhere. Let me look."

"Don't just look, Malcolm. Find!"

Maitland waited at the other end of the line while Malcolm Capshaw searched through various drawers in his desk until he found something. Capshaw picked up the receiver again.

"You still there, Boris?"

"I'm waiting, Malcolm."

"It seems her only relative is a cousin in Herefordshire, some obscure village in the country."

"Give me the address."

"What are you going to do, Boris?"

"Hopefully, I'm going to get you out of the shit again, Malcolm, that's what I'm going to do."

Maitland gave Capshaw no chance to reply, the line went dead. Capshaw sat quietly at his desk for a few minutes. He neither knew nor wanted to know what Boris Maitland planned to do. Whatever it was, he was certain that Charlotte wouldn't be wanting to come back to work for him. For now it was better that he kept his mouth shut and allowed Boris to solve the problem. He was good at that. Malcolm Capshaw believed it was time to find a new secretary anyway.

Chapter 34

Walter Graves was becoming increasingly bored and irritated. The surveyors had found nothing, despite Graves feeling that they were close to the right place. It had to be somewhere in the area they were now searching with the GPR. If they didn't find it soon, his job would become increasingly difficult. He knew that they were no longer fooled by the Excalibur story and assumed that Cutler thought that he and his people could somehow outwit him and turn the prize over to the authorities. Their conversation in the van that morning hadn't helped him much, being mostly concerned with the mysterious 'Lucius', whoever he may be. That at least was one question that Graves was determined to find an answer to very shortly. As soon as the team broke for lunch Graves excused himself, saying he had urgent business in town that couldn't wait, and promising to return in an hour.

He left them eating sandwiches and drinking tea and headed back to Glastonbury, his intention being to speak to Mrs. Cleveley and elicit information about Lucius. As he drove his car phone rang and Graves pressed the hands-free button, allowing him to talk as he drove. He was surprised to hear the voice of Boris Maitland who informed him that there was a problem at Capshaw's end of the operation and that Graves was to do everything he could to facilitate an early conclusion to the operation, whatever the cost. Maitland waited long enough for Graves to give him his assurance that he would do everything in his power to achieve a speedy resolution to the search, and the line went dead.

Graves sighed. It appeared Malcolm Capshaw hadn't been as clever as Graves had originally thought him to be. Whatever happened Walter Graves knew that he had to do whatever was necessary to ensure that he personally walked away from this job without a stain on his character. His future in both his fields of expertise depended upon it. As he neared the Rowan Tree he decided to bring certain parts of his plans forward, which might prove difficult, but felt he was being left with very little choice.

Annette Cleveley was delighted to see the 'nice historian' again. She welcomed Graves like an old friend and invited him into her office for a cup of tea, which he gladly accepted. She wondered if he'd come to see his 'friends' again, but he assured her that he'd just left them hard at work. No, he told her that he was trying to trace a friend who was supposed to meet him here. This friend had left his wife quite recently after discovering she was having an affair with his best friend and would probably be travelling incognito, using a false name so that his wife couldn't find out where he'd gone. Graves wondered if anyone new had checked in over the last couple of days, it was strange he said, that his friend hadn't phoned him, and Graves had especially recommended the Rowan Tree to him because of the lovely friendly landlady who ran the guesthouse.

Mrs. Cleveley was flattered, as Graves intended her to be, and replied that the only new guest who'd arrived in the last two days was another friend of Mr. Cutler and his people. She was more than excited to discover that her new guest was, like Mr. Graves, another professor of history.

Graves pressed her to tell her the gentleman's name. After all, as another professor of history there was a chance that they might know one another as their paths may have crossed over the years. Perhaps, he'd said, that they may even have worked together at some time in the past.

Mrs. Cleveley was happy to reveal the name of her new guest, and Graves thanked her very much, but told her that he'd never heard of the gentleman, and that they obviously didn't know each other at all.

Women, thought Graves as he drove back in the direction of Maiden's Farm. *A bit of flattery and most of them will tell you anything, even sell you their bodies if the price is right*, this last thought coming as he remembered Mrs. Cleveley's buxom daughter Claire from his last visit to the Rowan Tree. As for Lucius Doberman, Graves had lied to the proprietor and landlady of the guesthouse. He did in fact know the learned Professor, not personally of course, but by reputation. What on earth was such a scholar doing here, how did he know Cutler, and how dangerous could he be to the operation? Cutler, Fortune, and Corbett were one thing, but the sudden and inexplicable disappearance of one the country's leading historians would certainly raise a stink in all the wrong quarters as far as Graves was concerned. The whole thing was getting out of control, and if there was one thing that Walter Graves prided himself on when he was involved in a job, it was always being in total control.

From now on, he was going to have to be very, very careful about every step he took along the road to the recovery of the prize he was seeking, and he would have to keep a more than close eye on Professor Doberman. He could prove to be the proverbial 'fly in the ointment' and one that Graves could well do without.

Graves drove back to the farm where he spent most of the afternoon revising and re-revising his plans until he thought he might just have thought of a way to bring the job to a successful conclusion. First of all, he would have to make some slightly more in-depth preparations for the future of Miss Sally Corbett as his original plan would now be unsuitable. He needed somewhere more secure, and he knew just where to look in order to find just the right place.

A series of tunnels and passageways running beneath the ruins of Glastonbury Abbey, stretch out and into the land beyond. What they were originally designed for is a matter for conjecture, but Graves considered making use of the ancient passages for his scheme to bring Cutler and Fortune to heel and bend them to his will. It would need careful planning and forethought and time was running short. He would have to excuse himself from the search once again and make his way beneath the grounds of the abbey in order to make his preparations.

Joe seemed unperturbed by Graves's announcement that his important business would mean him having to disappear for the rest of the day. In fact, all three surveyors welcomed the news. Graves smiled to himself as he drove towards the old abbey. They might think they were clever, but Cutler and his amateurs could never hope to beat a true professional at his own game.

"What d'you think he's up to, boss?" asked Winston.

"Your guess is as good as mine," Cutler replied, "but I'll lay odds on it not being anything designed to improve the quality of our health."

"Do you really think he intends to harm us then, Joe?" Sally asked. She wasn't the kind of woman to be easily scared, but for the first time a slight tremor was audible in Sally's voice.

"I don't want to think it, but yes, Sally, I really think that Walter Graves is capable of the worst kind of violence."

"Listen, boss," said Winston. "I know we don't have much in the way of evidence, and Graves hasn't done anything overtly criminal as far as we can see so far, but surely we should be at least talking to the police. We can warn them of our suspicions about Graves and they can maybe keep an eye on him, and *us* come to that."

"Look, Winston, what do want me to tell them? That we suspect this man, who is a fully accredited professor of history, is leading us in a bogus search for King Arthur's sword Excalibur? Not only that but we've lied to the local authorities, telling them that we're looking for evidence to support a Biblical theory. We think that Graves is really looking for something else, though we haven't a clue what it is, although we think it's connected to a ship that sunk over sixty years ago, and a body we discovered in a field near Glastonbury and then helped to cover up again so we could continue our search. What proof do we have that he intends to harm us? Theories, that's all we have, Winston. Until Graves shows his hand we can only go along with the pretence and try to find out what this job is really all about."

"What about the gun? You could tell them about that," Sally said, hopefully.

"Yes, I could, Sally. Then what? Graves might have a legitimate permit for the weapon, I may have been mistaken, I'm not sure any more. I'm starting to doubt myself a little. Also, the police need a reason to search Graves or his room, I've told you that before. They can't just go blundering in and trampling all over his so-called 'human rights', so we've nothing to present them with."

"Oh well," Winston re-entered the conversation. "It was just a thought, boss. I s'pose we're just gonna have to watch each other's backs real close, eh?"

"Real close, as you say," Cutler confirmed.

"In that case, you'd both better promise not to take your eyes off mine for a minute," said Sally.

"Sally girl, back or front, it'll be a pleasure to keep an eye on you." Winston laughed.

Winston's humour could be infectious, and the mood between the three of them visibly lightened. They spent the rest of the afternoon in a fruitless search. Graves didn't return to the farm at all during that time. He phoned Cutler on his mobile to tell him that he'd been detained in town and would meet them at the farm at nine o'clock the following day.

As they drove back to the Rowan Tree that evening Cutler and his team were still blissfully unaware of the small transmitter that clung to the underside of the rear wheel arch of the van. Walter Graves was frustrated, however, by the fact that the survey team's conversation on their way back to the Rowan Tree was unusually muted, as though a cloud hung over the cab in which they rode. Apart from a couple of references to Lucius Doberman and what he may have discovered during the day, little else was said that bore any relevance to the matter in hand. Winston Fortune was obviously trying to cheer everyone up and produced a string of banal and cheesy jokes that wouldn't have been out of place at a children's birthday party. Graves was relieved when he heard Fortune announce, "Here we are then folks," and the sound of the van's engine died in the background. With a sense of relief Walter Graves turned his receiving unit off, though he really wished he could find a way of hearing what was discussed when they met up with Doberman later that evening.

As it was, he had to be content with returning to Meare Manor, where, after a shower and a meal, he retired to his room to finalise his strategy for the following day.

Chapter 35

In contrast to the previous evening, Lucius waited for Joe and the others when they arrived at the guesthouse. The professor sat at a table by the window, the last rays of the evening sunshine bathing him in an almost sepulchral light as they filtered through the curtains and reflected from the polished surface of the table. Once again, both Joe and Winston couldn't help themselves from making the 'Dracula' connection where Lucius was concerned, especially when he rose to greet them, his height causing him to stoop slightly as he offered his right hand, and Joe and Winston found themselves looking into his eyes. The black jacket and crisp white shirt did little to dispel those thoughts, and neither man would have been surprised to see a pair of sharpened fangs appear when Doberman's lips parted in a smile.

They were snapped back to reality by Lucius's warm greeting, and all thoughts of the Prince of Darkness were once again dispelled from their minds.

"Joseph, my dear boy, Winston and Sally, welcome back. Come, sit down. I know you have to go and shower and change out of your grubby working clothes, but please come and join me for a minute or two. I promise not to keep you too long."

Cutler and the others sat as Lucius had requested, refusing his offer of a drink.

"My friends, it has been a most interesting day. As I indicated to you earlier Marcus did indeed get back to me with some news relating to your Mr. Graves. I thought you would like to hear what he had to say before going to your rooms."

"We're all ears, Lucius," said Cutler. "What have you found out?"

"Well, as I said, your Mavis did a good job with her limited re-sources, but Marcus was able to extract more relevant information from the Dean of Graves's college. It appears that Walter Graves is very well connected in many ways. He came to the college with the highest of references, some of them from very unexpected sources, including the British Museum and a number of highly respected philanthropists and educational bodies. He is, in fact, slightly older than I am, but keeps himself in superb physical shape with daily workouts in the college gymnasium. He is regarded as something of a genius in his field, though his academic stature has always been held back by his predilection for disappearing for weeks or months at a time in order to pursue various 'research' projects as he de-scribes them. The college were a little unhappy at having to agree to allow him these extended absences when he joined them, but there was apparently a great deal of pressure brought to bear on the college authorities to give Graves the position with their fac-ulty. Where that pressure came from the Dean was not prepared to say, not even to Marcus.

Bearing this latest information in mind I would have to say that it merely confirms what we have already thought, that there is far more to Walter Graves than at first meets the eye. Oh yes, and there was one other thing. The Dean had no idea that Graves was in Glas-tonbury, and had never heard of any document relating to Excalibur. He was under the impression that Graves is in the Scottish Highlands, carrying out a historical research project into the decline of the Crofting industry north of the border. I fear, my friends, that great care must be taken in any dealings with the man."

"Pardon me, Lucius, I don't mean to be disrespectful, but I think we knew that already, man," said Winston.

"Yes, it's new information, but it does just reinforce what we've already deduced for ourselves," Cutler added.

"Yes, well, there it is anyway. I'm sure you'll agree that the man is definitely not to be trusted under any circumstances. I'll be glad if we can solve this mystery and get you all away from the man as soon as possible," said Doberman.

"Oh, Lucius, you're quite a sweetie really, aren't you?" said Sally.

"I just don't want any of you getting hurt, my dear," he replied. "I fear that Mr. Graves might be far more dangerous than any of you imagine."

"You've already told us that you think he's going to bump us all off when the job's done. I don't think you can get much more dangerous than that, can you?" asked Cutler, with a wry smile on his face.

"Hmm, you have a point, Joseph," said the professor. "Look, I just wanted you to know what Marcus had discovered. You're all tired. Go and get changed and I'll meet you here when you're ready and you can tell me about your day in the field with Graves."

Cutler and the others agreed to return within the hour, and left Doberman nursing his glass of Scotch. As hot water burst from the shower jets in his bathroom, Joe Cutler stood and let the water refresh his body. He wished the warmth of the water could do the same for his mind. He was bloody sick of trying to work out what the hell they were all doing here, and why he'd allowed things to go this far. He felt as though he'd put them all in danger by accepting Capshaw's contract, and for what? He didn't even know what they were supposed to find and even if he did and they were successful, it was highly likely that Graves would put a bullet in each of their heads, and that would be the end of all of them. As he stepped from the shower and pulled a towel around himself, Joe Cutler concluded that he was probably the biggest fool in the world. Now somehow he had to defeat Graves and Capshaw in their wicked aims, and keep his friends safe at the same time. He didn't know how he was going to guarantee that safety, but his sense of responsibility for those who worked for him gave him a steely determination to ensure just that. Neither Graves nor anybody else was going to hurt his people, oh no, Joe Cutler would do everything in his power to prevent that happening. Just let them try, that was all!

The conversation over dinner that evening centred mostly on the possible connections between the *SS Livara*, the missing ship's officer Hogan whose body presumable lay not far away in a Glastonbury field, and the Maitland family. Lucius and the others could easily understand the connection between old Samuel Maitland and the ship's owner Harry Blandford. Put simply, Maitland had provided Blandford with the stake he required to start his shipping company. In the days before easily available bank loans and finance companies virtually throwing money at people many East Enders utilised the services of people like Maitland. Despite their criminal activities men like Maitland often saw themselves as benefactors to the local community, many of whom would regard the crime bosses with a degree of affection. They might rob from the rich, but they'd never hurt 'their own' people, or so the train of thought went.

The problem was, what could Maitland have to do with the *Livara?* Financing its purchase was one thing, but what interest did he have in it on the night she was torpedoed. Then again, according to his granddaughter, Blandford had paid the loan back in full long before the *SS Livara* sailed on her last voyage, so Blandford certainly

---

wasn't in debt to Maitland, unless he owed him a debt of gratitude, and used the ship for carrying contraband of some sort across the Atlantic. But the ship was empty of cargo, at least as far as the official records showed. Then there was Hogan. Why was he killed, for it was blatantly obvious his death wasn't caused by natural causes; why else would he have been buried in a field? Finally, *who* killed him? He was an ordinary merchant marine officer as far as was known, so what could he have known that would induce someone to take the most drastic of actions by disposing of him?

These were just some of the questions that Lucius, Joe, Winston and Sally considered during the evening. Unfortunately, they were unable to provide answers for any of them. Lucius did inform them that his final e-mail of the previous day was still to produce any results, but that he would rather not say anything about it until his contact came back to him with a reply.

It was Sally who came up with what was perhaps the only plausible theory of the evening, or at least it was the only one that seemed to fit the facts as far as they knew them.

"Perhaps," she said, as the night wore on and the other customers had all left the bar, "it might have gone something like this. What if the *Livara* wasn't really empty? Let's say for the sake of argument that she was carrying a cargo that the government wanted to keep secret. That would explain the extra men on board. They were sailors, or marines or whatever they used in those days, sent on the ship to guard whatever she was carrying. When the ship went down, the cargo was lost and the authorities didn't want to own up that they'd lost it, whatever it was. So, when they listed the men as missing it was just what they wanted in a way that the destroyer sunk because they could put those extra men down as having been on the warship and no-one would connect the military with the *Livara*."

"But some civilian clerk put the men down as having been lost on the freighter and no-one noticed at the time because no-one would have been checking those figures as there was a war on!" This came from Winston, who was rapidly warming to Sally's theory.

"But where did Hogan fit into all this, and why was he murdered so far from Bristol, where the ship was docked?" asked Joe Cutler.

"I don't know, Joe. My theory doesn't quite stretch far enough to work out what he had to do with it or why they killed him." Sally looked a little crestfallen at not being able to add that particular piece to her puzzle.

"And what has our search here in Glastonbury got to do with whatever was on that ship?" Winston asked the question as he tried to think of an answer himself.

Lucius Doberman who had been sitting quietly listening to theory after theory during the evening suddenly became quite animated as he exclaimed: "Actually, I do think that Sally's on to something. Whatever was on that ship is here, buried near Glastonbury. I still can't be sure where Hogan fits into the picture, but everything else about Sally's idea makes sense. The fact that those extras on the ship were Naval personnel fits with Sally's theory that the government, or at least the Military were involved, but what could have been so important that it was worth covering up its loss for all these years, without any official mission being launched to recover the cargo, and how and why did it end up in Glastonbury? I suspect that was where our Mr. Hogan came into the picture. Someone, and I suspect it was the Maitland's grandfather, made sure that the *Livara's* regular first officer met with the little 'accident' that made him unfit to sail and he then arranged for an officer who was probably on his payroll to take his place, and help smuggle the cargo off the ship to a prearranged location. Maybe Hogan tried to double-cross Maitland, I really don't know, or maybe he was just killed to ensure his silence, but I think we are very close to solving the mystery of the *SS Livara*, and with it, the equally mysterious reason for your being here in Glastonbury."

Lucius Doberman rose from his seat and reached across the table to take Sally's hand in his own and plant an old-fashioned gentlemanly kiss on the back of the hand.

"Sally, I must congratulate you, dear girl. You have exercised your brain in the most productive fashion and have produced our most workable theory to date. I shall be very surprised, indeed, if your hypothesis is far from the truth when we eventually unravel the final clues in this mystery."

"In other words, Lucius, if Sally is right, we've just got to find an unknown cargo from a ship that sunk over sixty years ago, and while we're at it avoid being killed by a gangland hitman, and then also try to discover why the government didn't want anyone to know about it in the first place?"

"Precisely, Joe," said Doberman enthusiastically, "though when it comes to your third point, I rather think that I might be the best one to solve that particular riddle. Leave it to me. I have someone in mind who might be able to put two and two together to make five in our case."

With that, the conversation gradually drifted into a series of repeats of the points already raised until the weary quartet decided to call it a night and each headed off to their own rooms.

This night was a little different to the one before, however. The distance in knowledge between the good guys and the bad guys was shrinking by the hour thanks to Sally's new theory addition.

Chapter 36

Charlotte woke to the sound of birdsong coming from just outside her window. It was the unmistakeable serenade of a blackbird. She stirred lazily, feeling safe and warm beneath the daisy patterned quilt that adorned the bed in Jenny's spare room. As she turned over in bed to look towards the brilliant shafts of morning sunlight that were creeping through the curtains, Charlotte realised she hadn't felt so relaxed in a long time, certainly not since she'd begun working for Malcolm Capshaw. She knew that she had to keep at least one step ahead of her employer, or face what may be potentially painful consequences.

Her reverie was broken by a knock on the bedroom door. Jenny's cheerful face peered through the space, smiling at the sleepy eyed Charlotte as she sat up in bed.

"Good morning, sleepy head," she grinned at Charlotte. "Ready for some breakfast?"

"Oh, Jenny I'm sorry. I must have slept longer than I expected to."

"No need to apologise. You must have needed the sleep. Wrap yourself in that dressing gown behind the door and come and join me in the kitchen."

"Thanks, Jenny, I won't be long," said Charlotte as she pushed her feet out from under the bedcovers and stood, stretching and yawning.

The two cousins were soon sitting at Jenny's kitchen table enjoying freshly percolated coffee, croissants, and waffles drenched in traditional English honey. Charlotte hadn't felt this good in ages and wished she could stay longer in the sleepy little village, enjoying the hospitality and companionship of her relative, but of course, she knew that wasn't possible. She had to go, and go soon, the only question to answer was where to? She'd think about that later, and be gone by the following day.

They cleared away the paraphernalia of breakfast together and afterwards Jenny announced that she had to go into town again that morning to deliver a recently completed painting of Hereford Cathedral to the verger of the church in the village of Credenhill, a few miles away.

"May I see it?" asked Charlotte.

"Of course," said Jenny, going through the door to her studio, beckoning Charlotte to follow.

It's beautiful," Charlotte exclaimed as Jenny revealed the canvas to her. "You're so talented, Jenny."

"I'm glad you like it," said Jenny as she wrapped the framed painting in thick brown paper and then tied it with strong string to protect it on the short journey to the church. "You're sure you don't mind me leaving you?"

"Of course not. I'll be fine."

"Oh yes, I'm expecting a delivery of some very special paints I ordered via the internet. Will you listen out for the postman please? He'll need a signature for the package."

"Yes, now you go and deliver your painting. I'll be here when you get back, with the kettle on for a good cup of tea."

Jenny left minutes later, and Charlotte was left to her own devices. The cottage was quiet and peaceful and she suddenly realised that the blackbird had returned to his branch on the beech tree in the garden, singing his cheerful song once again. Charlotte walked into the small cosy sitting room and peered out of the window into the garden. As she looked up at the tree she could see the blackbird perched on one of the lower branches, his head arched upwards as though he were projecting his song as far as he could. Charlotte could almost feel the sheer joy he must be feeling on this warm sunny morning, and she actually envied the little bird, for it was free to come and go, to sing his song of joy and happiness as he pleased, unfettered by the bonds that held her to the daily grind of everyday human existence.

Her enjoyment of the blackbird's symphony was broken by the sound of someone knocking on the door. Assuming the postman had arrived with Jenny's package, Charlotte hurried from the sitting room to the front door of the cottage. Without thinking, she opened the door wide expecting to see the smiling face of a ruddy-faced countryside postman.

Instead, a man with short, almost cropped bleached-blonde hair and emotionless and penetrating blue eyes stood in the doorway. Before Charlotte could say or do anything, the man roughly pushed her in the chest, sending her spinning back into the hallway. She fell backwards as her feet caught on the legs of Jenny's telephone table, and landed face up on the floor. As she tried to catch her breath, the blue-eyed man loomed above her prone figure and in a voice that sent tremors of fear through every nerve ending in Charlotte's body he spoke quietly and menacingly:

"Hello, little whore. It's time to play."

Jenny arrived home two hours later. Finding the front door ajar, she assumed Charlotte had gone into the garden, perhaps to sit and enjoy the morning sun.

"Hi, Charlotte, are you there?" she called as she walked into the cottage and closed the door behind her. Silence. "Hey, cousin, have you gone back to sleep? I'm back."

Still receiving no answer Jenny tried both the kitchen and the sitting room, but there was no sign of Charlotte. Thinking she must have gone back to bed for a nap Jenny made her way upstairs and opened the door to the spare room.

The dead, sightless eyes of Charlotte Raeburn stared up at her from the bed. Her cousin's wrists had been bound with her own stockings and tied to the wrought iron headboard on the bed. Her legs were splayed wide apart and there was blood between her thighs.

The compulsion to scream welled up in Jenny's throat, but just as the sound was about to erupt from her lips a hand reached round her neck and closed over her mouth. She tried to struggle, but the man had his other arm around her body and held her in a vice-like grip. Jenny could do little more than kick her legs backwards in an attempt to fight off her assailant.

"One scream and you're dead," whispered a voice from close to Jenny's ear. "Do you understand?"

She did her best to nod.

"I only came here for your little whore of a cousin. Keep your mouth shut when I take my hand away and do as I say and you won't get hurt. Nod if you understand."

Jenny did her best to nod again. The hand released its grip on her face and the man placed both his hands on her arms, gripping her tightly. Jenny snatched the deepest breath she could. Fear coursed through her veins as she stood almost paralysed while the man moved her round until she was face to face with her cousin's murderer.

The steel blue eyes of her assailant stared into her own soft brown eyes, and Jenny's fear level tripled. The man pushed her back until the backs of her legs were against the end of the bed, then with one push he propelled her backwards and she fell onto the bed, next to the lifeless body of Charlotte. As the blonde-haired man bore down on her and his hands began to tear at her clothes Jenny tried to fight back. She vainly kicked out with her legs, but he struck her viciously in the face with the full force of his right fist. As stars exploded in her head, Jenny sobbed and gasped for breath.

"You said you wouldn't hurt me. Who are you?" she asked plaintively, through her tears as her dress was torn from her body.

The man didn't even pause in his rush to remove the last of Jenny's clothes.

"You can call me Karl, my pretty little whore, and by the way, I lied," came the reply as she felt her legs being pushed apart and then another fist smashed into Jenny's face.

Chapter 37

Walter Graves was waiting for them as usual as Joe and the team arrived at Maiden's Farm to begin yet another day's search for the elusive prize that Cutler and his team had as yet failed to identify. Over breakfast that morning Lucius Doberman had proposed an addition to the theory first propounded by Sally and on which he had elaborated the previous night. An entire ship's cargo would surely have been too big to simply spirit away and hide beneath the ground in the depths of the countryside. Plus, if it were so important and had gone missing then why did the Navy put those additional men on board the *Livara* to guard what would have been an empty hold? Doberman thought that only a *part* of the cargo had gone, and that was what they were searching for. What that cargo was he hoped to identify through his mystery contact later that day. As Joe had observed, whatever it was it must be of a very high value if it all fitted into one coffin sized box, and was worth all the trouble that the Maitlands, Capshaw, and Graves had gone to in order to retrieve it.

Graves had been listening to the conversation in the van as Cutler and the others drove to the farm. What he heard made him realise that Cutler and Doberman were getting perilously close to working out the secret of the *Livara*. Winston had been in ebullient mood, praising Sally for her wonderful theory, and Cutler had echoed that thought. Cutler had also been excited at the thought that Professor Doberman might be close to discovering what the *Livara* was carrying on the night she sank. If that were to happen then Graves knew that all could be lost. Cutler and Doberman would no doubt take steps to recover the prize themselves, possibly with police protection, and Capshaw's anger would be unbelievable in its ferocity.

That settled it as far as Graves was concerned. He had to move to ensure Cutler's continued co-operation, and he had to move today. Graves heard the laughter and the high spirits from all three of the surveyors in the cab as the van neared his BMW. They were confident that they had him backed into a corner. Let them be! In a few hours Graves would be back in total control of the situation and Cutler and Fortune would be doing just as he wanted. Doberman would do little without them, of that Graves was sure, so he just had to focus on his plan and by the time Cutler saw Doberman again, the professor's information should be neutralized.

After an hour of fruitless searching, the radar not detecting so much as a tree hole, Graves suggested a break as the sun was rising higher and the day becoming hotter. Cutler and Sally came in from the field and Winston stepped down from the control centre in the van. There was something of an atmosphere between Graves and the others, no matter how hard they tried; it was evident that the relationship between historian and surveyors was becoming strained. Graves knew that time was running out. The level of suspicion from both sides was rising by the day and something or someone would crack before long. The time to act had come. He made his decision as they all sat on the grass sipping the tea that Sally had poured from her flask. As luck would have it, Joe Cutler played right into his hands as they put the tea mugs away and prepared to start their search of the next grid.

"It's getting really hot down there in the field. Why don't you take a spell in control, Sally? I'm sure Winston won't mind working up a sweat with me in the open air."

"Hey, man, no problem. Just like home, eh?"

"Such chivalry," said Sally jokingly. "Thanks, Winston."

"No sweat, Sally girl," he laughed at his unintentional pun.

Joe and Winston made their way back to the search grid as Sally climbed into the van ready to handle the control. Graves appeared to be making a telephone call and called to the men, telling them he'd follow them in a few minutes. As soon as they were out of sight Graves made his move.

He unlocked the BMW and removed the Ruger from its customised hiding place under the driver's seat. Sally was seated in front of the control screen in the back of the van, but turned round when Graves's shadow blocked the flow of light into the vehicle's interior. Her face froze in terror as she found herself staring down the barrel of a gun for the first time in her young life.

"Not a word please, Miss Corbett, and please be so kind as to dispense with the earpiece and step down from the van," Graves instructed her.

Sally did as he asked, and as her feet touched the ground Graves made her turn round and put her hands behind her back. These he swiftly secured with cable ties, and Sally was ushered to the BMW, where she was deposited in a lying down position on the back seat.

"What now, Mr. Graves?"

"What, no, *why are you doing this to me?* Or, *'what's this all about?'* I am disappointed, Miss Corbett. I thought you'd have made some pretence at playing the innocent. You are quite a little actress after all, aren't you?"

"You know what we were saying?"

"Just a simple little bug, my dear, nothing elaborate. It was easy to attach it under the wheel arch of your van. I must admit some of the things you've all said about me were a little unfair and unflattering. I'm not an absolute monster you know."

"So why am I tied up and lying on the back seat of your car then, you bastard?"

"Oh dear, I'm sure there's no need for such language, Sally, my dear. I'm only doing my job you know."

"Yes, and a bloody dirty job at that, Graves. Are you going to kill me now, or later, or what?"

"Oh, not yet, my dear, not yet. Your friends Joe and Winston still have a job to do, and they'll do it much better if they know your life depends on them doing it right and handing over the prize without giving me any trouble."

"They won't do it, Graves. They know you plan to kill us all so why should they help you when they know you're going to kill me anyway?"

"Human nature, my dear Miss Corbett, that's why they'll do it. As long as they know you're alive and they think there's a chance that they can still beat me and rescue you, then they'll do exactly as I ask them to. Believe me, I've seen it all before, they'll co-operate alright. Now, I think that's quite enough chatter for now"

Sally gagged as Graves suddenly produced a roll of duct tape and drew a length of the shiny grey sticky material across her mouth, giving her no chance to communicate further with him. Fifteen minutes later she found herself shackled to the wall of a subterranean tunnel that appeared to be hundreds of years old. The iron shackles that held her in place against the wall were relatively new, but the tunnel itself smelled old and decayed, and Sally hoped that this cold dark tomb-like place wouldn't prove to be her last resting place.

"I'll be back later with something for you to drink, my dear. First I have a call to make, and then I must speak urgently to your dear Mr Cutler. Do make yourself comfortable while I'm gone."

With those parting words, Graves spun on his heel and was gone, into the darkness which now enfolded Sally like a cloud. With the tape firmly in place over her mouth she couldn't scream or call for help. Sally Corbett cried into the darkness. She'd never felt so alone and afraid in her life. The stone floor was hard and uncomfortable and she hoped that Joe or Winston or anybody would come and rescue her from the nightmare.

Chapter 38

"Sally girl, where you gone?" Winston asked, speaking into his headset. "Sally, are you reading me?"

Joe Cutler came over to his side with a questioning look on his face.

"Something's wrong, boss, Sally's not responding," said Winston, worry lines etching his normally happy and cheerful countenance.

"Sally, this is Joe, please respond," said Cutler, also trying to raise Sally on the mobile intercom.

"You're right, Winston. There's nothing wrong with our equipment, we tested it this morning. Where's Graves? I haven't seen him since we came back after tea."

"Neither have I, boss. I got a real bad feeling 'bout this."

"Come on, Winston, fuck the search, we're heading back to the van."

The two men made it back to the van in less than ten minutes. It was empty. There was no sign of a struggle. Whatever had happened to Sally had at least been free of violence, or so Cutler surmised. That didn't mean, however, that violence wasn't waiting just around the corner.

"Graves's car is gone, boss."

"The bastard's taken Sally," said Cutler, strong venom etched in his voice.

"If he's harmed her I'll fucking kill him myself," Winston snarled.

"You'll have to take your place in the queue," said Cutler, feeling helpless as he stood looking into the empty van.

The sun picked that moment to disappear behind a large bank of cumulus that drifted high above them and the greying effect of the sudden change in the colours of the land perfectly matched Joe and Winston's mood. Anger, fear and a rising tide of the need to do something, but not knowing what took hold of both men who would have done anything at that moment to take Sally's place wherever she was.

As the cloud bank continued to obscure the sun a sound reached their ears from a little way along the farm track and both men instantly recognised the shape and colour of Graves's BMW as it bumped its way towards them.

"I swear to you, boss, I'm gonna kill the bastard."

"No you're not, Winston. In fact, you're not going to say or do anything, is that clear? I'm still in charge of this company, and I'll do the talking when he gets here, is that also clear?"

"Yeah, right, I suppose so," said Winston, grudgingly. "But if he tries anything..."

"Winston!"

"Yeah, okay, boss, say and do nothing. Leave the talking to you. Don't worry, I've got the message."

"I hope you have because if we're wrong, assuming of course that Graves has got her, then we might be putting her life in danger. Just remember that and hold on to your temper."

"I said okay, boss."

Graves pulled up a few yards from where the two men stood and stepped from his car as if he were doing no more than going for an afternoon stroll in the country. He nodded a greeting to Cutler.

"Mr. Cutler," he said.

"Mr. Graves," Joe replied, mimicking Graves's nonchalant manner, hoping to sound as equally disinterested as the historian/hitman.

"I'm sure you don't need me to tell you that Miss Corbett has become my unwilling guest for a while whilst you've been hard at work. I must say she's been most co-operative so far. I just hope that you and Mr. Fortune here will be equally as accommodating."

Winston Fortune almost made a forward move as though to lunge at Graves, but Cutler caught the movement from the corner of his eye and quickly laid his hand on Winston's arm, holding him back. "No, Winston."

"I'm sorry, boss," Winston apologised.

"I hope your boss here has explained to you that any pre-emptive action against me could prove disastrous for your friend Sally, Mr. Fortune. After all, apart from anything else, you have no idea where she is, and unless I return to tend to her needs in a short time, she will start to become very uncomfortable, if you know what I mean."

Winston merely growled in reply.

"What do you want from us, Graves? We're already carrying out your search for you, what more can we do? Why snatch Sally?"

"Shall we say for insurance purposes, Mr. Cutler? Yes, I think that's a good way of putting it. You see, I'm well aware that you know you're not here to find Excalibur. That was of course just a blind, a ruse to get you here and have you carry out the search for what we're really looking for."

"You mean the *Livara's* cargo," said Winston in an attempt to rattle Graves.

"Oh yes, you think you're very clever don't you, Mr. Fortune? Thanks to the little bug I placed in your van I've been aware that you made some connection with the *Livara* some time ago, but I think you're bluffing. You still have no real idea what you're here to find, have you?"

"Whether we do or not, it doesn't explain why you've taken Sally," said Cutler.

"Let's just say that you and your little team have come a bit too close to discovering the truth about your job here. I can't take the chance that you might do that and then go running to the police."

"We didn't go to the police when we found Hogan's body, did we, why should we go to them now?"

Cutler's mention of Hogan's name at last brought a response from Graves, who appeared visibly shaken for a moment.

"You seem to have found out more than I was aware of, Mr. Cutler. I congratulate you. It will not, however, serve to do you any good. You have a few clues, and have gleaned certain facts concerning the case without being able to join them together into a coherent pattern. I say again, you have no idea why you are here."

"Then tell us you bastard. At least let us know what this is all about."

"Perhaps in good time, Mr. Cutler. For now, you and Mr. Fortune will do exactly as I say, and continue searching for the item in question. When it's found and in my safe keeping, Miss Corbett will be released from her place of captivity and you will all be allowed to leave."

"Yeah, like we should believe you, man. You're going to kill us all once you've got your hands on whatever it is you're after. Why don't you admit it?" Winston was getting angrier by the minute despite the threat of violence that now simply emanated from Graves as he stood facing them, legs apart, his body language that of a man in total command of a situation. As if to reinforce that control Graves reached his right hand into the inside pocket of his jacket and withdrew the Ruger, which he now pointed at the two men in front of him.

"For now, Mr. Fortune, I can only suggest that you take me at my word if you want to see Miss Corbett again. The future is another matter, and we shall discuss it when the time is right. Now, do we have a deal?"

"We don't have much choice do we, Graves? But I'm warning you now, if anything happens to young Sally there'll be hell to pay, and that's a promise."

"Fine words, Mr. Cutler, fine words, but I think you'll agree that you're in no position to make threats. Now listen to me. We've almost mapped out and searched the whole area where we expected to find the item. There are only two sectors left, one of which should yield what we're looking for. The map left by those who buried the item was so obscure and indistinct that we've had great difficulty making any sense of it at all, but at least we knew where to search within a couple of square miles. Believe me, I can smell success, if not tomorrow, then the next day. You may take the rest of the afternoon off to prepare yourselves for an early start in the morning and to allow you to fully assimilate all that's happened today. Do not try to double-cross me or call the authorities or Miss Corbett is likely to meet with an unfortunate end. Oh yes, please give my regards and professional compliments to Professor Doberman, won't you? I understand he's the source of most of your more accurate suppositions and surmises. I'm afraid even he can't help you now, Mr. Cutler. I have the upper hand in our little duel of wits, and I intend it to stay that way."

Joe and Winston were left standing in the field as Graves simply turned away from them, got into his car and drove away, leaving them looking at each other as though stunned.

"Bastard," was all Winston could say.

"Fucking murderous shit," Joe added as the gleaming BMW disappeared in the direction it had arrived from, dust from the track forming a cloud in its wake. In seconds Graves was gone from their sight. The two men climbed dejectedly into the van, Winston fired up the engine and they drove in silence back to Glastonbury, to the Rowan Tree and Professor Lucius Doberman. Joe was downcast and fearful for Sally, but he still believed that somehow the learned scholar could just be their last chance to solve the mystery and save Sally Corbett. Something in the way Graves had talked when he mentioned Doberman's name made Joe think that there was a bit of apprehension evident in Graves's manner. Maybe he'd imagined it, but he thought not, and if Graves did have an Achilles heel, then Joe could only pray that it went by the name of Lucius Doberman.

Chapter 39

Doberman was stunned by the news of Sally's abduction. Far from displaying signs of being an 'Achilles heel' where Graves was concerned, he appeared to display an air of defeatism and regret.

"I shouldn't have come here," he said disconsolately as the three men sat on the bed in Cutler's room. Privacy had now become their watchword, no drinks in the bar while Sally was in danger. "If I hadn't encouraged you to continue with this foolhardy search, made you go to the police instead, maybe Sally wouldn't be in this predicament."

"Oh come on, Lucius, it's not your fault," Cutler said, soothingly. "You know why we didn't go to the police and you agreed with our reasoning. We had nothing, no evidence at all. You know as well as we do that the police can only act *when* a crime has been committed, not just when someone suspects one is *going* to take place, especially when they don't know what that crime might be."

"Even so, dear boy, I do feel partly responsible for Sally's plight."

"Listen to me, Professor," Winston spoke sternly but with respect towards Doberman. "If it weren't for you, man, we wouldn't know half the things we know now. You've helped us more than you know and if we can get Sally out of the fix she's in and find whatever

Graves is looking for then we'll have you to thank for pointing us in right direction."

"I'll second that," said Cutler. "Come on, chin up. Sally isn't dead yet, and I don't intend to let anything happen to her. She'll be safe as long as we let Graves think we're still doing what he wants. He's too clever to bump her off before we've found what he's looking for. We might insist on proof that she's alive, and as she's his big bargaining tool he won't want to lose her until we've found the prize he's after."

Joe's confidence seemed to have an uplifting and motivational effect on Doberman who seemed to cheer up slightly after the re-assurances from both Cutler and Fortune. The professor appeared to be deep in thought for a moment or two, and then he smiled at them. After those few minutes of hesitancy and discouragement, it appeared the old Lucius was back.

"You must forgive my temporary display of weakness. I have allowed my concerns for Sally to deflect me from the reality of our situation. If we are to help the dear girl then I think the time has come for us take decisive action, gentlemen," he pronounced gravely.

"What are you suggesting, Lucius?" asked Cutler, pleased that their new friend had recovered his intellectual composure. A clear thinking Lucius Doberman was far preferable to the muddle-headed unconfident man who had sat wringing his hands a short time ago.

"What I'm suggesting is that we go to the authorities and bring them up to date with the happenings here in Glastonbury."

"But Graves said Sally would be in danger if we did that," said Winston, horrified that Doberman could suggest such a thing.

Cutler said nothing. He wanted to hear the rest of Doberman's proposal. Joe knew that the professor always had a reason for what he said or did and was prepared to hear him out before pronouncing judgment on his plan.

"Listen, Winston," Doberman went on. "Sally is already in danger. That fact is inescapable. Also, as Joe said, Graves won't do anything to harm her as long as he needs you two to do his dirty work. He's no idea yet how long it will take you to find what he's looking for and you will certainly want assurances that Sally is alive and well during that time. He's ruthless, I agree, but he's no fool. To do anything to Sally at this point would be counter-productive to his aims. Wouldn't you agree?"

Winston had to concede that the professor was right. Graves couldn't harm Sally without harming himself and his cause. Only a fool would dispose of their strongest bargaining tool, and that was exactly what poor Sally was at this moment.

"But if Graves sees the police crawling all over the place…"

"He won't, Winston, trust me. I'm not without influence you know, nor is Sir Marcus. I'm sure that between us we can convince the chief constable to allow a discreet police operation to be conducted without Graves or Capshaw becoming suspicious or knowing that we've talked to the authorities at all."

"And in the meantime?" asked Joe.

"In the meantime, you and Winston continue to play the parts of Sally's loyal and worried friends. You go on with the search and leave any liaison with the police to Marcus and me. That way there'll be no way that Graves can discover that you're in contact with them, which technically of course, you won't be."

"But won't they want to speak to us?" asked Winston.

"Don't worry about that. As I said the chief constable will be approached, apprised of the facts, and it will also be made clear to him that Sally's life could be in danger if you are known to have spoken to the police. I'm sure that Marcus and I can convince him that we are in command of sufficient facts to facilitate his beginning the investigation without direct contact with the two of you, for the time being at any rate."

"Lucius, I just hope you're right," said Cutler. "What you say makes sense, but there's still a risk to Sally whichever way you put it."

"But don't you see, Joe, that's just what I've been saying. Sally is already at risk, but that risk is hardly compounded by us contacting the authorities, because Graves needs her, and as long as we handle things my way there's little or no chance of him even knowing that the police are involved."

"What do you think, Winston?" asked Joe.

"I gotta say I agree with the professor. I know I was against it from the start, but his plan seems to be our best option if we want to beat that bastard Graves and get Sally back in one piece."

"Okay, Lucius, make the call," said Joe.

With the agreement made, Lucius announced that he would phone Sir Marcus Farthingwood from his own room when they parted and set things in motion. It would be best, he hinted, if Marcus was the one to contact the chief constable. His name, reputation and title could all help to open doors that might otherwise remain locked to other mere mortals. Cutler agreed to leave that decision in Lucius's hands.

Winston suggested a drink before Lucius went to make the call and Joe Cutler removed a bottle of single malt whisky from his bedside cabinet. He poured each of them a large measure of Scotch. While Joe poured the drinks Winston switched on the television. The evening news had just begun. Lucius proposed a toast to success and they all sipped from their glasses. Joe Cutler suddenly looked aghast as a picture appeared on the TV screen.

"Turn the sound up, Winston," he ordered. "I know that face."

Photographs of two women were being shown on the screen. The newscaster had already begun the story, but the men were soon able to catch the essence of it.

"...*were found today in a cottage in the picturesque village of Stretton Sugwas near Hereford. The cottage belonged to Jennifer Lees, and the second body was identified as that of her cousin Charlotte Raeburn, who was visiting her at the time. Miss Raeburn was the secretary to multi-millionaire businessman Malcolm Capshaw, who, when interviewed at his office in Stratford-on-Avon this afternoon, was said to be distraught at the news of his employee's brutal rape and murder, and that of her cousin. Police inquiries are continuing.*"

"Bloody hell!" Joe exclaimed. "That's the girl who showed me into Capshaw's office. I met her, talked to her, now she's been murdered."

"I think that we must assume that the poor woman's death is not just coincidental to whatever is happening here, Joe," said Lucius. "Somehow she must have incurred the wrath of her employer and I fear that Miss Raeburn has been silenced to protect Capshaw's interests, or that of the Maitlands."

"Lucius, I don't want to appear paranoid, but I really think you should put the whisky down and go and make that phone call."

"Why did you have to kill them both, you fucking idiot?" Boris Maitland ranted at his brother. "I told you to make sure she didn't talk to anyone until the job was over, I didn't mean for you to murder the bitch, or her bloody cousin. Do you realise what a hornet's nest you've stirred up? I thought you had more brains than that brother."

"She was asking for it, Boris. She was nothing but a whore, and so was that cousin of hers. They could have been sisters to look at them, and by God, they were fucking scared before I did them I can tell you."

"And what about Malcolm? Do you think he's going to be pleased that we offed his secretary and his mistress? Jesus, Karl, we need him on our side, not against us."

"Oh come on, Boris. Little Malcy'll do just what we tell him to, you know he will."

"I just hope for your sake that you're right because we're too close to the prize now for anything to go wrong."

Malcolm Capshaw picked up the telephone with a trembling hand and dialled the Maitland mansion. Boris answered the phone on the second ring.

"Boris! What the hell's going on? You said you'd take care of Charlotte, not bloody send that brother of yours to rape and kill her, or her cousin. Don't deny it, Boris. It was that little shit of a brother of yours, wasn't it? He's been after Charlotte for ages and this has got his sadistic stamp all over it."

"Malcolm, for God's sake calm down. Yes, it was Karl, and no, I didn't order him to do it. He acted on his own initiative to solve a problem for all of us. It might have got a bit out of control..."

"A bit! Do you realise that I'm going to have the cops crawling over this place in the next couple of days, just when we're getting close?"

"Look, Malcolm, you had nothing to do with her death, so you just play the bereaved employer, all sympathetic like, and let them run rings around themselves. We'll get through this, don't be such a worrier."

"I can't help but worry, Boris, but I hope you're right, that's all, because you know that if I go down, you go with me."

"I hope that wasn't a threat, Malcolm, because I don't take kindly to being threatened whether you're an old friend or not."

"I'm not threatening you, Boris, just stating a fact. We're too closely tied together on this job and if the cops find out about me they're bound to figure out your involvement, that's all I'm saying."

"Good, as long as that's clear," said Boris. "Now you just go and carry on as normal and leave everything else to me."

Malcolm Capshaw replaced the phone on its cradle and realised that he was shaking all over. This wasn't how he'd intended for things to work out.

In the Maitlands' home Boris who had defended his brother's actions to Capshaw now turned the full force of his vehemence on his brother, who by his actions had put the job, and everyone involved in it in serious jeopardy. It was nearly an hour before the shouting in the library stopped and Karl Maitland stormed out of the house and drove off at breakneck speed in his yellow Ferrari, dust and gravel joining with his exhaust gasses to form a cloud in his wake.

A lot of people were reaching boiling point, and very soon the lid would have to blow on the mystery surrounding the search at Glastonbury.

Chapter 40

Despite her fear and anxiety Sally was relieved to hear Graves's footsteps as he returned along the tunnel. He had a light with him, a halogen powered emergency lantern, and as the beam shone in her eyes Sally blinked against the glare.

"How are you, Sally?"

"What do you care, Graves?" she retorted angrily, adrenalin fuelling a bravado at odds with her inner fears.

"Ah, poor little Sally. Let me say that I care far more than you think young lady. Hopefully it won't be long before your friends find what we're looking for and you can go home."

"Liar," she snapped. "You intend to kill us all, don't you, you miserable bastard?"

"As you wish, my dear," he replied. "We really must do something to make you more comfortable, my dear Miss Corbett."

Graves bent down to where Sally was shackled to the wall and removed a key from his pocket. In seconds, her wrists were free of the heavy burden of the iron manacles and she winced as Graves manhandled her to her feet. Her legs were shaky from having been confined in a sitting position for so long and her feet tingled as the blood rushed to them through her previously constricted veins. The burning sensation lasted only for a short time and she stretched her toes in her shoes as full feeling returned.

"Come with me, young lady," said Graves as he took hold of Sally by the left elbow and began to propel her along the tunnel.

"Where are taking me?" she demanded to know, "or are you going to finish me off now?"

"Wait and see," said Graves, "Just wait and see."

In the bar, and over dinner that evening, Lucius Doberman filled Joe and Winston in on the gist of his phone call to Marcus and his subsequent talk to the Chief Constable of the county.

"Marcus was in total agreement with me, and called Chief Constable Harvey at his home, (don't ask me how he got the number) as soon as we finished talking. He called me back a few minutes later. Seems the chief constable was most accommodating when Marcus explained the situation to him. He asked Marcus to request that I phone him straight away, which I did, and Harvey was very attentive when I explained the situation to him. Obviously, the Maitlands are known to the police even out here in the shires, and Harvey would love to help put them behind bars. He's liaising with the Met in London, and putting together a covert surveillance operation. Plain clothes detectives will be on hand within the next hour to keep a watching brief on all of us and to tail Graves from his hotel wherever he goes. If he's got Sally hidden anywhere nearby, which is likely, the police will find the location and release her as soon as Graves leaves her unattended. Harvey is also getting in touch with the police in Stratford so that tabs can be kept on Malcolm Capshaw, and I think we can safely assume that the net is gradually closing on our bad guys."

"What do we do in the meantime?" asked Joe.

"Like I said, Joe, just carry on as normal. Let Graves think he's still got the upper hand. You and Winston should be able to drag the search out long enough for the police to locate and release Sally, then they can move in on Graves and the others."

"Man, I just hope this works out for us and for Sally," said Winston, shaking his head from side to side. "I really hope it does."

"Trust me," said Lucius, "it will."

The telephone rang in Walter Graves's room at Meare Manor. He reached across the bed and lifted the receiver. He wasn't pleased when the voice of Boris Maitland boomed down the line at him.

"I presume you've heard the news, Graves?" he asked.

"I heard," said Graves, waiting to hear what Maitland had to say rather than volunteering an opinion.

"Karl was impetuous, but it's done now. I want you to step on the gas down there. Get Cutler and his people working flat out, at gunpoint if necessary. I want it found tomorrow. Just to be sure, I'm sending Karl down there, when he gets back from his sulk. I tore him off a strip earlier."

"Too right," said Graves, again keeping his conversation with the crime boss to a minimum.

He wondered why Maitland was being so open about his displeasure with his brother, then realised that Boris was trying to let him know that he would have Karl under control by the time he reached Glastonbury.

"I'll have him there sometime tomorrow so be sure you're ready for him when he arrives," said Maitland. "He'll want to see some progress."

"I'll be ready," said Graves in the same monosyllabic tone he'd used throughout the conversation.

"Good," was all Maitland said before ringing off and leaving Graves holding a silent phone in his hand.

"Hmm. Looks like things are going to get very interesting in the morning," he said to the unlikely guest sitting relaxing in the chair in the corner of his bedroom.

"We're going to need all the sleep we can get tonight."

The other simply nodded in agreement as Graves rose and poured two large brandies.

Chapter 41

Morning arrived in a haze of mist, damp and vaporous as a cloud. It seemed to cling to the fabric of everything living or artificial, plants, people, buildings, cars. The forecast was for a fine sunny day, and it would be once the sun had burned the mist off, but for now, Glastonbury was grey and quiet, as though the souls of the monks whose sandaled feet had trod the Abbeys' vaulted halls so many years before had returned in the night to haunt the streets of the ancient little town.

Joe Cutler shivered as he pulled the curtains open and looked out upon the mist shrouded vista of the street that met his eyes. Was there malevolence in the air? It certainly felt like it to Cutler. He couldn't say why, but he just knew that something was going to happen that day and there would be trouble before the sun set in the evening.

The same all-pervading air of gloom and despondency seemed to have infected his two companions as they sat together around the breakfast table. Winston was as quiet as Joe could ever remember him being, and even the normally effervescent Lucius was more subdued than Joe had previously witnessed.

"Whatever's going to happen, it's going to happen today, I know it is," said Joe as he sat endlessly stirring a cup of coffee that had long ago turned cold.

"I think you're right, boss," said Winston. "I've got a bad feeling."

"You're letting the dismal weather cloud your judgement," said Lucius. "I agree that things are looking as if they're coming to a head, but we must remember that the police are going to be tracking you every inch of the way. I'm sure everything will be alright."

"I just hope you're right, Lucius," Joe said thoughtfully.

Little more was said as the two surveyors took their leave of Lucius Doberman and set off for Maiden's Farm. They agreed to phone and inform him of any developments that took place as soon as they happened during the day. As he had on his first day in Glastonbury Lucius Doberman stood on the street outside the Rowan Tree and watched as the van carrying Cutler and Fortune disappeared from view. He turned and walked back into the guest house and within minutes was involved in a surprisingly long telephone conversation with his friend Sir Marcus Farthingwood. What Marcus told him that morning would significantly change Doberman's view of the whole scenario in which he'd found himself.

Walter Graves answered the knock on his door, wondering who could be disturbing him this early in the day. He wasn't due to set off to meet the surveyors for an hour and he wanted to complete his preparations for what could be a difficult day ahead.

The blue-eyed belligerent figure of Karl Maitland pushed passed Graves and strode into the centre of the room. Graves hadn't expected Karl to arrive in town this early.

"Well, well. Now who's this little beauty?" asked Karl, as he took in the sight of Graves' overnight guest sitting in the chair next to the window.

"This is Miss Sally Corbett," said Graves, "one of Mr Cutler's survey team."

"And very nice, too, if I may say so," Karl leered at Sally. "Have you had the pleasure yet, Graves?"

"Don't be disgusting, Karl," Graves replied. "Miss Corbett is my guest."

"Oh, that's a new name for it. She's just another tart, like the others I saw off yesterday."

"You really are a disgusting piece of filth, aren't you, Karl?" said Graves with a look of hatred in his eyes.

"Who the fuck do you think you're talking to, you slimy little bastard?" Karl thundered at Graves. "Just remember who pays your damned wages, you prick!" Graves stepped back as Karl Maitland pulled a handgun from the waistband of his trousers.

"I'll show you who's in charge here," the younger Maitland screamed at Graves. "I'll have this little beauty for a start and then we'll go and deal with her two playmates at the farm."

Karl took his eyes off Graves as he moved two steps closer to Sally. It was two steps too far.

"I wouldn't do that if I were you," said Graves with malice in his voice.

Karl turned back to face Graves and found himself staring down the barrel of Graves's Ruger.

Graves didn't say a word as he pulled the trigger. Karl Maitland staggered back in shock as a hole appeared in the centre of his temple, and the impending shock of his own impending death registered in his steel-blue eyes in the two seconds it took for the sadistic younger brother of the powerful Maitland clan to fall to the floor, his body slumped at the feet of Sally Corbett, who was too shocked and surprised by what had just transpired to even think of screaming.

Graves made sure that she was alright before he picked up the telephone. He spoke softly into the phone and Sally couldn't be sure who he was speaking to, but he eventually replaced the receiver on its cradle and turned towards her.

"I think it's time we finished this," was all he said as he took Sally by the arm and led her from the room where Karl Maitland's body lay growing colder by the second.

"What about him?" Sally managed to gasp as Graves closed the door behind them.

"Room service will deal with it," he grinned at Sally as they started down the stairs and out into the swirling morning mist.

Cutler and Fortune had set off earlier than usual for the farm and were already scanning the terrain beneath their feet as the sun began to burn off the mist that lay like a flat horizontal cloud over the surface of the field. There was no sign of Graves, which puzzled them both, but they wanted to take advantage of his late arrival. Perhaps they'd find whatever they were looking for before he arrived. That would make the whole thing easier, and give them some leverage to use against Graves. If the treasure, whatever it was, were in their hands they would have something to trade for Sally's safety.

As Cutler walked the second line in the grid they'd marked out he suddenly stopped and called to Winston in the control centre in the van.

"Winston! Get down here and bring the spades."

"You reading something, boss?"

"Yes, and it's big enough to be a grave."

"I'm coming, boss."

They began to dig and after half an hour of excavation Cutler's spade hit something solid.

"Here, Winston, we've found something."

Together, they cleared the last few inches of soil from the surface of the object and slowly revealed a box very similar to the one that had held the body of James Hogan. They soon managed to excavate a channel around the find that allowed them to access the sides of the box. It was Winston who made the surprising discovery that there was a second box buried beneath the first one.

"We're going to need something to prise it open, Winston" said Joe. "We'll have to check the first one before we access the lower box. Let's get the crowbar from the van while we get our breath back."

The two men were sweating profusely as they hauled themselves from the hole containing what they assumed to be the prize they'd sought for the last two weeks, even though the contents of the boxes were still a mystery to them. Shaking the dust and soil from their clothes and boots, they felt a degree of satisfaction that they were so close to solving the mystery.

"What do you think's in them, boss?" asked Winston.

"Why, gold, of course, Mr Fortune. What else were you expecting?"

They whirled round to see the face of Walter Graves grinning at them. His left hand had a firm grip on Sally's elbow, and in his right hand, hanging loosely at his side, was a gun!

Chapter 42

"Graves!" Winston spoke first as Joe looked in horror at the gun in the historian's hand.

"If you've hurt one hair on her head, Graves, I'll bloody kill you with my bare hands if I have to," Cutler blurted out.

"Joe, no, you don't understand," said Sally as both Cutler and Fortune assumed a defensive stance, ready to react to any threatening move from Graves.

"No, Joe, you don't" said Graves, releasing Sally's arm. Joe was surprised that Sally made no effort to move away from Graves. She remained by his side.

"What the hell's going on here?" asked a confused Winston. Sally's attitude was at odds with that of a kidnap victim. She was too calm.

"Please, Joe, let him explain," Sally implored.

At that moment, the piercing sound of a police siren could be heard approaching from not far away. The sound was soon followed by the appearance of a police car which pulled up at the end of the track about 40 yards away, disgorging four officers who slowly made their way up the shallow incline towards the gathering in the field.

"He can explain to them," said Joe as the police officers drew closer.

Graves made no move to get away; instead, he stood quite still, the gun at his side as they waited for the officers to arrive.

"Am I glad to see you?" Joe shouted when he was sure that the policemen could hear him clearly.

"Mr Graves?" one of the officers shouted in reply.

"I'm Graves," said the man in question.

"My name's Inspector Murray, sir. I was told to expect you here."

"What the fuck? said Winston. "Will someone tell us what's going on here? Why don't you arrest him? He's a killer and a..."

"Winston!" Sally shouted at her friend. "He's not one of the bad guys. Will you please just listen to him for a minute?"

Stunned by Sally's outburst Winston and Joe fell silent as Graves finally moved, not towards them, but off to one side with Inspector Murray. After a hurried conversation Graves turned back to face the two perplexed surveyors.

"Gentlemen, you must forgive my subterfuge and my behaviour towards you over the last few days. In my job you can never be sure who you can and cannot trust. You could have been in the pay of the Maitlands, or freelance treasure hunters, the only thing I knew for sure was that you were no friends of Malcolm Capshaw."

"But who the hell are you then if you're not one of them?" asked Joe Cutler.

"I'm a humble servant of Her Majesty's Government, Mr. Cutler, a special investigator for the Treasury, and my job for the last few years has been the tracing and recovery of certain, shall we say, missing articles either belonging to H.M. Government, or the governments of our allies? You'd be amazed at the monetary value that lies beneath the ground or in hidden vaults and illegal bank accounts around the world. Why, what you're standing on at the moment has an estimated value of around £7,000,000."

"Seven million pounds!" Winston was stunned, as was Joe by Graves's revelation of his true identity and by the staggering value of the gold they had just unearthed.

"But where did it come from, and what had the Maitlands and Capshaw to do with it?"

As they spoke a second police car arrived down the lane and four burly constables approached with spades in their hands. They soon joined two of the original officers in helping to dig the two boxes free from the earth. Joe and Winston hardly noticed them. Together with Sally, they allowed Graves to lead them to the side of the field where they all sat in a circle on the grass. Graves continued his narrative.

"In 1940, the war was going particularly well for Germany, not so well for the British. The government decided to take the drastic measure of transferring a proportion of the country's gold reserves out of the country to prevent them falling into the Nazi's hands if the Germans launched a successful invasion of this country. Canada was our largest Commonwealth ally, and the National Depository of Canada was thought to be the ideal location to store the gold. It was far enough from these shores to ensure that the Nazis would never get their hands on it and it could be used to finance a government in exile and a liberating re-invasion of the country if the need were ever to arise.

To avoid arousing the suspicions of any potential spies, it was decided to ship the gold across the Atlantic on an ordinary freighter in one of the many convoys that plied the route at the time."

"The *Livara!*" said Joe.

"Correct. Unfortunately, the Livara's owner Harry Blandford was an associate of old Samuel Maitland, the grandfather of Boris and

Karl, and he had arranged to be kept informed of any 'likely' targets for his enterprises that might be carried by the ship. Maitland was heavily involved in the black market and even a case full of tinned peaches could have brought him a handsome profit in those days. Usually, he had the odd seaman bribed to pass information on to him, but eventually he thought it wise to have someone in authority, an officer on board who would have been privy to more lucrative information."

"Hogan?" Joe said.

"Precisely. That was just bad timing as far as the government was concerned. They had no idea that Hogan was involved with Maitland. They'd probably never even heard of him. They chose the *Livara* at random from the list of ships due for convoy duty, but owing to the importance of the cargo it was thought prudent to inform the Captain and his officers of the ship of the nature of that cargo and to explain to them the necessity of a contingent of marines being placed on board for the duration of the voyage. Hogan, of course, went running to Maitland with the information just as fast as his treacherous legs could carry him, and Maitland laid out his plans to relieve the government of a proportion of the gold.

The gold was ferried from London to Bristol in a convoy of trucks and when they stopped for a break along the way, Maitland's men were waiting. They ensured that the rear truck in the convoy had a puncture, then as it lingered behind while the driver and guard changed the tyre, they struck. The bodies of the two soldiers were found in a ditch three days after, the truck abandoned nearby in a disused quarry. The six men who carried out the hijacking included James Hogan. The plan was to bury the gold somewhere it could be retrieved later, after the hue and cry died down. It was too heavy and the boxes too bulky to transport back to London without fear of discovery. Unfortunately for Hogan, Sam Maitland didn't want to take the slightest chance that he might be tied to the crime through Hogan, so he gave orders for Hogan to 'disappear' after the theft. After all, many seamen simply failed to turn up for a voyage and were quickly replaced and forgotten about. That's how Hogan ended up in the field, killed by his own confederates. By all accounts, no-one mourned his passing."

"What about the rest of the gold?" asked Winston, interrupting Graves.

"The rest of the gold reached Bristol safely. When the theft was discovered, it was assumed that word of the transfer had leaked out, and rather than load it onto the *Livara*, it was placed on board the *Dominion Princess*, another ship in the convoy that was due to sail without an outward cargo. To deflect any wrongdoers from the gold's new location, it was decided to allow the marines to remain aboard and sail on the *Livara* as planned. No-one would know that the gold was safely loaded on board the other ship until it docked in Canada."

"Did the *Dominion Princess* reach Canada?"

"Yes, Joe, it did. The gold was returned to the UK after the war, but the theft of the two containers comprising 100 bars of gold in total was never made public. It was thought that such news would have had a detrimental effect on national morale though the crime was never forgotten in official circles. I've already told you its value at today's prices."

"But why wasn't it found until now? And how did the authorities know that Sam Maitland was behind the theft? More to the point, why didn't he have it dug up as he'd planned?" asked Winston.

"I don't know why, but the men who carried out the theft chose this as the burial place for the gold. Maybe it was because it was the first town they came to after the theft that was near enough to their route. Anyway, one of them drew a map showing where they'd buried it, but he wasn't very accurate and nothing was to scale.

Worse, there was no starting point on it apart from the mention of the name Glastonbury, and a general layout of the land around what today is Maiden's Farm. He also forgot to put the obligatory 'X marks the spot', just to compound things. Then, as if to make things worse, the thieves caught a train to Bristol. There was an air raid that night and the train was struck by a German bomb. The men were in the third carriage and were all killed, except for one. He survived long enough to relate some of his tale to a doctor in the hospital who wrote it down in a notebook, and then foolishly tried to sell the book to Sam Maitland. The doctor met with an unfortunate end, as did the surviving thief, who died mysteriously in his hospital bed while recovering from his wounds."

"That's the notebook you've been carrying around," said Sally. "You showed it to me in your room last night."

"You stayed in his room last night?" Winston was incredulous.

"Actually, Sally spent much of yesterday chained to a wall in one of the old tunnels that run under the town," said Graves. "Once I was sure that you were all on the level I transferred her to my room at Meare Manor, where she slept most comfortably in my bed, while I curled up in a chair."

"There's one thing that bugs me," said Joe. "How did you know when the Maitlands would start looking for the gold? They could have been searching for it for years."

"They were, Joe. The police have had them under surveillance for years. Both Sam and the boys' father set searches in motion that never bore fruit, and when Karl and Boris set up Capshaw to lead the hunt this time we were ready for them."

"But how did you know they'd send for you?" the question came from Winston again.

"I've spent years in what we call 'deep cover', Winston. You'll have heard of that. The business of me having a problem in the Falklands, leaving the army, the history degree and the Indiana Jones lifestyle all gave me a perfect background and cover to hunt down various big time currency thieves and embezzlers. I'd done work for Capshaw before and when the Maitlands came calling it was a foregone conclusion that they'd want Walter Graves on the job. A private investigator named Silas Bowling who I was supposed to kill for Capshaw is safely living in an MI5 safe house as we speak."

"What about the men who died in some of your previous 'investigations'?" Joe asked.

"None of them were premeditated killings, Joe, I assure you. I only killed them when it was a matter of necessity, in self-defence. I'm not as cold-blooded as you think. As for you, if you'd found the gold I'd have arranged for you to stay in a safe house until we had the others in custody. I had orders from Capshaw to kill you if you'd succeeded."

"So I assume that now you've found the gold you'll be arresting the lot of them," Winston inquired.

"Well, Karl is dead, and Capshaw will be picked up later this morning, and Boris will be spoken to at length."

"Hang on," said Joe. "Boris will be *spoken to* at length? Won't he be arrested along with...wait a minute. I've been wondering who you were on the phone to so much when we were working. How come you knew so much about the original theft and the Maitland's business affairs? Boris Maitland is working for *you*, isn't he?"

"In a manner of speaking, Joe, yes he is. You see, Boris learned a long time ago that crime doesn't really pay. Most of his businesses are 100% legitimate; it was Karl who was the real career criminal in the family, and he's dead now, and believe me Boris won't mourn his brother for a minute longer than is necessary. Oh yes, there'll be the usual London gangland funeral with horse drawn coach and all, but after that I think you'll find that Boris will soon forget his little brother. Anyway, Boris approached the Treasury some years ago with a proposal regarding the 'family legacy' as he called it. If he helped us to find the gold, the treasury would pay him a percentage of its value, and the country gets the rest. A deal was struck and the rest, as they say, is history."

"But what about those two young women in Hereford?" Joe asked.

"Ah, yes, so unfortunate. Boris wanted Karl to take the Raeburn girl back to London where he would have spoken to her and if necessary paid her off to make her forget about her involvement with Capshaw, and ensure her silence. He didn't know that Karl had crossed the border into murderous sexual psychosis, and Boris was more than furious when he found out what his brother had done."

"Did he ask you to kill Karl?" asked Winston.

"I think I'll remain tight-lipped on that question if you don't mind, Mr. Fortune."

"Don't you think he's like a real-life James Bond?" Sally asked the others, as she stared admiringly at Graves.

"What happened to Indiana Jones?" laughed Joe.

The policeman in charge of the digging party called out to Graves.

"Sir, I think you might want to take a look at this."

Graves motioned for the others to follow him, and a few seconds later they were staring down at the contents of the first box.

"Wow," said Joe.

"My God," said Winston.

"Beautiful," was Sally's response as the sun reflected a brilliant yellow glow as it beat down on the rows of gold bars that had lain beneath the earth for so long, and that had cost so many lives.

"Your share of the finders' fee should put Strata Survey Systems on its feet for quite some years to come, Joe," said Graves quietly to Cutler.

"You mean I actually get paid for this?"

"All of you will, even Lucius Doberman. I'll make sure of it," said Graves, reaching out a hand and shaking the one Joe Cutler offered in return.

"I couldn't have found it without you."

As if on cue, a car screeched to a halt at the bottom of the lane. The tall distinguished figure of Lucius Doberman came running up the slope towards the others. He arrived, out of breath, arms flapping like a wallowing seagull, and the words simply tumbled from his mouth as he babbled; "Joe, you'll never believe it. I phoned Marcus, and he phoned the chief constable who phoned someone in Whitehall and they all phoned each other back and then Marcus phoned me back and told me the most amazing story…"

Epilogue

Malcolm Capshaw was arrested later that day and subsequently sentenced to a ten year jail sentence for incitement to murder and various financial offences thanks to information secretly provided by Graves and Boris Maitland. Boris's cover was protected by the authorities and he continues to be a source of invaluable help to the police in their fight against organised crime. His cover, if anything, is better than anything Walter Graves could ever have hoped for.

Lucius Doberman returned to Oxford, and still keeps in touch with his friends from Strata Survey Systems and is often an honoured guest at parties at Joe Cutler's home. Like Joe, Winston and Sally, and all those concerned with the case of the *Livara's* gold, he was asked to sign the Official Secrets Act, and he can never discuss the case or his involvement in it with anyone apart from those who played a part in the recovery of the treasure trove.

Winston was well rewarded and bought a houseboat where he soon settled in with his new friend, a Skye terrier which he named Lucius in honour of Doberman. Joe gave him the official title of Deputy Managing Director of Strata Survey Systems, while Sally bought a house and continued to work for Joe in her new capacity as Operations Director.

With his share of the finder's fee Joe Cutler was able to expand the business and soon found himself employing a total of ten people working from his office on the brand new industrial estate just outside Cheltenham. The business continued to grow with contracts arriving from some unexpected sources. Joe surmised that one or two of the contacts he'd made during the Glastonbury mystery may have encouraged certain organisations to place some of that business his way.

Mavis Hightower was at last a true 'office manager' with a filing clerk and an office junior at her disposal. She still 'mothered' Joe and the others and used her share of the reward to take a round the world cruise with her friend from G.C.H.Q. Betty Hunter, after buying her nephew a new car.

Not long after her return to the office, her head still full of the memories and mental images of that wonderful six weeks at sea, Mavis answered the telephone. She listened carefully to the voice that spoke in measured tones at the other end of the line, asked the caller to wait a moment while she checked to see if Mr. Cutler was available, and then switched the call to 'hold' as she buzzed through to her boss and said, almost unable to keep the excitement out of her voice:

"Joe; Walter Graves is on the telephone for you. He wants to know if you'd be interested in helping him with a little job...?

The Author

Winner, Best Author, The Preditors & Editors Readers Awards 2009, and also Winner of Best Children's Book, and Best Artwork for *'Tilly's Tale'* (under his Harry Porter pseudonym), and with a Top Ten Finisher Award for his thriller *'Legacy of the Ripper'*, Brian L Porter is the author of a number of successful novels. His works include the winner of The Preditors & Editors Best Thriller Novel 2008 Award, *A Study in Red - The Secret Journal of Jack the Ripper* and its sequels, *Legacy of the Ripper* and the final part of his Ripper trilogy, *Requiem for the Ripper*, all signed for movie adaptation by Thunderball Films (L.A.), with *A Study in Red* already in the development stages of production. Both *A Study in Red* and *Legacy of the Ripper* were awarded 'Recommended Read' status by the reviewers at CK2S Kwips & Kritiques.

Aside from his works on Jack the Ripper his other works include *Pestilence, Purple Death, Glastonbury, Kiss of Life* and *The Nemesis Cell*, and the short story collection, *After Armageddon.*

Brian has also become thoroughly integrated into the movie business since his first involvement with Thunderball Films LLC and is now also a Co- Producer on a number of developing movies, as well as being a screenwriter for many of the movies soon to be released by ThunderBall Flms. He is also the co-creator of a new docu-drama TV series, *Jack the Ripper, Reality and Myth* having also written the screenplay.

He is a dedicated dog lover and rescuer and he and his wife share their home with a number of rescued dogs.

Printed in Great Britain
by Amazon

75907468R00176